36 HOUR DATE

KELLY SISKIND

First edition: published under the title Licks April 2018

Second edition: CD Books November 2019

ISBN 978-1-988937-05-2 (ebook edition)

ISBN 978-1-988937-04-5 (print on demand edition)

❀ Created with Vellum

PRAISE FOR KELLY SISKIND'S ONE WILD WISH SERIES:

"Addictive and refreshing." ~ Rebecca Yarros, #1 *New York Times* bestselling author on He's Going Down

"I devoured this book." ~ *USA Today* bestselling author Brighton Walsh on He's Going Down

"It was impossible not to lose my heart (and occasionally my breath) from this sexy, smart, wholly consuming story." ~ Bookgasms Book Blog on He's Going Down

"Siskind knows how to write characters that have off-the-charts chemistry." ~ RT Book Reviews on Off-Limits Crush

"Funny, charming, and hot as hell." ~ author Beth Anne Miller on Off-Limits Crush

"Sexy, funny, and at times heart-wrenching. I loved every moment!" ~ author Rachel Lacey

"An emotional rollercoaster, with sexy highs and what-will-happen-next lows. The perfect mix of romance, friendship, self-discovery and mystery." ~ *USA Today* bestselling author Stefanie London on 36 Hour Date

ALSO BY KELLY SISKIND

One Wild Wish Series:

He's Going Down

Off-Limits Crush

36 Hour Date

Over the Top Series:

The Snowflake Effect

One Degree of Perfect

Slammed into Focus

Showmen Series:

New Orleans Rush

Don't Go Stealing My Heart

The Beat Match

The Knockout Rule

The Bower Boys series:

Fall in love with the Bower brothers! A decade after being forced into Witness Protection, they're finally allowed to return home and fight for the women they lost.

Visit Kelly's website and join her newsletter for great giveaways and never miss an update!

www.kellysiskind.com

CHAPTER 1

Nine Years Ago
Aka Ground Zero for Gwen's Worst Terrible Fuck-up

Gwen

Dictators and loan sharks needed to rethink their torture methods. Sure, waterboarding and sleep deprivation could break a man. Pulling out fingernails and smashing kneecaps were reliable interrogation techniques. But if you really wanted to make someone suffer, to reach into their chests and yank out their proverbial hearts, simply force them to scroll through Facebook.

All seemed innocent at first. I sat on my too-hard chair and stared at my laptop, ignoring the Hello Kitty stickers affixed by the previous owner. The usual images floated by:

Fake smile.

Fake smile.

Kissy face.

Cat playing piano.

Drunk shirtless dude.

My attention darted between my laptop's flipping snapshots and my silent Blackberry, a cup of Jägermeister poised at my lips. Jägermeister was the butthole of birthday drinks. It tasted like cough syrup and bad decisions. It was a reminder of the bile-marinated blackout that would forever remain unspoken. An event that would *not* be repeated tonight.

Yet here I was, drinking Jäger, because underage beggars couldn't be choosers, especially at 10 p.m. on my nineteenth birthday, while alone in my apartment, wondering why my best friend hadn't texted me. The fact that we hadn't spoken in over a year should have been a clue.

I sipped the Jäger and grimaced.

Fake smile.

Faker smile.

Pouty face.

Cutest baby koala on the planet.

Drunk frat boy…in a diaper.

And how did Facebook know which bra I was wearing? I peeked into the front of my gray V-neck and back at the sidebar advertisement. That was seriously creepy. And depressing. The black lace looked miles better on the model than on my less-endowed 34Bs, but the sight had me imagining my breasts and my former best friend's large hands, our naked bodies, and a whole lot of heat.

A needy moan slipped past my lips.

Since the man in question had forgotten my birthday and had probably blocked my number, that particular scenario was as likely as me wearing pink nail polish. Not that I deserved a guy like August Cruz.

I poured another shot into my Badass Bitch mug and did the thing I pretended I wasn't going to do: I clicked on August's timeline.

A new profile photo filled my computer screen, and I bit my lip. The most pathetic sigh deflated my posture. His wavy dark hair was shorter these days, clipped at the sides and messily styled. His glasses were different—thicker frames than he used to wear, obscuring the gold flecks in his hazel eyes. He seemed to have bulked up, too. Unless his Lawn Enforcement Officer T-shirt had shrunk.

His clothing choice exacerbated my tipsy melancholy.

Had he worn that shirt because I'd given it to him? Did it remind him of me nipping at his heels and tossing clippings at his face as he'd cut our neighborhood lawns? Odds are it was nothing more than a comfortable relic—a T-shirt that would wind up in the trash one day, forgotten and cast away. Like me. Unless he'd consciously chosen to post the image, hoping I'd see it.

My next sigh was more heartsick than wistful.

I'd been down this unrequited-love road before. I'd walked it so often a permanent path had been forged behind my stinging eyes. I missed how August's rumbling laugh would infect me with giggles. I missed the way he'd dribble a soccer ball around me in an athletic blur. How he'd sit behind me, arms and legs around my torso, teaching me to play guitar.

I missed the only person who could soothe me when my mother's anger had burned through my lonely house.

These thoughts weren't new, but his profile photo and that T-shirt jostled them, a violent shove that shook my foundation. A strange awareness overtook me. He *must* have chosen that image on purpose, knowing I'd see it and think of us. He *must* have launched that sign through cyberspace so I'd catch it. It seemed obvious now—*Jägermeister obvious*, but whatever: August must miss me as much as I missed him.

I had to reach out and tell him I understood him and his subliminal message, the way only I could. Considering his stupid girlfriend, Kayla Morgan, was evil incarnate and the reason everything with August had gone to shit, she probably treated him like crap. I should have singed her blond hair in chem lab when I'd had the chance. Instead I'd let her vicious words infect my mind, poisoning all thoughts of August.

We'd been friends back then, Kayla and me. At least I thought we'd been. *You drag him down,* she'd told me. *You're too needy. He pities you.*

Her words had hit their mark, feeding my insecurity. Fear of being a charity case had caused me to curl in on myself. Since I didn't do things half-assed, I shoved August away with the quietest silent treatment known to man...and Kayla, my supposed friend, gave him all the noise I'd sucked from his world.

She was still on his profile page. Still his girlfriend. I snarled at her picture filling my computer screen and grabbed my phone before my Jäger courage wore off.

Heart pounding in my throat, I pulled up August's name and rushed off a text. My fingers trembled as I typed, **I'm sorry.**

Who is this?

His quick reply almost had me launching my cell. My pulse went haywire, my hands too shaky to reply. But this was good. This was *right*. Of course he replied promptly. He wore the T-shirt! Fate was finally on our side.

Although he'd only been ten minutes away the past year, studying at SFSU while I killed myself cracking the books at San Francisco's City College, he'd felt so far. Not tonight. Not now.

I took a breath, then two more. I blinked away my Jäger fog and steadied my hands. **Hardy har har**, I wrote.

No. Seriously, August replied just as quickly. **The only Gwen I know hasn't spoken to me in a year and a half.**

His words were a knife in my chest, and the same wave of remorse I'd battled since I'd cut August from my life crashed over me. This wasn't the time to cower, though, the way I had the past year. This was the time to take charge of my life, beginning with an apology.

My thumbs went to work. **I'm sorry I was a bitch our last year of high school.**

Which time?

That knife twisted deeper.

Every time. All the time.

God, I wished high school had been the raging party promised in classic eighties movies. Instead it had consisted of me sinking into a jealous despair as I'd battled my mother's dictatorship and had struggled to get into college. I'd worked two jobs. Student loan applications had dogged me. All the while, my neighbor and best friend had coasted through life, then and now.

August's mother loved him. He had a father he actually knew and siblings to bond with, including an identical twin who had his back. Grades came easy to him. His soccer scholarship meant paying for college wasn't a stress. He played a mean guitar and had a crowd of hangers-on—friends who fed on his cool factor like pilot fish catching scraps from a powerful shark.

August had always had everything. I'd had nothing in high school but him.

Now I didn't even have that.

You ignored me, he shot back. *Stopped returning my calls and texts.*

Infection set into my festering wound.

I know. I'm the worst person.

Not good enough. You don't get off with a weak apology. What you did fucking hurt.

A heart transplant would be needed now. Or a heart amputation. Was that even a thing? Could a person live without her heart? Remorse fisted my rotting organ.

I knew I'd hurt August—I'd destroyed myself in the process —but hearing it firsthand had the burn in my eyes turning liquid.

He deserved some answers. *I was jealous. Your life kept getting better, and mine got harder. I felt like I was slipping into your shadow. I was resentful.*

What kind of bullshit is that? I never treated you as less. You were the most important person in my life, and you walked away like I meant nothing.

A tear leaked out, but I dashed it away. I wasn't a crier. I never let my emotions overrun me. Unless August was involved. He was also right: my actions may have made sense back then, but they had been a load of bullshit. The notion of dragging him down with my depressing life and crappy situation had seemed worse than shutting him out. It had been the wrong choice.

But it wasn't why I'd kept those invisible bricks stacked between us.

My fingers moved before I could stop them, before I could take a breath and collect myself and decide on the smart thing to say.

It was also because you started dating Kayla.

I stared at my sent message and smacked my forehead with the heel of my hand. *What the hell is wrong with me?* There was no ctrl-alt-deleting that horrifying confession. My stomach twisted, courtesy of the Jäger and my stupid fingers.

Kayla Morgan was still his girlfriend. Facebook reminded me of that painful fact daily. And I just kind of admitted I'd had the hots for him.

August didn't post much, but Kayla loved tagging him at every opportunity: selfies with her arm around his waist, candids of him studying or sleeping, captioned with things like: *I tuckered him out.* I would then "caption" my rude gestures with colorful expletives, all shouted at the screen. (Proof of Facebook's torture potential.) My roommate, Clean Your Damn Area Claire, would make a throaty sound and roll her eyes, then tell me to *clean my damn area.*

I stared at my silent phone, bouncing my heel, chewing my lip, wishing I could reverse time and suck that message back into my traitorous fingers.

His eventual reply didn't help: **What does Kayla have to do with this?**

Now he wanted me to bleed for him, eviscerate the guts of my hidden affections. All I managed was a partial truth.

I was jealous of her too. Because of her, we spent less time together. It wasn't rational. I'm sorry and I miss you.

I should have been more honest, admitted the depths of my feelings for him back then. My feelings for him now. Regret knotted my noodley insides as I waited for his reply. I contemplated moving to Mars or the jungles of Africa, a place where Facebook and stupid crushes wouldn't derail my life. My phone vibrated with August's reply.

You should never have dated Jared. Things would be very different now.

Holy hell.

Did that mean he'd wanted me in high school, too? Had we both read each other wrong? Jared and his leather jacket had been a distraction and nothing else, even though he'd barely kept me from fantasizing about August. The effort had been so dismal I'd broken up with Jared during prom.

Could I have spent that time kissing August's perfect lips instead of inhaling Jared's Axe Body Spray?

I typed a frantic reply, then deleted each letter. This was big. Huge. Like "winning all the blue jelly beans in a blue jelly bean counting competition" huge.

I'd been in Intro to Psychology with August's twin brother, Finch, all semester, staring at him with unhealthy longing. Aside from sharing August's dark hair, ridiculous bone structure, and gold-flecked hazel eyes, my belly had never flipped around him. The hairs on my neck had never shivered. That hadn't stopped me from ogling Finch, pretending and wishing he were August —the only man I'd ever truly *wanted*.

Up until one minute ago, I was sure my August ship had sailed, any chance with him destroyed by my childish behavior, but he was staring at his phone now, somewhere in San Francisco, not far from me, waiting on my reply.

This was do or die. This was the shot I never took.

This was my perfect birthday wish come true.

Holding my breath, I wrote out a careful reply, ensuring no typos waylaid my intentions. Brutal honesty was what this called for. Jäger honesty.

I dated Jared because you hooked up with Kayla. I had feelings for you back then and couldn't be around you guys.

I reread my reply. It didn't say how I *still* had feelings for him. Massive, crushing feelings. But it was more than I'd ever admitted. I swallowed hard and sent my heart through cyberspace.

One second passed. Two lumbered by. Five, ten, *fifteen* seconds dragged.

Heart pummeling my chest, I shot to my feet and paced. My eyes darted wildly, unable to focus on the guitar neck protruding from under my bed or my overflowing laundry basket or my King Kong Green Day poster. I felt like a science experiment, all vibrating molecules and firing synapses, a cataclysmic event away from full meltdown.

No message answered me. Not a one. The air in my lungs turned to glue. If I had a paper bag, I'd breathe into it.

Unsure what to do, I plunked down on my chair and scrolled through Facebook, a futile attempt to distract myself. It was either that or fill my bathtub with Jäger and go for a swim. The flipping images blurred, one annoying smiling face after another, until one particular face had my mouse stilling and my eyes bugging.

Kayla. Kayla tagging August in one of her flirty posts.

I wanted to slap my laptop shut and forget I'd ever sent that text or opened this Pandora's Box of awful, but I couldn't stop from leaning closer and studying the image. The glue in my lungs hardened into cement. I blinked several times, but Kayla still filled the screen. Her hand faced me, a band on her wedding finger.

The comment above read: *Guess who got a promise ring?*

———

Dazed and confused (not in the good way), I pushed into The Barking Owl. The student bar was jam-packed, sweaty bodies abundant, heat and pop tunes stuffing the pulsating room. An elbow jabbed me. Someone used my shoulders to keep from falling. Even in the oppressive space, I was relieved to be away from my computer and treasonous phone.

The second Kayla's post had sunk in, I'd hidden my Blackberry. There'd been no need to read whatever reply August would send. The sweet guy he was, he'd for sure let me down gently, and I'd marinate in my embarrassment, followed by a therapy session with my pals Ben & Jerry.

Better to cry on Jack Daniels' shoulder than poor Ben's.

"Gwen!" A waving hand caught my eye. When I noticed the hand was attached to Finch, I cursed the birthday gods for making this the suckiest birthday in the history of sucky birthdays.

My mother's curt phone call this morning had been as warm as a polar bear's ass. I used to get a yearly birthday card from my aunt, but those had vanished when I'd turned twelve. My grandparents pretended I didn't exist, and I'd just confessed my love to a boy who'd already given his girlfriend *a promise ring*. A freaking promise ring. Like it was 1950.

Now I had to spend the night looking at his identical twin.

A Jäger-bath and Ben & Jerry's chaser sounded better and better, but that involved actual effort.

Grumbling, I maneuvered toward Finch. Not an easy feat. A foot from my goal, some oaf in a Warriors jersey stumbled and dumped half his beer over my boobs.

"What the hell?" I attempted to shove him off, but the giant barely budged.

"Sorry about your shirt." His sleazy smirk suggested he wasn't particularly sorry.

I pinched the front of my sodden V-neck, the thin fabric

fighting me as I peeled it off my chest. I could now add wet T-shirt contestant to this year's birthday of awesome. "Next time you wanna waste your beer, pour it over your head."

His lewd smirk graduated to vulgar. "It's not a waste if I get to suck it off you."

College students sure were classy.

Rolling my eyes, I flipped him the bird and squeezed toward Finch's spot at the bar. Considering most students crammed into the overheated room were underage, the San Francisco fake ID racket must have been thriving. Tonight mine was a godsend.

Finch squeezed my hip and raised his voice over the music. "Glad you made it."

I peered at him, unsure why he seemed to be on his own. "Did we have plans?"

"You didn't get my text?"

If it had been sent after I'd humiliated myself with his brother, his message would be buried with that damning evidence. "I haven't checked my phone in a bit."

"Then I guess this is fate, and I get to buy you a birthday drink."

I tried to smile at his sweet effort. When we were kids, he'd raised hell with August and me, but as we'd gotten older, August would often tell him to get lost. Finch would sulk, but I'd been too focused on his brother to insist he tag along. Alone time with August had been a valuable commodity.

The past year and a half, though, after having cut August from my life, Finch had been more present. The two of us were at the same school now. He'd make an extra effort to check in on me, inviting me to lunch, the library. He and August seemed to have drifted since high school, but my childish silent treatment meant I couldn't ask August why, and there was an unspoken rule between Finch and me: August was a classified subject. Any mention of him or his name would disqualify our friendship.

A friendship I'd begun to count on. Finch even remembered my birthday.

"What can I get you?" he asked.

"Shot of Jäger."

He cringed. "Who the hell drinks Jäger?"

"I do, apparently." Because Jäger was the butthole of birthday drinks, and today was a butthole of a birthday. "I should order a double."

His gaze dropped briefly to my wet T-shirt, to the now-visible black bra that had looked miles better on the Facebook model. He leaned closer. "Are you drunk, Gwen Hamilton?"

I met him the rest of the way, our noses an inch apart. "Not wasted enough."

The people and music and laughter swirled around us, so loud and distracting that for a second I was sure it was August's Roman nose nearly touching mine, his lips within biting distance. His scruffy jaw. His firm chest. But there was no scar on Finch's chin. August's scar had been acquired the night we'd snuck into the abandoned Wheeler home. Finch didn't have an untamable lick of hair that always shot heavenward or callused fingers from endless guitar sessions. He hadn't written songs for me while lying in the grass and staring at the sky.

But Finch was good for a laugh.

"You're lucky you found me." He pretended to tighten an invisible necktie. "We may have grown up neighbors, but I don't think you know I have a PhD in intoxication."

I rubbed my palms together in eager anticipation. "Do tell, Dr. Cruz."

"Well, if you're aiming for *sad* wasted, I'd suggest we start you off with tequila shots, followed by a keg of beer. If it's giddy wasted you're after, Long Island Iced Tea should do the trick."

"I was thinking more pissed-off wasted." Insane wasted. *Furious* wasted.

If I hadn't been so pathetically insecure during high school, I could be getting giddy wasted with August, instead of shooting the shit with his brother. The horrible choice to cut August off was a wake-up call if I'd ever heard one. Never again would I let a missed opportunity slip by. I wouldn't coast through life, cowering at challenges, afraid to rock the boat. I would scare myself. I would push my boundaries. I would make life my bitch.

Finch nodded sagely. "If pissed-off wasted is your mission, then stick with the nasty Jäger."

I almost did just that, but drinking more would dull this painful ache. I deserved to suffer every jab and twinge, each unforgiving pang. This was my fault. I should have admitted my feelings to August years ago.

Instead of walking the easy road of inebriation and oblivion, I ordered a Red Bull.

An insane amount of sugar-laced caffeine later, I stood in the crowded bar feeling more alone than when I'd been at home. The string of Red Bulls had done their job. I was painfully sober, and my revved brain kept reliving every different decision that could have resulted in a different outcome. Not this crappy outcome.

I was angry at myself. I was angry at August. And Finch was here for the entire show, doing his Finch thing, teasing my surly scowl and telling god-awful knock-knock jokes until I cracked a smile. Some song about booties blared. Two chicks acted out the lyrics, putting on a show for the bar. August barely glanced at them.

Dammit. Finch. *Finch, Finch, Finch.*

I kept doing that—thinking, wishing he was his brother.

Finch and his easy grin were facing me, like they had been all night. His chest rubbed my arm as he yelled in my ear about his summer backpacking plans, his voice battling against the loud tunes. I nodded automatically, barely hearing him.

Warriors jersey dude, who hadn't passed out yet, danced suggestively while ogling the bootie girls. The giant waste of space tripped into me again, sending my clutched Red Bull to the ground. Finch glared at him. Frustrated, I bent down to retrieve the fallen can being kicked to-and-fro like a pinball. Finch had the same instinct. At the same time.

Our heads smacked together.

"Fuck." I pressed my palm to my forehead.

"I'm not sure it'll help with the headache, but we could try."

We could…*what-the-what*?

Finch and I were crouched inches from a sticky floor covered in spilled beer and pretzel bits, a forest of legs surrounding our shoulders, and he was eyeing me like he wanted a closer inspection of my black bra.

What the hell?

I was strung out on Red Bull, my heart pounding a mile a minute, and my vision turned hazy. Blurred with sadness. I found myself craving more contact. Touch. Comfort in someone's arms. No matter how hard I looked at Finch, he didn't become August—the only person I wanted to fill that role. Did it matter?

Finch was nice, fun. He was the only one with me on my birthday, and he wasn't hurting in the handsome department, clearly. If August didn't want me, why not have fun with his twin?

Because August might find out and be upset, my unhelpful conscience whispered.

If August had really pined for me in high school, the way he'd sort of admitted, he'd have confided in Finch back then, when they'd been close. He might be pissed if Finch and I hooked up. But August had a girlfriend *with a promise ring*. A life that didn't involve me.

My decisions weren't his concern.

Tired of my lame wallowing, I grinned at Finch, returning his flirtations. I turned my brain to silent as we walked to my apartment. I moved on autopilot as I fitted my key into the door and dragged Finch inside. I closed my eyes when our shirts hit the floor, his bare chest pressed to mine.

His lips searched for purchase. "So long," he murmured. "I've wanted you so long."

My belly cramped at those needy words. Passionate words. Words I longed to whisper to August. *I've wanted you so long.* He wasn't here, though, and I was lonely. So, so lonely. Finch was undressing me, showering me with kisses. I tried pretending it was another man's mouth on my skin. *August. My August.* If I couldn't have the man I wanted on my birthday, I would steal a moment of abandon from his twin. Pretend. Dream. Live the lie.

It was a wasted effort.

The sex was mechanical, motions gone through, our bodies fitting together, my mind somewhere else. My faked orgasm sped the whole affair along. Finch, however, whispered endearments, hips relentless in pursuit of his pleasure. I was glad when it was over. And sad. Guilt returned as Finch kissed me gently and went to deal with the condom.

Did he have a thing for me? Had he been crushing on me the whole time I'd been crushing on his brother? Did August know? It was likely why Finch had been so attentive this year, and here I was, only wanting a mindless night. God, what a mess.

Letting him down after this would be another painful blow.

A knock at the door cut through my worry, and I groaned. Last thing I wanted was a witness to this sham, but Clean Your Damn Area Claire must have forgotten her key again. That emo girl would lose her black fingernails if they weren't attached.

Tossing on an oversized tee, I stood and breathed through the fog of bad decisions this night had become. I couldn't even blame the Jäger.

Unable to swallow past the lump in my throat, I hurried to the door and yanked it open.

I nearly passed out.

August Cruz was in my doorway, at my apartment, a crazed look in his stunning hazel eyes. "Happy birthday," he said, a slight pant to his words, as though he'd run here.

Then he kissed me. Callused fingers gripping my jaw, he

crushed his lips to mine, devouring me like I was air in an airless world. This wasn't mechanical. This wasn't pretend. This was the love of my life twirling his tongue around mine sensually, moving his lips and body the same way he played guitar: with animal abandon.

It was too good. He was too good. And I let it all go on too long. I somehow managed to push him away. "You gave her a promise ring," was the first thing I said.

Not, *I slept with your brother.* Not, *your brother is in the next room.*

My brain cells had vacated the building.

He winced. "You saw that post?" Before I could answer, he breathed harder, talking over himself. "I'd bought that ring for *your* birthday, and she assumed it was for her."

He tugged at the back of his dark hair. "It's just, I've been thinking about you nonstop lately. Not sure why now—maybe it was your birthday coming up or the school year ending—but I knew I needed to set things right with you. I'd decided to end things with Kayla tonight. I got your address from your mother and planned to face you, then you sent me that text. And it was like…the whole thing kind of floored me."

Creases sank into his furrowed brow. "I'm sorry I lashed out at first. I wasn't expecting for all that shit to resurface. But I think it's good, you know? That we cleared the air. Now we can finally do this, be together. Because this thing with us?" He prowled closer and lifted the ring in question. "It's always been you, Gwen. No one holds a candle to you."

That's when Finch walked into the living area, nothing on but his boxers.

That's when I realized the extent of my Worst Terrible Fuck-up.

CHAPTER 2

Present Day, 12 p.m.

I couldn't remember names to save my life. I sucked at *Jeopardy* and Trivial Pursuit, and every video game ever created, but I could play guitar in my sleep, and if there was an Olympic procrastination event, I'd take gold.

Gear slung over my shoulder, I joined the melee of sweaty men gathered around the soccer field. Being a full-time musician —touring, writing, recording—left me little time for my old obsession, but I missed soccer. The quick footwork. Working with a team. Plus finding a pick-up game meant I could put off the real reason I'd returned to San Francisco.

Handshakes were passed around for a game well played. Others, like me, readied to hit the field next. The grins and laughs brought me back to my high school days playing in the

California Regional League. It also forced a montage of a giggling Gwen front and center.

Her shoving grass down my shirt as I dribbled around her.

Me tickling her while she tried to steal the ball.

I ground my teeth, something I'd been doing too much of since returning here. Since avoiding Gwen, specifically. Considering she was the reason I'd flown home, I needed to get over myself, or I'd end up with a hefty dental bill.

I tossed my gym bag next to the clothes piled near the field. A game was what I needed. Sixty minutes to focus on nothing but marking an attacker, stripping the ball from him, and executing clean passes. Sixty minutes to forget why I'd cut my European tour short, and to pretend tomorrow's April 12th date didn't still affect me.

My molars worked harder, as though chewing that memory into sludge. I even spat out a wad of saliva, but my tongue still tasted bitter—bitterness laced with guilt, the latter emotion new when it came to Gwen. But when she learned what I'd done, she'd have more right to punch me than the retaliation I'd unleashed on Finch nine years ago. Not that I regretted the sting of my fist connecting with his nose.

Jaw locked, I yanked my cleats from my bag. I nearly snapped the laces tying them up. *I'll call her after the game*, I told myself. *Meet her face-to-face and say what I came to say, then get out of town.*

Unless this was like the April my second album had been due to the record label. That procrastination-athon had involved walking the Paris streets and a ridiculously clean apartment, forcing me to mainline coffee as I busted out the album in five endless days.

If I didn't get my head together, I'd have to ransack my hotel room like a bona-fide rock star, then spend my avoidance time tidying up.

Tired of my looping frustrations, I swept aside thoughts of Gwen and tried to enjoy the sun on my back. It was a welcome change to Germany's recent drizzly spell. The fresh air beat the smoke-filled clubs I'd played the past year, the stage spotlight nowhere near as nice as the California sun.

Sunshine. Soccer. No insane tour schedule. Maybe being home wasn't so bad.

"August, man…where'd *you* come from?"

I spun around and smiled in earnest. "Owen. Shit. How long's it been?"

The big guy shook his head, looking equally as surprised to see me. "Too long. Way too long. Last I heard, you and your guitar were winning over Europe."

I ran my left thumb over my callused fingers. "Not sure about the winning part, but it pays the bills."

"Modesty doesn't suit you. I've seen YouTube videos. There were screaming girls."

I shrugged off the comment, never comfortable with praise. I may not have hit it big in the U.S., but my European audience had grown steadily, my singer-songwriter style hitting the mark with them. Downloads had recently shot through the roof, my fan base building, tours getting longer. And lonelier. Not that I could complain. Most musicians would trade their spleens to make a living doing what they loved.

"What about you?" I asked, happy to deflect. Last thing I needed was him asking why I was in town. "Thought you were living in D.C."

I glanced at the tattooed guy beside him and offered a nod.

Owen dragged a hand through his sandy hair, mopping up sweat along the way. "I was, but it seems like a lifetime ago. Been living here over a year now. Traded in my finance job for a woodworking business."

"Dude, are you trying to be an asshole?" The tattooed guy drew my attention, his grin a contrast to his snarky comment.

I took in his rough exterior, catching a glimpse of familiarity under his dark scruff and shaggy hair. I squinted and leaned closer and…no fucking way. "Jimmy?"

He motioned to his yellow jersey. "Is the color throwing you off?"

I snorted. It may have been twelve years, and we may have worn red when the three of us had played soccer together, but the change in jersey wasn't what had thrown me off. Teenage Jimmy had been a clean-cut pretty boy, not a tatted up, scruffy man. "You did something different with your hair, I think."

He barked out a laugh. "Nailed it. My girlfriend likes applying conditioning treatments."

We shook hands and pounded backs while I digested this biker version of Jimmy Giannopoulos. It wouldn't have been such a shock if I'd kept in touch with the guys, but who had the time? Owen and Jimmy were a couple years older than me, had gone to different high schools, but we'd played in the regional league together. We'd been close. Staying connected into adulthood was still tough.

The only social media I suffered through was to promote my music, never wasting hours scrolling through Facebook or Snapchat or Twitter. The meager news I'd hear about old friends came through accidental run-ins, the odd person attending my shows.

Owen massaged his shoulder. "If you're in town awhile, we should go for a beer."

This visit would be as short as possible, unless I decided to learn how to knit or speak Japanese before facing Gwen. "I'd love to catch up, but I have some things to take care of, then it's back on the road."

At least I sounded confident about getting shit done.

Arriving here around the anniversary of Gwen's epic betrayal wasn't helping matters. The event may have been part of the reason I'd quit school and had become a musician, something I could thank her and Finch for, but the betrayal had festered a long time. I'd managed to block Gwen from my life the past nine years, but missing her mother's recent funeral had felt wrong. I'd also found myself remembering our good times lately, more than rehashing that one awful night. Barely being civil with my brother was a whole other wreck, everything easier to ignore when across the globe.

The sooner I saw Gwen, the sooner I could put her—and all of it—behind me.

Instead I was winning my procrastination-athon.

"If you change your mind," Owen said, "let me know. This guy"—he elbowed Jimmy—"lives in Napa now, but he's around plenty. We can coordinate soccer next time. Sign up for the same pick-up game."

"You running the winery now?" I asked Jimmy.

He nodded. "My brother and I took it over. We're doing some rebranding, and I'm organizing Napa festivals on the side. Actually…" He bobbed his head as though having an internal conversation. "Any chance you'd play at a function? It would be great exposure for the festivals."

Committing to anything in San Francisco made me itch, but I offered a vague, "Sure, we'll work on it."

We all traded numbers as Owen's brother, Emmett, joined us with his boyfriend—a pompadour-styled guy with more ink than Jimmy. A few short minutes of reminiscing settled me, but it was a reminder my life now was full of transient people, acquaintances. Not friends who remembered how I drank myself sick on tequila and had puked on Samantha Walsh. No one in Europe had a clue I'd streaked through Delores Park. These guys did. Built-in history. Easy banter.

Owen smiled at someone over my shoulder, then headed toward his gear. I turned to check out the recipient of that affectionate look, and my internal organs slammed on their brakes.

Gwen.

The two girls beside her were watching the guys leave, but Gwen's eyes were locked on me, and my pulse rocketed, like I'd already played my soccer game, had run a marathon, had summited Everest, my oxygen thinning at a rapid rate. I wanted to drop to my knees and apologize for what I'd done. I also wanted to tell her *her* actions had devastated *me*, but if she'd listened to my first angst-ridden album, she'd be well acquainted with my resentment.

That didn't keep me from soaking her in.

Even from my distance, I could tell her arms were defined in her slim tank top, suggesting she worked out a lot. She'd always been athletic, but this was a body honed through years of exercise, work. Her hair skimmed her shoulders, shorter than I'd ever seen it, her face a bit more angular. She still exuded casual style. Effortless. Unpretentious. Drop-dead beautiful.

Swallowing became an effort.

As did hiding the desire one look from her inspired. It echoed through me, the vibrations like reverb blasting from my guitar. It wasn't cool. I replayed how catching my brother in his boxers had sickened me, that smug grin on his face. How often I'd pictured him and Gwen in bed together, unable to stop. My lips compressed and my nostrils flared.

That was better. That was how I was supposed to feel.

Angry. Resentful.

Gwen sat on the bleachers, gaze locked on me, piles of unaired dirty laundry between us. If I had to write a song for the haunted anguish in her eyes, I'd title it: "Shame's Window."

———

Gwen

My two best friends were trying to talk to me—Ainsley snapping her fingers in front of my face and checking for vitals, while Rachel asked what was wrong. I couldn't focus on anything but the man talking to Owen and Jimmy.

And I did mean *man*.

August hadn't noticed me yet, thank God, the small mercy allowing me to study him. Unlike the boy I'd grown up with, this August had shoulders a swimmer would covet and a jaw that could cut diamonds. The cords on his neck stood out. His thighs and calves belonged on a Greek statue. Glasses no longer shielded his hazel eyes, but I wasn't close enough to test if the gold flecks in those stunners still reduced me to a soppy mess.

That didn't keep my body temperature from spiking to lava levels. Even more alarming was that he seemed to know Owen and Jimmy, the three men slapping backs and talking like old friends.

Considering Rachel and Ainsley were the better halves of those two hunks, this could be world-ending bad.

Rachel leaned forward and stared at my catatonic face. "Do we need to call a doctor?"

"It's him," was all I managed.

Ainsley, the always stylish fashionista, crossed her legs and smoothed her floral dress. "Him who?"

"August," I said.

The sound of my friends sucking in shocked breaths should have been amusing, but amusement was no longer in my emotion arsenal. They knew August had been my first love, but the details of why we'd never hooked up had remained in my high-security vault. A *Mission Impossible*, booby-trapped vault.

I should come clean and finally confess what I'd done, explain how I'd lost August for good, ruining his relationship with his brother in the process, but the words blockaded my throat.

The girls were the closest thing I had to family, to sisters. They knew how estranged I'd been from my mother before cancer took her last month. They'd listened to me speculate endlessly about who my father might be, while cursing my mother for keeping the information secret. They were the most important people in my life. The idea of them learning my Worst Terrible Fuck-up gutted me.

Ainsley ogled the love of my life. "Was he that hot when you knew him?"

"He's filled out," I murmured.

August's back was to me now—a well-built, muscular back—but he glanced over his shoulder as though sensing me. His eyes widened in recognition, and that lava in my veins steamed and bubbled. When a shadow eclipsed his features and his body stiffened, that molten liquid hardened into ice.

"I need to go." Barely glancing at the girls, I rushed away from the soccer field, worried I'd puke on the grass or start bawling. I never cried. Ever. Not even at my mother's funeral. And I hadn't thrown up since my first CrossFit workout and the one hundred pull-ups that had bested me.

Yet, here I was, ready to puke or bawl.

Nine years should be long enough to get over my Worst Terrible Fuck-up (aka my WTF night, an appropriate acronym), but some guilt-ridden disasters were eternal.

Hence my nausea. And my stinging eyes.

I should have contacted August after what I'd done, offered some sort of explanation. I'd dialed his number so often the digits had practically been imprinted on my fingers. I'd even practiced what I'd say, every night, every morning, repeating my apology on a loop: *I slept with your brother because I loved you and the idea of never having you had destroyed me.* But shame had kept the words inside. Disgust with myself. Then too much time had passed.

Nine years, to be precise.

Nine years of remorseful silence.

Now he was in town.

August was supposed to be on tour, *not* that I'd memorized his tour schedule. I didn't know every word to every one of his songs, either. I didn't own two T-shirts with his face plastered on them or have a poster of him pasted inside my closet door like a lovesick teenager. Nope.

I barely knew August Cruz existed.

Chewing my cheek raw, I drove to my mother's as I'd planned. Seeing August wouldn't derail my day, my week, my life. Definitely not. Nothing had changed, including how I'd torn out his heart. If the songs on his first album were any indication, he probably owned a Gwen voodoo doll he disemboweled daily. The titles sure were cheery:

"The Destroyer."

"Love is Hate."

"Dressed in Lies."

"I Don't Need You."

"Torching History."

My personal favorite: "Girl with the Black Heart."

Those stabby lyrics had punctured my heart on repeat. They affected me to this day. God, I was pathetic, unable to let that idiotic night go.

I parked and marched toward my mother's home, but couldn't keep from glancing at the neighbor's bungalow. That particular habit was as grating as my workout playlist filled with August's songs. His family no longer lived there, but I always paused next to the lemon-yellow house. The current owners didn't tend their lawn, dandelions ruling most of the grass. August wasn't there to tame it. To tame me. To sneak into my room and sing me to sleep.

If I didn't stop obsessing, I'd have to lobotomize myself.

I forced myself inside and exhaled. Silence. Blessed, blessed, silence. It enveloped me, calmed the uglies nicking at my dark places. A normal woman would be bereft in here, sad to see the quilt draped over the reclining chair that hadn't reclined in months, the unused cherry dining table, the lack of pictures on the taupe walls. But my tear ducts were as empty as the vacant bungalow.

And empty was A-okay.

I mentally stuffed thoughts of August into a dynamite stick, blew it to smithereens, then stomped up my mother's stairs.

Boxes lined the hallway, most rooms bare but for the larger items to be appraised. All was neatly sorted, tagged, stacked. Forty-five years of Mary Hamilton eating Raisin Bran, working as a receptionist, watching *Murder She Wrote* reruns, while either ignoring me or criticizing my clothes or grades or music, all tucked inside brown cardboard.

Life reduced to bundled boxes.

It was a reminder living was more important than collecting. The organization of it had fed my recent restlessness.

Her bedroom was a different story.

Where the office, bathroom, and guest room were stripped bare and catalogued, these beige walls barely contained a tsunami of disorder. I'd upturned every dresser drawer, had flipped her mattress. I'd searched her books for hidden compartments, had even cut away sections of her taupe rug, sure she'd hidden some piece of her past before she'd died.

A memento. A diary. Any clue to who my father was.

No such luck.

But if I lost my adoption agency gig, I could photograph the wreckage and place a Craigslist ad: Goon for Hire.

My exhaustive search had been fruitless. I'd all but given up. Today was supposed to be about stemming this damage, packing it away, cleaning up. But I'd promised myself I'd find my father this year. Before my birthday.

Before tomorrow.

I stared blankly ahead until a vague pounding registered. The sound grew in decibel and frequency. I was so zoned out, it took a stupid amount of time to realize someone was at my front door. I dodged the upstairs boxes, side-to-side, like I was racing through an obstacle course, hurried down the stairs, and yanked open the door.

"There's something going on with you, and I'm not leaving until you tell me what." Rachel, with her freckled skin, big brown eyes, and J.Crew ensemble, attempted severity by crossing her arms. Bambi would have better luck moonlighting as Godzilla.

I matched her wide stance. "Look at you, being all bossy."

"I'm going for no-nonsense."

"Try harder next time."

Her attention dragged to the house next door. She studied it as though it might instantaneously combust. Exactly how I felt. I wasn't sure if Rachel's bad cop routine was hurting or helping. "Come on in, Sherlock."

She followed me into the living room and surveyed the organized mess. "Wow. Looks like you're almost done."

"Just my mother's room left." Which I wasn't about to show her. "I'd offer you a seat, but it might get dicey." We eyed the boxes barricading the couch and dining chairs.

She dropped her purse, plopped herself on the hardwood floor, and patted the space in front of her. "This will do fine."

I remained standing. "What if I'm not ready to open the vault?"

She straightened her posture. "Then I'll chain myself to the sofa and stage a sit-in until you crack."

"You'll miss Jimmy."

"He'll visit."

"I won't provide wine."

"I'm due for a detox."

I glared at her, and she smiled back. The woman was battle ready.

Normally I hated to lose, even in a battle of wills. With no siblings growing up, a "no electronics in your room" rule, an early curfew, and a mother who had vacillated between depressed and antagonistic, I'd kept busy by competing against myself.

I'd play solitaire on my bedroom floor, over and over, refusing to sleep until I'd win a round. When August would smoke me in backgammon, I'd throw a temper tantrum and force him into another game. I'd run sprints at ungodly morning hours, determined to make my high school track team and win our meets. Blisters had been my badge of honor.

These days I was relentless in CrossFit, bettering my endurance, my strength, my speed, all to beat myself.

I could shore up my defenses now, win this battle of stubbornness against Rachel, and keep the details of my WTF in my secured vault, but the shock of seeing August this morning had weakened my stronghold. Maybe caving to Rachel would help me rebuild it.

"Thing is," I said, settling in cross-legged, facing her, "I kind of fucked up in college."

She gathered my hands in hers. "Tell Auntie Rachel everything."

Her already large eyes widened as I admitted my shame: pushing August away our last year of high school, the birthday texts, telling him I'd been jealous of him and his girlfriend, the "promise ring" misunderstanding, sleeping with his brother. Him walking in afterward.

"You should have seen his face," I went on, my voice thinning under the weight of that awful memory. "He looked at me like I'd murdered his family. I mean, disgust doesn't even begin to cover it. Then August and Finch got into it, shoving and yelling. Saying crazy stuff about me, like August and Finch had had an agreement about me or something. I don't know. It all happened so fast and I was in shock. But the part where August broke Finch's nose with a right hook and told me I was dead to him is crystal clear."

The confession tasted as sour as it sounded, and that burning returned to my eyes. I bit my tongue to steady my emotions.

Rachel didn't release my trembling hands. She squeezed them tighter. "Did you talk with him after that night? Apologize and explain things?"

I shook my head. More shame swamped me.

"No wonder you're upset. First your mother, then seeing him —any rational person would run for cover."

"This has nothing to do with my mother," I said quickly. "I told you, I'm not sad about her." This worsening emptiness couldn't be because of Mary Hamilton. You couldn't mourn someone you didn't love, or even like.

Rachel pursed her lips as though she didn't believe me. An understandable reaction. When she'd lost her father years back, the tragedy had gutted her. It still did. But he had never treated her like she was a mosquito he couldn't shake. An irritation. A problem to squash.

My mother couldn't glance at me without curling her lip. She'd refused to tell me who my father was. She'd hated the man, that much had been clear, and I'd obviously been a reminder of him. She'd been estranged from her parents, too, robbing me of grandparents—although those two subscribed to a special brand of wacky. She hadn't even spoken to her sister in over a decade. Mary Hamilton wasn't built to foster relationships.

No. I hadn't mourned my mother's passing. Right or wrong, good or bad, relief had come with that eventuality. Except it meant I'd never discover my father's identity.

I'd also lose the challenge I'd set for myself last year.

Three hundred and sixty-four days ago, I'd sat in a bar with Ainsley and Rachel, and the three of us had agreed to make life-altering wishes. Resolutions to change our lives by our next shared birthday.

Meeting the girls the night we'd all turned twenty-one had been my saving grace, the three of us coincidentally wasted in the same bar seven years ago. After my WTF, April 12th had become a black hole of a day. Since meeting the girls, it had turned from an approaching death sentence to a celebration.

Every year we drank and laughed and had fun, but last year had been more meaningful, the wish to learn my father's identity a huge one for me. I was sure I'd make it happen.

Then my mother died.

"No," I said again, more vehemently, "I'm not sad she's gone. I'm pissed at her for screwing me up, but not sad."

"You're not screwed up. You're the strongest person I know." She released my hands and squeezed my bicep teasingly. "And the craziest, but in a good way."

"Jumping out of airplanes isn't crazy."

"It's certifiable. As is rock climbing without a rope. And bungee jumping. And surfing insane waves."

She had a point. But after my WTF night and hitting the Grand Canyon of rock bottoms, I'd vowed to stop living my life afraid. *Scare myself. Make life my bitch.* Those had become my mottos. Aside from being stupid good fun, adrenaline was the only outlet that drowned the unpleasant voices in my head. Which meant I should have marched over to August Cruz earlier and apologized. That would have shot my heart rate through the roof.

If I'd finally confessed the extent of my feelings toward him nine years ago, my heart would probably have burst through my chest.

Texting back then that I'd been jealous of Kayla hadn't been the same as saying *I loved you so much in high school it hurt to breathe.* I wasn't about to lay that crushing truth at his feet now, not when one look at him stirred those dormant feelings to life. He did, however, deserve a grovel fest complete with bended knee.

Yet I'd run away.

I picked at my stubby nails. "Maybe I should drive back. Drag August out of the game and beg his forgiveness."

"Might be awkward timing," she said drily.

"Is there good timing for this sort of thing?"

"I'd go for something less public."

I dropped my head forward. After dealing with my mother's illness and death, I figured I was due for some good karma. I'd considered dating again, hoped my luck would turn around and I'd meet a non-asshole. Instead, August Cruz had been thrust back into my life. The opposite of an asshole, but he'd never see me as anything but a traitor.

This wasn't how I'd expected my twenty-seventh year to end. Not by a landslide. Especially after how it had started. "Ainsley told me you guys fulfilled your birthday wishes this year," I said. "Which I'm thrilled about—you both seem so happy. But I was stupid enough to wish for the impossible."

"To meet your dad?" Compassion filled her voice.

I nodded, touched she knew me well enough to figure it out. We'd written our wishes down last year, hadn't shared them aloud. We'd needed accountability, assurance we'd work toward our goals. Then I'd tucked the folded papers in my purse to be opened at our next birthday, which was tomorrow.

"Not fulfilling mine's been eating at me," I said. "Worse with tomorrow's deadline—which I know is silly. There's no timeline on something like this. But I thought setting the date would make it happen, that I'd at least learn my father's name. So I think that's messing with my mind, and seeing August didn't help. He used to help with reconnaissance work, childish investigative stuff with the two of us sleuthing to find my dad. It all just kinda sucks."

She tucked my hair behind my ear. "It sucks big fat donkey cock."

I snorted at her uncharacteristic dirty humor. "Way to channel your inner Ainsley." A girl who got her rocks off embarrassing others with inappropriate jokes.

"Anything to make you smile." A job well done. Her tone sobered. "I'm glad you told me what happened with August. I get it if you want some alone time to wallow, but Jimmy and I are meeting Ainsley and Owen for early drinks tonight, before we head to different events we have. A little 'day before birthday' celebration. You should—"

Knocking cut her off, another intruder. So much for my blessed silence.

Groaning, I pushed to my feet and headed for the door. If someone was selling Girl Scout Cookies, I'd buy the whole lot and drown my stress in cookie goodness. But it wasn't a Girl Scout. It was a sweaty August.

CHAPTER 3

1 p.m.
35 Hours until Gwen's Birthday Wish Expires

August

I swallowed past the history gumming up my throat and offered a tentative smile. "Hey."

Fucking *hey*. Three letters. One syllable. Not exactly eloquent for a guy who poured his heart into verse. Nine years of deafening silence will do that to a man, a lifetime of my favorite memories torched by one disastrous night.

And all I had was *hey*.

Gwen's jaw unhinged, not a sound coming out. Mine almost dropped, too. It had been one thing watching her from afar on the field, but this? Her body was as strong and toned as I'd thought, lean muscles defining her arms. Her tank top accentuated her tight stomach, the curves of her breasts. I'd almost had my hands on those soft swells, my mouth, my tongue, my *teeth*.

Too bad she screwed my brother.

Except that fiasco wasn't why I'd bailed on my soccer game partway through, why I was standing on her mother's doorstep now, in workout shorts and a soccer jersey, sweat cooling into clammy patches on my skin.

What happened nine years ago was history. Painful history, but history nonetheless.

Curling my hands into fists, I wrenched my eyes from her body and focused on her face. Her hypnotizing eyes scattered my thoughts. "I'm sorry about your mother."

She blinked, as though rousing from a dream. "My mother?"

"I should have called. Come in for the funeral."

Before she could reply, the brunette from the bleachers poked her head through the door and offered her hand. "I'm Rachel, Gwen's friend. I think you know my boyfriend Jimmy."

Gwen had friends I no longer knew. She probably had a boyfriend, too. A life beyond the neighborhood we grew up in and years we'd shared. A sudden cramp seized my gut. Probably a stitch, after-effects of splitting on my soccer game without stretching, coupled with all things Gwen. The faster I got this over with, the faster I could breathe easier.

Unfortunately, I couldn't stop staring at Gwen's pink lips, how the lower one was slightly fuller, with that damn freckle on the left.

I shook Rachel's hand. "I'm August. Jimmy and I played soccer together as teens. It was nice catching up."

"Well…" Rachel glanced between Gwen's still-gaping mouth and my divided focus. "I need to get going, but—"

"No, you don't." Gwen clutched Rachel's elbow.

"Yes, I do."

"But we have that thing."

Rachel patted Gwen's shoulder. "Later. Our thing is later. Meet us for drinks." She kissed Gwen's cheek and nodded to me as she slipped past, leaving us to stew in our tension.

Gwen wrapped her arms around her middle.

I shifted on my feet, wishing I wasn't in sneakers and shorts. Nowhere to shove my restless hands. Hands that wanted to erase the deep furrow sinking between Gwen's green eyes. It had always been like this with Gwen, my need to comfort her an embedded impulse. I also wanted to rail at her, our history bubbling below my skin. "Sorry if I smell," I said, tamping both reflexes and grasping for conversation. "I was playing soccer."

She cleared her throat. "Considering I saw you there, and you're sweating on the front step now, I put two and two together."

"I see your sarcasm is alive and well." The edge to my tone was also a living, breathing thing. A sharp rasp in my throat.

The crease in her brow deepened. "Sorry. This is awkward."

To say the least. I could have done this over the phone, called her a week ago, before my procrastination-athon had begun, but this wasn't the type of news you dumped on someone from afar, no matter our strained past.

She peered at me intently. "Did you swap your glasses for contacts?"

"I had laser eye surgery."

"Oh." She looked at her toes, at my knees, at the yard beyond me. "The lawn isn't as nice as when you lived there."

I followed her line of sight to my childhood home. I could practically see a path between our front yards, a trail forged by memories of a giggling Gwen and water fights and nights lying in the grass, her head on my lap, my hands itching to stroke her hair. The vivid flashbacks fisted my heart and squeezed.

"The house looks smaller," I said. Not *I miss you.* Not *why did you ruin us?* Not *I did something you'll never forgive.*

She kept her eyes on the house. "You're just bigger."

"Did the gutters always slant like that?" This I could do. Talk about nothing instead of our past and the reason I was here.

"Doubt it."

"It needs an overhaul."

"The paint job certainly needs love."

The word *love* drifting from her lips had me rubbing the stitch still twisting my side.

I'd thought we were destined for each other, Gwen and me. The type of soul mates who'd gone through hardships, but could never stay apart. Her nineteenth birthday was supposed to have been the start of our time. Our new beginning. It had been the exact opposite, and I needed to remember that. Not give life to the overpowering connection tugging at me while we talked about laser eye surgery and the deterioration of childhood homes.

Her focus finally settled on me. "How'd you know I was here and not at my apartment?"

"Shot in the dark." Wasn't sure yet if it was lucky or unlucky, not with these confusing feelings jumbling my insides.

She didn't invite me in, or apologize for what she'd done all those years ago, but the jade in her eyes shimmered, a hint of pooling tears. Gwen didn't do tears. She was tough, made of self-determination and independence. Built by an indifferent mother and lack of affection. But the vulnerability behind her rigid posture was palpable…as was something else.

Her face softened, wistfulness in the lift of her brow, mixed with desire? Yearning?

If the emotion pouring from her eyes were a song, it would be titled "First Love."

It rocked me. All our history, and it only took one look, one mundane conversation, and I was imagining my lips on Gwen's, her in my arms, our painful past erased. Exactly why I hadn't contacted her after receiving her mother's insane letter. Why I'd missed the funeral. Why I'd delayed coming here: I'd never gotten over Gwen Hamilton.

That awareness didn't erase the sting of betrayal simmering in my gut. Both sloshed together, stirring into a queasy concoction.

When it came to Gwen, I couldn't see straight.

"Can we talk?" I nodded toward the house. I needed to move, break this spell. Apologize for what I'd done, then get away.

Arms still hugging her belly, she stepped back. I walked past her and our arms brushed. Just a whisper of skin against skin, but enough to spark each of my follicles. *The Zap*, I used to call it —a stupid, infatuated teen who'd go gaga, one graze from her zinging all my nerves to life. *Fire. Thirst. Hunger.*

Some things never changed.

I focused on her and Finch instead. Gwen the Deceiver. Gwen the Traitor.

That Gwen was familiar. That Gwen I could talk to without wondering if she felt this indelible connection, too. But the boxes filling the too-familiar space shot me with an injection of guilt. She probably did this alone, packing her mother's life away. Unless her friends had helped her, or a man. Likely a man. My cramp knotted tighter, turning my sloshy insides into a trash compacter.

I readied to tell her about the blasted letter and get away from her and this uncomfortable ache, but she swiveled, and said, "I'm sorry about that night."

Dammit. Not what I could handle right now. "It's ancient history."

If I said it, maybe my heart would believe it.

"It's not. Not for me, at least. I was too embarrassed to contact you after. It's the worst thing I've ever done, my biggest mistake. I don't even want to explain it, because it makes no sense. Absolutely none. And I won't make excuses, but I want you to know how sorry I am."

She didn't want to explain it? Not even try? "Why don't you give it a shot, Gwen? Give me the abridged version. The bullet points of why you fucked Finch."

She swallowed convulsively, and I tensed down to my toes,

barely refraining from punching the wall. This was *not* why I'd flown home. This wasn't about me and my bruised ego.

Why the hell couldn't I just let it go?

She sucked on her bottom lip, a move that had more fire driving through my veins. Different fire. I couldn't keep from glancing at her slim hips, her long legs, how the bottoms of her camouflage pants skimmed her calves, the material tough but sexy. Like Gwen. Nine years of nurtured anger threaded with remorse over what I'd done, and tangled with this *thing*. This gripping attraction and wistfulness—a deep missing of this woman from my life—leaving me lightheaded.

I was such a mess around her. "Forget I asked that. I don't want to know. The reason—"

"Because I was lonely, August. That's the abridged version. The ugly truth."

"Jesus, Gwen." There was no couch to fall onto, unless I wanted to scale boxes. Nowhere to brace myself for the conversation we'd avoided for nine years.

"I know. I'm an idiot. But I saw that stupid Facebook post, the ring on Kayla's hand, and I freaked out. I'd just admitted I'd had feelings for you—all those years and I finally found the courage to tell you. I couldn't face you after that."

"So you sought out Finch? To hurt me?"

"No, God, never." She reached for me, but curled her hands into fists. "I was hurting back then. Like really hurting—sad and lonely, about you and my mother. I had no one close in my life, and I chose the wrong way to self-medicate. It's a childish excuse, but it's all I've got. Everything I did that night was wrong."

Understatement, but I'd thought I'd dealt with it. Yet here I was, the wounds feeling fresh once more. "All you had to do was wait. I was ready to forgive you for cutting me from your life *for a year and a half.* Why couldn't you have waited one fucking night for me?"

"I don't know. I was a stupid kid with no real family and few friends, and enough self-loathing to keep half the therapists in the country employed. I didn't think you'd ever feel what I felt. And you and Finch looked so much alike. I wanted to pretend, even for a moment, that you were mine, which is really warped. It just got so twisted."

Beyond twisted, and my head spun.

For nine years I'd believed her texts that night had been lies. She'd ghosted on me our last year in high school. Had ignored me until her birthday messages. Then she'd slept with my brother, as though she'd gone out of her way to toy with me. I'd assumed her actions had been a form of retaliation—a way to punish me for who the hell knew what? For having loving parents? A scholarship? More friends?

"Not sure what to do with that," I said, my voice scratched up. I wasn't sure what to do with any of this.

Her chin wobbled. "I don't expect your forgiveness. I know there's no chance for us. It's done. I just wanted to apologize. I should have said it back then."

No chance for us. Her words were threaded with such loss, like she'd toss a penny into a pond and wish for it to be otherwise. Like she'd take me now if I offered myself up. The regret pooling in her glistening gaze was enough to fill the Pacific.

All I'd ever done was try to make Gwen happy. I'd taught her guitar, to touch her and sit close, but a creative outlet was valuable, something to distract her from her cold house when I wasn't around. I would invite her to my family dinners. We'd sneak into each other's rooms, to play cards and backgammon and argue if Superman or Wolverine would win in a flat-out brawl. We had spent endless hours together, searching for clues to find her father.

Then she tossed me and our history away like it had been nothing.

Not an easy pill to swallow, but I'd coped by believing everything had happened for a reason. Walking in on Gwen and Finch had led to more hours writing music, less studying. Deferring my courses. Traveling. Putting everything into song. Without that devastating blow, I could be living in San Francisco, working some nine-to-five, ass sore from warming an office chair, singing karaoke instead of originals.

But if fate had guided my folly in showing up at Gwen's that night, then why had it brought me here now, after what I'd done? Why was I feeling this intense longing when the information I came to share would shatter her?

She was shaking slightly, gnawing on her lip like it was her job. I jammed my hand through my hair. All this time, all this pain, and she'd slept with my brother because she'd been irrevocably lonely. Not to hurt me or push me away. She'd done it to cope with her abandonment issues.

It still stung…but less. I was also tired of holding a grudge.

"Apology accepted," I said, ready to leave our past in the past. "The history isn't as ancient as I let on, and it would do me good to put it to bed." But the comment had me picturing Gwen in a bed, *in the present*, those strong thighs around my waist, my cock buried inside her. Lust tapped a beat up my spine.

Tainted history and all, my attraction to her hadn't lessened, and delaying my reason for being here only made it worse.

She stepped closer. "Do you mean it?"

"Mean what?"

"You can move on from what I did? Forgive me?"

I didn't recognize the hesitancy in her voice. Teenage Gwen hadn't had a tentative bone in her body. "It's been nine years. I'm not holed up in my apartment, wallowing in self-pity."

She tilted her chin down—eyes wide, head cocked—giving me her *don't bullshit me* expression. *This* Gwen, I knew. "'Girl with the Black Heart'?" she said.

Busted. Writing an album full of hate songs had been excellent therapy. The fact she knew it also meant she'd been keeping tabs on me. "Have you been listening to my music?"

She shook her head quickly. "No. Of course not. I'm more of

a metal girl. I just read the song titles somewhere." But her nose twitched. The same tic that followed a Gwen fib.

"Liar."

"Says you."

The idea of her lying in bed, my music filling her room, pleased me more than it should. I shouldn't be joking with her, either. Or were we flirting? Nothing was going according to plan. Including my bitterness that resurfaced. "You should give it a listen. It's a how-to on dealing with a broken heart."

She inhaled sharply. I expected her to bite back, the way her sarcasm used to match mine blow for blow. Her tone quieted instead. "Since when does mending a broken heart involve dousing a girl in gasoline?"

"Not a girl. Her shadow. It was about torching history you can't shake. And I thought you hadn't heard the song."

"I maybe saw the lyrics online."

"Which line is your favorite?"

She opened her mouth, likely to tell me off, but she flattened her lips. A twinkle backlit the wariness slitting her eyes. "It's tough to decide between the part where you stomp on my ashes or the line where you say my soul is black." She punctuated the gibe with a shaky grin.

There was nothing amusing about that dark song, or my state of mind when writing it, or how I wanted to tear Gwen's clothing off now and release this tension and attraction for good. "I like the part where I watch your shadow burn."

Her nostrils flared. "You should write Hallmark cards."

I barked out a laugh, so loud and sudden we both startled. This acerbic bantering was unexpected. I didn't think I was capable of banter with Gwen, brusque or otherwise. We'd excelled at mocking each other back in the day, jabs that had been more sweet-natured than this barb-laced jousting. Still, that nostalgia returned with a vengeance, reminding me of our once-easy friendship.

As though reading my mind, she pressed her hand to her breastbone. "You have no idea how much I've missed you."

An ache spread through my chest. "It's been a long nine years."

An eternity. So much had changed, yet so much hadn't, our past still between us, but less potent. If I'd come for a different reason, maybe we'd have a chance at friendship. *A chance to unleash my lingering angst a different way,* a wicked voice murmured. But her mother's letter had been burning a hole in my wallet for two months, that fragile paper folded and unfolded so often it threatened to rip.

Not that I needed to read it again. I had the damn thing memorized.

Dear August,

I am dying. As a dying woman, I have a request. Below is the name of Gwen's father. She has always wanted to know who he is. I ask that you be the one to tell her, be there for her when she finds him.

It had seemed like a simple request, but nothing with Gwen was simple. Not the way reading the letter had made me want to hop on a redeye and fly home and scoop Gwen into my arms to hold and protect her while she finally met the man she'd searched out her whole life. Not the way I'd stuffed the note in my wallet and had skipped Mary's funeral, hoping the sudden pain of missing Gwen would disappear. The final line had made it so much worse:

Remember what I told you on Gwen's nineteenth birthday.

That's how she'd ended the letter, as though I hadn't lived the last nine years wondering why she'd said what she had that day. I'd called her for Gwen's address, and she'd given me more than I'd hoped to hear. An earful that had made me believe Mary Hamilton had cared for her daughter more than she'd let on.

Gwen stood before me now, one hand still on her chest. So many emotions—affection, shame, every secret and hope we'd ever shared, and something like uncorked *desire*—swirling in her green eyes. Unless I was projecting my overwhelming feelings onto her.

Ignoring the cocktail of emotions shaking me up, I dredged up my fortitude and prepared to admit what I'd done.

But someone knocked on the door.

CHAPTER 4

1:30 p.m.

34 ½ Hours and Counting…

Gwen

When had my mother's house turned into Grand Central Station? The knocking persisted, but I didn't budge. August looked a second from combusting, as though an internal war waged behind his sharp expression, and the intensity in his eyes sucked me in. Twin hazel tractor beams.

I'd never thought I'd see tenderness on his face again, but it had been there. A semblance of it, at least. There'd been anger, too, at first. That man had every right to spit in my eye and launch a flaming shit-bomb at my door. But the hint of longing under his tight features, the way his gaze had dipped down my body, skimming my curves, had been wholly unexpected.

And likely nonexistent.

I for sure imagined the heat in his perusal, the way I'd imagined every love song he'd ever written had been about me. Because I was certifiable. Crazy for August Cruz, always had been, always would be. Lovesick until the day I die.

A breather was in order. Space to remind myself this man had actually written hate songs about me. "Don't go anywhere," I said, terrified he and his tractor-beam eyes would disappear from my life again.

He offered a stiff nod.

I had no clue why he'd come, but I didn't care. August was in my childhood home, joking with me, offering me forgiveness. I hadn't felt this giddy since I'd forced Rachel and Ainsley into Playworld's bumper cars. (I'd cracked up while ramming them. Margaritas had been involved.) This wasn't a giddy buzz, though, the tingling in my limbs more dizzying than cackle-inducing. Facing your worst mistake and greatest love in one fell swoop came with a bevy of side effects.

Functioning in a daze, I managed to open the front door. The Girl Scout I'd hoped for earlier still hadn't appeared. In her place was an Asian man with a clipboard in front of his face and a battered red suitcase at his feet. He peered over his notes. "Ms. Hamilton?"

I had to tilt my head back to meet his eyes. "Depends which Hamilton you're after."

He checked his notes and motioned to the suitcase. "Mary Hamilton. On behalf of Greyhound bus lines, I'm returning her lost luggage."

I raised a skeptical eyebrow at the roughed-up suitcase, one of those hard-shell types with dents and skid marks, the outside covered in band stickers. I snickered. "You must have the wrong Mary Hamilton."

But I'd have paid money to see her at a Billy Idol concert. The bold stickers splashed across the suitcase would have horrified her.

He frowned at his papers and prattled off our address and the name again, scratching at his neck until a red mark bloomed.

"Look," I said, cutting him off. "Mary Hamilton was my mother. She was a forty-five-year-old dental office receptionist who died last month, not a teenage band groupie. There must be a mistake."

Again with the neck scratching. "Sorry...I should have explained fully." He blinked as though he had a loose contact and nudged the bag forward. "This is from a batch of luggage we recently found, that went missing in 2001. They had been locked in an unused storage facility. We're returning the lost items."

Luggage from 2001? Was this guy for real? "My mother didn't travel. I'd never even seen her pack an overnight bag. She barely—"

"Was she related to a Doris Hamilton?"

I stumbled back and braced myself against the door. "What did you say?" Doris was my grandmother. Linked by DNA, not any form of relationship, but still...I'd have fallen on my ass if it weren't for the strong presence behind me. A large body. August with his hand on my lower back.

"Doris Hamilton," the man repeated. "Her name was also listed on the luggage tag, but Mary Hamilton's was the main contact."

My mother.

Lost luggage.

Billy Idol.

2001.

Breathing became an effort. "And you're saying this was hers? From seventeen years ago?" I would have been ten or eleven back then. I'd have remembered having a band groupie for a mother.

"Mary Hamilton," he said again, slowly, loudly, as though I was hard of hearing. "From 2001."

If it weren't for August looping his arm around my waist, I'd be eating pavement right now: face first, teeth chipped, bloody nose. Balance eluded me.

"Do you need us to sign something?" August took over, showing me where to write my name, behaving like a coherent adult. He led me inside afterward, just him and me and this shocking suitcase.

He gripped my hips and turned me to face him. "This is pretty nuts."

"This isn't nuts. This is like digging up the time capsule from your yard, only to discover the Barbie you disfigured by swapping her legs with Spider-Man's had come to life to take over the globe."

He smirked. "Barbie-Man was awesome."

"Barbie-Man was a horror. Barbie-Man as an immortal bent on world domination would be catastrophic."

He smiled fully, the creases around his mouth and eyes filling with affection. Wooziness swept through me again, and I clasped his wrists. Scents of sweat and clove and man drifted from him, an unfamiliar cologne. As a boy he'd smelled of fresh-cut grass and his mother's fried chicken. To this day, I couldn't pass a lawnmower or fast-food chicken joint without sighing.

He inched a fraction closer, his smile slipping into something darker. His warm breath skimmed my hair. I'd swear his grip on me tightened. "Barbie-Man was scary because you scalped her. You ruined what I was trying to create."

Was that another dig? Him reviving how I'd ruined *us*? He had said he'd forgiven me, but laying nine years of resentment to rest wasn't easy, and I deserved every quip and wisecrack. Yearned for it, actually.

His grip on me grew hot and heavy—something else I yearned for. "If I'd known you had an artistic vision in mind, I wouldn't have acted so rashly." I might not have slept with Finch.

His thumb moved a fraction, a slight drag downward, and his attention fastened on my lips. "You would have defaced her one way or another. You were always impulsive like that."

"That doesn't change how scary that suitcase is." How terrifying being close to August was.

He cast a searching glance at my face, as though reading the double-entendre in my words. "This is uncharted territory. We always fear what we don't know."

I couldn't be sure if he was talking about me or the suitcase-bomb dropped on my life, but I met his probing gaze, taking in his full physique. He really had filled out the past nine years, the sleeves of his soccer jersey cutting into his biceps. Strong veins mapped his tanned forearms and big hands. He had a bold Roman nose, thick eyelashes. Darker circles cradled his hazel eyes, but they upped his hot factor, broodiness always a turn-on for me. The hint of stubble dusting the severe cut of his jaw didn't hurt either.

It also didn't hide the scar on his chin.

I'd sat with him after he'd sliced it on the Wheelers' broken window, the two of us having snuck into that abandoned home like we'd been FBI. Always messing around. We'd sat facing each other afterward, on my bedroom floor, our knees touching, my hand on his face as I held a wet towel to the gash. We were fifteen then, and I'd wanted to kiss him.

I was one day from twenty-eight now, and I wanted to *devour* him.

There was no way this big, gorgeous man returned the sentiment, but his hands were on my hips, the slightest tremble to his grip. What could he see before him but a betrayer?

Disoriented, I eased away from him and knelt in front of the case. "You know what this means, right?"

He cleared his throat. "You might learn your mother was an eighties club kid?"

Not even close. I still couldn't believe this was happening, that August was with me for this wild turn of events. Who got lost luggage returned after seventeen years?

I wanted to unpack the man behind me as much as I wanted to dissect this new treasure. Find out every country and town he'd toured, what cool foods he'd eaten in Japan, if writing music felt as cathartic as it seemed, if being on the road was lonely or exhilarating. We weren't there yet. Not close. Not friends, even. We might never get there.

Better to stick with safer topics, like why this suitcase fascinated me.

Hands on the hard plastic, I glanced at him over my shoulder. I was about to tell him there could be clues about my father in here, but the hope taunted me, the hours I'd spent ransacking my mother's room proof I was grasping at straws, wishing for the impossible.

With August here, though, the impossible no longer seemed unattainable. Still, I latched on to his humor instead. "You nailed it, but if Mary Hamilton loved the rave scene, *I'm* an arachnid scientist with a penchant for mayonnaise."

I got off on bungee jumping and would kill to surf a fifty-foot swell, but drop an eight-legged critter near me or force mayonnaise down my throat, and I'd scream bloody murder.

August's good humor returned. "I ruined you, didn't I?"

"You were an evil mastermind." Who'd hidden a trove of plastic spiders in my room and had snuck gross mayonnaise on my turkey sandwiches. He'd also ruined me for men, unbeknownst to him, my history littered with nothing but assholes until my dating hiatus this year. No one had ever compared to August.

I kept my focus on the suitcase, grounding my wobbly hands on the cool metal, still aware of my former best friend behind me. His sneakers scuffed the floor. To leave? Walk out of my life again? I'd taken care of my mother's funeral arrangements on my own, had dealt with her will, was packing her life into boxes.

But this…

I didn't want to unearth more of her past alone. I didn't know how to ask for August's support. I kept talking instead. "As far as I know, my mother never left San Francisco. Never took so much as a weekend getaway. And I was eleven when this supposedly went missing. I'd remember her traveling, wouldn't I?" It also seemed weird it turned up today. With August. The day before my birthday. "Why am I nervous to open it? This is worse than skydiving."

"Since when do you skydive?"

His question proved how far we'd fallen away from each other. He didn't know me now, the woman I'd become. When I didn't reply, he said, "It's just stuff, Gwen. Nothing in there can hurt you."

He was wrong about that. "Says the guy who grew up with a great family."

"It wasn't as peachy as it seemed. Nowhere near what you went through, but we have our issues."

I almost turned at his bitter tone, but I didn't want to acknowledge the part I'd played in their family discord. I also couldn't look away from the suitcase. "Will you stay while I open it?"

I had no right to ask August for anything. He probably came by to clear the air between us, find the closure we both clearly needed, or to reinstate his anger—fodder for his songwriting. (He could name his next gem "Girl Who Can't Forget the Past.") Some nerve I had, asking him for support now.

"Of course," came his quiet reply.

I stayed focused on the case, couldn't look at his expression as I faced my mother's history. But he was here. *Of course.* He would let me lean on him. *Of course.* He'd forever be the only person who could calm me. *Of course.*

"Thank you," I whispered.

I heard him move, felt the heat of his palm on my back. Magnetically, I curved forward, rounding my spine into his tender touch. I closed my eyes.

Three extended beats later, he moved away, my serenity leaving with him. "Take your time with her stuff," he said. "I'll make myself at home."

Easier said than done in a packed-up house, but August

knew these walls as well as me. He'd been the one to make pencil marks in the pantry every year I grew taller. He moved that way now, toward the kitchen, farther from me. The distance felt physically painful. I also appreciated it; he always knew what I needed.

I examined the relic before me. Billy Idol stickers. INXS. Depeche Mode. I traced the stained graphics, beyond baffled. Maybe someone had lent my mother the case. Someone who'd enjoyed music and had let loose. Someone who hadn't shuffled through a quiet life.

Afraid to disturb its contents, I eased the suitcase on its side and opened it. A musty smell hit me full force. I rubbed my nose, but the stale aroma stuck to my nostrils. Seventeen years of confined clothing.

Clothes I couldn't believe had belonged to my mother.

Sitting cross-legged, I pulled out one item at a time: a neon windbreaker, high-waisted jeans, a micro-mini skirt, bright tank tops that would fit Barbie-Man. She would have been twenty-eight when this went missing, not sixteen. The styles were as baffling as the concert stickers, until I noticed the *Rolling Stone* magazine below, from 1990.

The year I was born.

Could these contents and band stickers have been from then? They certainly fit the bill, but that wouldn't explain the eleven-year gap between being packed and sent on a Greyhound bus.

More confused than ever, I spent time with each piece, smoothed the worn fabrics, tried to picture my mother in something other than black, white, gray, or beige. She'd kept her hair short, her shoes functional and flat. Whoever *this* Mary Hamilton had been, she'd had questionable taste, too, but colorful.

Two pairs of shoes were below her clothing. One was a cute set of beaded sandals. Sandals I'd actually wear. I ran my fingers over the blue beads, unsure how this miniskirt wearing, INXS-loving girl had had the color sucked from her life. Except the possible answer had my throat feeling thick. If the *Rolling Stone* date was the more accurate one, if these contents *were* from 1990, not 2001, then *I* was the thing that had sucked her color dry.

I'd been the child she hadn't wanted.

I clenched and unclenched my hands, unsure why my heart rate had picked up. I didn't love my mother. Miss her? Not on your life. She was unimportant, a barely-there blip on my ancestral radar. So why was I zoning out, staring at nothing while my lungs worked double-time?

Too much history had been unearthed today. August. My WTF. My crappy childhood. *August.* An unhealthy amount of time passed as I touched those sandals.

Eventually, I shook my head and reached for the other shoes. These were odd—soft black leather with laces and small square heels. Deep creases ringed the middles as though the arches had been bent every which way. Jazz shoes? For dancing? I snorted out a laugh. This was too much. Picturing my mother taking a bong hit was easier than imagining her shaking jazz hands. These couldn't belong to a woman who'd never listened to music.

I turned the soft shoes over, ran my fingers along the soles and laces. Inside the heel was a scribbled name: *Mary Hamilton.* My breath caught.

That tiny scrawl shot this reality home, confirming beyond a doubt these belongings had been hers. The mother I'd come to resent had lived a phantom life.

I moved faster, going through her toiletries (red lipstick, the woman had red lipstick!), sifting through her lacy underwear, and a bible. The bible made sense. From what I knew of my grandparents, they were religious. The zealot sort whose lives revolved around church. I set the book aside, along with every other article she'd lost. Nothing pointed to any friends she'd had, or a boyfriend. I still couldn't accurately gauge what year it was all from. It was just stuff, like August had said.

That didn't stop me from another exhaustive analysis, the same intense focus I used at my job.

When couples applied for adoption, I double, triple, and quadruple checked their facts, making sure babies were matched with the right parents. If Mary Hamilton had applied for a baby from me, I wouldn't have allowed her to adopt a Home Economics egg.

But every day, I made families whole. I helped babies land in loving homes, with caring parents who would nurture and protect them, everything I never had.

I applied the same extensive analysis to the artifacts before me. I turned every item of clothing inside out. I checked the edges of the suitcase. I flipped through the entire *Rolling Stone* issue, finding nothing but one dog-eared page: a "fancy" boombox advertising quality CD sound. Totally cool and retro, but not a clue to my father's identity or the suitcase's origin.

I started again.

Partway through my third pass, strumming teased my ears. August. I blinked at my surroundings, unsure how long I'd been searching through the case. A glance at my phone told me almost two hours had passed. Two hours, and August was still here. He must have found my old guitar among the boxes. My small pile of memories I couldn't part with.

He played a quiet tune, familiar soft notes: America's "Horse with No Name," the first song he'd ever taught me. The simple melody flowed with only two chords, easy to teach. August had sat with his legs around me, my back rounded against his chest, his fingers moving mine along the strings. I'd figured it out pretty quick, but had pretended to struggle—to keep him close, to keep his hands on mine, to pretend I'd been brave enough to spin and press my lips to his.

His choice of song pulled at me. The nostalgia in here must be getting to him, too. Forgetting the mess I'd made on the floor, I leaned on my hand to push to my feet and sneak a peek of him, only to realize my mother's bible had gotten lost under my debris. It caved slightly when I picked it up, the middle of it denting. Odd.

I shifted to my knees and opened the cover. "Holy shit," I murmured.

My pulse was back to hammering, a frantic tune drowning August's soft song. My mother, the apparent rebel, had cut out the interior of her bible like she'd been an undercover agent. Inside her hidey hole was a journal.

Carefully, I extricated the journal from its hiding spot and opened the cover. I grinned at the scrawled note:

If you're reading this, you've stolen my property.

Put it back or face the consequences.

The dates inscribed in the top right corner edged the grin from my face: 1989-1990. I reached out to touch the writing, but yanked my hand back.

This wasn't a coincidence. These dates matched the magazine and clothing styles. These contents must have been from that time. It didn't explain why the bag had gone missing in 2001, but not much about this suitcase arriving at my mother's door made sense.

What was startlingly clear was that I held a diary. One written by mother, encompassing the times during which I'd been conceived and born.

This could lead me to my father.

No matter how often I'd asked her who he was growing up, she'd clam up. No hints given, only bitter sneers or blank stares. Now I had a hidden journal from the year I was conceived. *Be careful what you wish for.* The cautious saying looped through my mind as I steadied my breath and shook out my hands, like I was readying to touch hot coals.

I may have spent my entire teenage and adult life desperate for this knowledge, but it suddenly seemed daunting. This journal had the power to rewrite my past and shape my future, and not all shapes were pretty. Still, I opened it.

I flipped the pages. Each was filled with writing, some with taped receipts or mementos, a *Dead Calm* movie stub. She printed her sentences, instead of writing in cursive, making her entries seem more youthful than the handwriting I recalled. More proof of the journal's dating.

August's strumming got louder, and I clutched my treasure to my chest. My birthday was tomorrow. That left thirty-three hours before the clock struck midnight. It meant I might not lose my resolution to find my father. Not that resolutions could be lost, and I was no Cinderella whose life would revert to pumpkin status, but Rachel and Ainsley had been so happy since fulfilling their wishes. I'd figured I'd lost my chance.

Now I had pages full of possible clues to find my father. Picking through them on my timeline was sketchy, but I never backed down from a challenge. I surfed on them, jumped off them, scaled them. This was no different.

And I might not have to do it alone.

I made my way to the kitchen, to August, my original partner in crime, and stopped outside the doorway. He had shoved boxes aside and sat on one of the two wooden chairs that had once circled the small breakfast table. The only talking that had occurred while I'd hunched on that seat had been when my mother would berate me for not cleaning the bathroom properly, or leaving my shoes askew by the door, or tracking mud into the house.

Listen for once in your life, she'd scold. Always calling me a disappointment.

The silent meals had been preferable, another reason August would invite me for dinner, where I'd barely eat. Overwhelmed with the laughing and teasing between him and Finch, their parents, and their little sister, Melody, I'd often forget about the food.

Shaking off the memories, I tiptoed closer to August. His eyes were closed, his fingers gliding over the fretboard like wind strumming leaves. I'd felt those callused fingers on my face once. His lips on mine. I still remembered the heat of his tongue and soft-wet press of his mouth. Or maybe I didn't. Maybe I'd relived it so often, I'd fabricated every glorious detail.

But the guitar in his hands was real. He'd bought it for me, his attempt to fill my stark life with vibrancy. When I'd get tired of learning, he'd go off on tangents, practicing riffs and licks while I'd imagine licking him. He wouldn't leave until I'd smile. He'd always done stuff like that, little-big things that changed my world, but the efforts had often been too overt, pity-filled attempts to fix me, like I was broken, a project, a challenge. They'd inflame my insecurity, leading me to pushing him away.

I wanted nothing more than for him to stay in my life now, any way I could have him. As a friend. As a partner in crime. *As more.*

My pathetic heart hiccupped at the impossibility.

That didn't stop me from testing my limits with him. "August." My voice was so thin and scratchy, he didn't open his eyes. I swallowed hard and said his name louder, with confidence.

His fingers kept playing, but he focused on me, eyelids hooded, intensity darkening his gaze. He moved as he strummed, a slight rocking of his shoulders. His sneaker tapped the floor softly. Normally, at concerts, August would wear threadbare jeans and slim T-shirts, *not* that I'd watched all his YouTube videos.

Even in workout shorts, a yellow jersey, and sneakers, he looked delicious. He also kept staring at me. He licked his lips. I couldn't feel mine. His mouth softened imperceptibly, tilting up in one corner, as though I *had* inspired every love ballad he'd ever written.

Unable to contemplate that unlikelihood, and my constant need to read into everything August—because I was more cuckoo than a store of clocks—I blurted the one thing I had no right to say. "Will you help me find my father?"

CHAPTER 5

3:30 p.m., 32 ½ Hours…

August

My fingers slipped on the guitar strings, a ridiculous fumble on the world's easiest song. I hadn't strummed "Horse with No Name" in an eternity. The simple tune came with too many memories. Here, in this house, I couldn't fight the pull.

I could practically feel Gwen wiggling between my legs as she'd struggle through the basic chords, no clue to the torture she doled out. I'd have to harness my fantasies back then, focus on my hippie aunt's unshaven legs or run soccer plays in mind to keep the action behind my zipper in check.

Hearing my name from her lips now zoomed me back to that time, those days, and my fascination with her. How Finch would wind me up or a lost soccer match would get me down, and Gwen would nag me until I was nestled beside her on the couch, watching *Gilmore Girls*, a show I'd never admit to liking. I'd toss popcorn at her face. She'd stick her stinky socks in my face.

And the world had been right.

Even now, all this chaos between us, somehow I was more right. I wasn't staring out a train window as foreign towns slipped past, melancholy lyrics teasing my fingertips. I wasn't dating a woman for a month or two only to lose interest, lose the connection, the attraction. Around Gwen, I felt grounded, yet alive. Still slightly resentful when it came to her, but I liked it—that fiery spark.

Until she said, "Will you help me find my father?"

A sour note plunked from the guitar, mimicking the dread churning my gut. My lungs pinched. How had I let things go this far?

Gwen prattled over my guilt-ridden silence. "I know I'm the last person you'd like to help. Trust me, I get it. But I found a journal hidden in my mother's bible, from when I was conceived, and something tells me it'll lead to my dad. If you say no, I'll totally understand, but don't you think it's odd? This case showing up before my birthday? After my mom died? With you, the same day?" Her eyes were wide, filled with hope.

I prayed my face didn't show the unease lurching inside me. *Right now. Tell her now.* Except I wanted more time with her, more of that turbulent grounding she inspired. An oxymoron maybe, but there was no other way to describe the storminess she stirred, all wild and unpredictable. Around her I smiled one minute, bit out cutting remarks the next, the space between filled with unease and a burning lust to show her what she'd ruined. What she'd stolen from both of us.

I wanted to fuck her, raw and rough.

It was a painful ache. It should also never happen, not with our history, but I couldn't shake the need to be around her, to learn her. The second I admitted why I'd come, she'd disappear from my life for good.

That pinching in my lungs worsened.

She kept talking over herself. "You know what? Forget I asked. It was selfish." She popped her left knee and fiddled with the bible in her hand. "You're busy and touring and probably have a thousand things to do, and I'm asking too much. I'm just glad you stayed. It's appreciated, and while you're here, I can at least give you this."

She placed the bible down and rustled through an open box while I stayed silent. I clutched the guitar with one hand, spun my pick around the fingers of my other. *Over. Over. Under. Under.* The smooth edges flew in a familiar pattern.

Gwen faced me, her neck and cheeks flushed. "I found a few mementos the past month, stuff I couldn't toss." She moved closer, by my knees, and held out a felt circle.

No matter my raging turmoil, I couldn't fight my laugh. "You still have that thing?"

"And our old class pictures, which I won't let you see."

"But you rocked those braces."

"It's more the frilly blouses my mother made me wear. They've all been burned."

I eased the guitar to the floor and smiled at the badge Gwen had made for me. In the middle, stitched with wonky black thread, it read:

August Cruz
Badass PI

She'd made them, one for each of us, when our neighbor's garden gnome had gone missing. Our sleuthing had never turned up the ugly statue, but she'd pull out our badges when we'd hunt down clues about her father. Those hours had often revolved around Gwen riffling through her mother's purse, finding stray business cards, then trolling the internet for leads, sure her father's name would turn up. We'd stalk men she'd find and show them photos of Gwen's mom.

All futile searches, but I'd loved the softness of the felt PI badge in my pocket. A connection to Gwen.

She stepped between my knees and placed the badge over my stuttering heart. "It was stupid to keep it, but..." She shrugged, flattening her palm on my chest. Her chest expanded as fully as mine, more color flushing her olive skin.

I spun the guitar pick around my fingers, faster, faster. My thoughts skittered as quickly. And *bam*, the Zap was back. An electric surge.

I wanted to latch my hands around her hips and tug her to me. Slip my hands down the front of her pants and stroke her silky heat, feel everything I'd been denied. Slam my cock into her, hard, fast, dirty. I also wanted to press my forehead into her abdomen and whisper how much I'd missed her.

Surprisingly, I didn't want to tell her off. Not anymore.

Especially since the anger I'd nursed hadn't been directed solely at her.

As twins at the same school, Finch and I had occasionally lusted after the same girls. He'd even fooled around with Kayla before we'd hooked up. I'd made sure he was cool with me asking her out before anything happened, but he knew how I'd felt about Gwen. I'd told him, grumpy and often, how worried I'd been to make a move on her and screw things up, lose her friendship.

Not just for me, but more for her.

I was all Gwen had. If I'd ruined that, she'd have been left with nothing.

I'd nearly pulled out my hair when I'd heard about her dating that Jared douche. I'd been miserable about it, and Finch knew. He'd even promised to look out for her after she'd cut me off, because I'd been worried about her. He'd agreed to my request. Not without asking for a favor in return. A doozy of a favor. I'd held up my end of our bargain.

Turns out "looking out for Gwen" translated to Finch as "banging her."

There was intent with that. Premeditation. Especially after what I'd done for him. It had ignited our growing tension, stress Gwen never knew about. I'd assumed Gwen had been screwing with me, too. That they'd gone out of their way to hurt me. Nine years later, she confessed her actions had been a result of her messed up childhood, her past warping her choices.

And here she was, hand pressed to my aching chest, affection in her eyes.

As though my limbs had a mind of their own, I anchored my hand over hers, flattening our palms. "Do you have a boyfriend?"

So tightly clasped against me, I felt her hand flinch. *I* damn well flinched: I hadn't planned to blurt the question that had dogged me since knocking on her door.

She bit her lip and shook her head. "Not for a while."

I exhaled heavily.

Her fingers dug deeper into my chest, her thumb sinking between my pecs, and my cock thickened. "Do you?" she asked, almost breathless. "A girlfriend, I mean. Women must throw themselves at you." She winced slightly, as though a headache had set in.

"No one important," I said. No one worth writing songs about, good or bad.

"Oh."

Oh, was right.

Oh, we're both single.

Oh, we're both still attracted to each other.

Oh, I might finally be able to work out my Gwen addiction in a rough session between the sheets.

Except my remorse resurfaced, the stupid decisions that had brought me here tamping the urge.

Trembling slightly, she pulled her hand back, and that silly PI patch clung to my shirt, an echo of our past. Heat echoed from her touch. A reverberation I'd felt for nine years. This connection was probably why I'd never had a real relationship. I could blame it on my music and traveling all I liked, but every woman who'd moved through my life had been a bridge, a transition that filled song gaps. Gwen was the refrain and chorus, the addictive hook that wormed into your mind.

A habit I was struggling to break.

Staying seated, I slowed my breaths and plucked the badge off my jersey. I tucked it into the waistband of my shorts.

She watched my every move, crossed and uncrossed her arms. "Rachel, who you met, wanted me to meet them for drinks in"—she glanced at the microwave clock, her hips still in grabbing distance—"a couple hours. I'd like to go home and read the journal a bit beforehand, but you could come, if you want. To the bar. Since you know Owen and Jimmy."

"You want me to meet your friends?"

"They're your friends, too." She huffed out an incredulous laugh. "Because, you know, today isn't strange enough, we also have the same friends. Which I totally don't get. How'd I never meet them?"

I thought back to those years, my hours split between playing guitar, school, soccer, and Gwen time. "We hung out after practice, nights when you were studying." Always cracking the books, struggling with her grades.

"The soccer guys," she mumbled, as though to herself. Then louder, "That's what you'd say: 'I'm going out with the soccer guys.'"

Guys who'd turned into men that Gwen now knew. We shared baffled looks.

It really was one hell of a coincidence. Fate, that sneaky little devil, toying with our lives—the way her betrayal had launched my music career, and her mother had launched me back into Gwen's life. Like both of us single now, launched together.

I still hadn't answered her about searching for her father, hadn't said yes or no or admitted my screw-up. There was also this unrelenting *thing* between us that went beyond fierce attraction and residual resentment, that maybe, *maybe* she'd always be the one for me. There'd been no one since Gwen. No one meaningful.

Here, with her, there was meaning in every breath and pause.

That left me existing in no man's land, wondering if those weighted beats meant Gwen and I still had a chance at…something, yet I was withholding vital information from her.

Unsure how to proceed, I nodded. "I need to shower and change at my hotel, but I can meet you there."

"Really?"

"Really."

"You're coming with me?"

"I'm coming with you." I hated that we'd been reduced to this—once inseparable, now questioning a simple outing with friends.

"Will you keep repeating everything I say?" she asked.

"Only if you keep stating the obvious."

She flicked my shoulder, and I squeezed the sensitive spot above her knee. She squealed, a sound I'd always loved. Happy Gwen. Giddy Gwen. She went to pinch my nipple, her go-to move, but I batted her hand away. I grabbed her waist and tugged her onto my lap, her back flush against my chest. Nowhere for her hands to roam. "You're getting slow in your old age."

She quit squirming. "You're getting faster."

And harder. She probably felt it, my erection free to roam in my workout shorts. Minimal contact was all it took. Like I was a teen again, my body always quick to respond to her. Needing to regain control, I eased her off my lap, but gripped her waist too long. Felt each of her lean muscles through her thin tank top. "You've been working out."

"CrossFit," she murmured while she stepped back and faced me, adjusting her camo pants. "But I'm considering taking up pole vaulting." Her eyes focused on my groin.

The pole in question twitched, and my mind was back to ricocheting, too much stimulus—good and bad—to focus on one thing. I could handle this, though. Subtle flirting while we figured out what the hell to do with each other. While I figured out my next move. "I'd think you were already a skilled vaulter."

"The poles I've used tend to buckle under pressure."

"Then I guess you need a steadier pole. Something longer and firmer?"

I imagined her cupping the length of me, stroking me until I roared. Fantasies I should curb.

She touched her collarbone, ran her fingers toward the dip at her throat. "I need a pole that can go the distance. The kind that can support my weight."

Her tone wavered from coy to uncertain. Trepidation that probably had little to do with me. The burden of her mother's lost luggage must be affecting her. Unclaimed baggage, filled with years of neglect. I cocked my head, hoping the motion would organize my jumbling thoughts. Sex. Want. Guilt. Ire. The need to take Gwen in my arms and whisper soothing words.

Our eyes locked again and the air snapped, the way an extended note vibrated and hummed.

Abruptly, she hugged her waist. "Is your number the same? Should I text you where to meet?"

"My number hasn't changed."

Gwen suddenly had. She was on the move, snatching up the bible and journal. She stacked them in the open box that had held my PI badge. Her shoulder-length hair dipped forward, a wavy curtain covering her face.

To avoid looking at me? To avoid this intensity binding us, whether we wanted it to, or not?

Not surprising with the day's craziness. I needed to stop thinking with my body, too. My bruised and battered heart. A shower would do me good. A cold one. An ice bath, maybe. Something to remind me why I'd avoided Gwen all this time, her ability to unbalance me powerful, the details I hadn't shared enough to end this reunion for good.

If I could nurse the anger I'd harbored the past nine years, it would help me confess about her father and move on. Stop pretending the two of us could water these fledgling feelings, grow something good out of them.

Watching her gather and pack a tiny box that represented her few good childhood memories silenced that notion. She'd endured so much growing up, too much the past month, me and this lost luggage adding to her stress. The grudge I'd harbored seemed childish now. We'd been kids back then. Stupid. Led by our fears, unsure who we were and who we should be.

Today, I was a lonely musician who missed his best friend. Today, I was a man struggling to tame his desire for his first and only love.

———

Gwen

I couldn't gather my paltry box fast enough. If I could eject myself from this overheating kitchen, that had shrunk with August in it, I'd strap myself in and brace for impact. One second I was ready to grab his *pole* and test how high it could make me jump, the next I couldn't stop remembering the rabbit hole I'd fallen into after my WTF.

Losing August back then had been a sledgehammer to my heart. For two years I'd wallowed, barely going out. Self-imposed isolation. Until I'd met Rachel and Ainsley. The girls had reminded me there was life after a shattered heart, but the extent to which I'd suffered wasn't something one forgot.

I was twenty-seven now, not nineteen, but the San Francisco fault line had nothing on my shoddy foundation.

One moment on August's *aroused* lap, and the cracks under my feet showed.

I shuffled across the white linoleum floor, glancing at him as he returned my guitar to its case. His strong back stretched his jersey, his shoulder blades shifting with each move. My Badass PI partner.

Of our investigative duo, he'd been the clever one, quick to decipher leads and solve problems as we'd hunt down clues. I was the sneaky one who'd sweet talked "suspects" and "informants," donning my meager acting skills.

Anything to spend more time with August.

He hadn't agreed to investigate with me today, only to join my friends for a drink. The possibility of combing the city with him sounded too good to be true, grinding on his pole sounded even better, but we'd spent the last nine years ignoring each other, angry and hurt. Me ashamed and pissed at myself. August furious with *me*. Not the kind of history suited to unearthing parental information that could trigger my own personal earthquake.

That didn't lessen my internal tug-of-war: I wanted him with me for this daunting scavenger hunt. I wanted him playing me songs, flirting with me, possibly *thrusting his pole inside me*. An electrifying and petrifying prospect.

Which meant I needed to focus on one sure thing: August and I were friends. We had been, at least. A relationship I wanted back. A fling might calm the fire one look from him stirred, but he could never be a one-night stand, and we'd never be more, certainly not today, with this journal and the challenging hours ahead of me.

Finding my father was priority one.

August trailed me from the kitchen. He wasn't even close, but I could barely breathe through the feverish grip on my lungs.

"So, we'll meet in a couple hours?" he asked.

Hopefully long enough to get these hot flashes under control. "Five thirty. I'll text you."

He opened the front door and reached toward me. "Give that to me."

I narrowed my eyes at him. "What?" My heart? My soul? He owned both already.

"The box. So you can lock up."

Right. The box I was holding. So I could lock up.

Even his simple gesture had me picking apart his intentions. The action also had me all thumbs.

What should have been a simple handoff of a small box went haywire when his hand brushed my arm. I squeaked and fell into him. The box tumbled to the ground, his arm came around my waist, and my hand grazed his *pole*.

He grunted, short and harsh. I should have moved my hand. A normal person who needed to be only platonic with her ex-best friend while she chased down leads on her ghosted father should have moved her hand. I *did* move my hand, but it was more of a needy slide.

Air hissed through his teeth. "Do that again, Gwen, and I'll toss you over my shoulder, take you up to your childhood bedroom, and live out the dirty fantasies that kept me up for most of high school."

Good Lord.

I jumped back and smacked my shoulder into the doorframe. My lungs had practically incinerated, burned up with my unquenched desire. Still, I managed to say, "I'm sorry."

"Don't be." He was breathing hard, too, and he smirked.

He wasn't a smirker. He was a hate-song writer. I couldn't get my head around it all. "What are we doing?"

"Honestly?"

"No, August. I'd like you to lie to me so I can continue acting like a moron. I don't even know why you came by or why you're in town." Most of his family lived in Chicago now. He didn't have a house here.

His lips tipped into a frown. "I'm not really sure anymore."

"Why you're in town, or what we're doing?"

He dragged a hand through his dark hair. The strands were shorter than they used to be, but they still had a slight curl, that one lick up top defying gravity. I itched to smooth it down. Touching him wasn't smart, and I was a smart girl. A together girl. A girl who needed to focus.

"I came home to take care of some personal business," he said cryptically. "As for us, I'd like to hang out this afternoon. We'll take it from there."

A loony laugh escaped me. "We'll take it from there?"

"Now who's repeating who?"

"You do know how weird this is, right? You and me hanging out and…" I glanced at his crotch, the loose fabric tented slightly. For a second, I wondered if that personal business had to do specifically with me, but the possibility was laughable. His brother lived here. He likely had music contacts in the area, too. Still, he'd shown up at my mother's door, looking for me.

He shrugged an unaffected shoulder, like our flirting didn't mock the laws of nature. "I've decided to stop analyzing it."

He bent to gather the few things that had tumbled from my box, and I froze. It was one thing to give him his Badass PI badge, but each memento littering the walkway—the only keepsakes I'd saved from my childhood—were all linked to the man bent over them. Every last one.

My first Wonder Woman comic—his gift when I'd won my track meet.

The *Die Hard* DVD he'd sent over when I'd been holed up with mono.

Every homemade birthday card he'd slipped into my locker.

He righted the box and returned the escaped items, but paused on each one. My throat closed. They were damning, hard proof I'd never gotten over him. The longer he lingered, the hotter my neck burned. Mortification over my obvious obsession with him winded me, along with hope he'd understand how important he'd been in my life.

Seeing as we'd never unleashed our monolithic sexual tension, *his* flirting made sense. A quick fuck could offer him closure, even though it would ruin me. This evidence wasn't simple flirting. This was proof of a deep emotional scar, years of missing him nurtured and splayed on flagstone.

I expected him to stand, make some excuse about a forgotten appointment or meeting. Flee the scene of the crime. Instead he placed my mother's journal over our memories and stood, facing me. "I have a picture of you on my laptop, from our trip to the zoo, with you making faces at the chimpanzees. I've switched computers over the years, had plenty of opportunity to delete it. I never could."

He smiled a sad smile, his gaze traveling over my face and landing on my lips. He licked his, a slow slide of his tongue. Then he turned and jogged to his car.

My heart jogged in time.

CHAPTER 6

5 p.m., 31 Hours…

Gwen

A frosty shower later, I pulled on dark jeans and a white tank top, ready to meet my friends for a drink. *Not* continue obsessing over a certain someone who'd be joining me. I would not admit to modeling five different outfits beforehand, when I should have been analyzing my mother's journal. I had *not* applied two different shades of lipstick before settling on a rosy gloss. I also *hadn't* performed these neurotic acts while listening to August's latest album.

Nope. Not me.

God, I was pathetic.

Looking in the mirror now, I barely recognized myself. My ruffled bangs swept to the side like usual, my chestnut waves as ordered as I could get them. My cheekbones still stood out, my right eye slightly rounder than the left, and the rock climbing scrape on my forearm still lingered. Put the facts together, and I hadn't changed one iota. But since adulthood, I'd never lost my mind over a man.

Here I was, cracked out over August.

Before this year's dating hiatus, I'd made an effort when meeting men, trying to look pretty, putting my best foot forward and all that jazz. Never had my efforts involved a frustrating fashion show and clothes-littered floor. It was time to get my act together.

I used my last half hour to curl on my couch and pore over my mother's journal, the analytical work more calming than I'd have thought. It was methodical. It gave my mind something to latch onto, other than the fact that August had saved a photo of me. Did he look at it often? Had it haunted him the way my keepsakes of him had haunted me?

I growled into my empty apartment, annoyed August had thwarted my focus again.

I focused harder and flipped more journal pages, frustrated when some stuck together, causing me to miss sections. Not that all my mother's random entries were gems. Her "I hate my mom" rant could have been written by me and most kids during their teen years, but Mary Hamilton's malice had stemmed from forced church attendance, a strict dress code, curfew, and TV limitations.

Partway through, a cutout of a ballerina stopped my flipping. A quick browse showed more dance pictures and corresponding entries, my mother writing things like:

Dancing is everything.

The music makes me feel alive.

I would rather die than not dance.

Those jazz shoes must have been her prized possession. I suddenly wished I hadn't left the suitcase at her house. I wanted to wear her shoes, experience that passion. The possibility puckered my mouth. There was no point searching for something that had died long ago. There was only the here and now. This reality.

Journal in my lap, I glanced around my small apartment. It was generally neat, the open kitchen and living area decorated in shades of blue and gray. My leather couch was comfy, the closets big enough to store my rock climbing equipment and diving gear. The slate walls were bare except for the surfboard and mountain bike taking up real estate. There were no family photos. No snapshots of birthdays or weddings or celebrations. My mother had only ever visited my place once, because I'd asked her over. That painful hour had involved both of us checking the time repeatedly.

Mary Hamilton may have had interests and passions as a teen, but that wasn't the woman she'd become. The only thing I wanted to find in these pages were clues to the man she'd slept with, a visual that turned my insides to *ick*.

Eye on the time, I studied the dance pages for a hint. A partner she'd waltzed with? A boy who'd picked her up from class? Assuming she'd taken classes. That part wasn't clear. What did repeat was the acronym TASC.

Tucking my legs under me on the couch, I searched my phone for the term and gawked at the landing page.

Tenderloin Arts and Spiritual Center: a community space in the Tenderloin district where art and culture and spirituality come together.

Spirituality? If I'd sipped the water on my coffee table before reading that, I'd have done a spit take. It was easier picturing my mother as a tattooed biker than getting spiritual in the Tenderloin—San Francisco's seedy epicenter. Granted the area was changing, theaters and music venues drawing different crowds, but those streets had crawled with drug dealers and prostitutes back then.

Oh, crap…*prostitutes.*

Visions of spitting water vanished as my mouth dried.

What if young Mary Hamilton had worked the street? What

if she'd run away from her controlling parents, only to wind up knocked up and devastated?

Be careful what you wish for.

I toyed with the journal's edges, debated closing it, choosing ignorance over truths better left unknown. It would mean giving up, and I didn't give up. I worked harder, did more reps, lifted heavier weights. All to reach my potential.

I'd set a goal for myself last year, and this journal was my chance to reach that target. Giving up was losing. Giving up meant failure. Giving up meant I'd have nothing to focus on besides August Cruz.

Nose back in the book, I scanned a few more pages and noticed a "him." No names or specific descriptions, just:

He watched me dance today.

I saw him at TASC.

When I spotted the intimate tidbit: *I'm dying to kiss him*, my hands shook. This was my first clue. A real lead, not the stupid window washer business cards I'd stolen from my mother's purse. There had been a boy at this TASC place.

Possibly my father.

Part of me wanted to keep reading, but the reality of August and these clues tumbling into my life so suddenly had my head ready to pop. What would I say if I met my father tonight? How was I supposed to act around August later?

Thank God I'd made plans to meet the girls, a reprieve I desperately needed. A chance to find my equilibrium and unload this drama before it intensified, even though August would be there, too.

Soon, he'd be sitting with us, possibly flirting with me and going on about his saved photo and *pole* like the two of us could forget our past. Even worse was the possibility of him *not* flirting with me and going on about his saved photo and *pole* like the two of us could forget our past.

I wasn't sure which option stressed me more.

———

Journal left in my car, I crossed the street to Sweet Pea, a cute bistro/bar we frequented. The barn-board walls and cramped wooden tables created a casual-chic vibe. I normally found the place relaxing, the country tunes not too loud. This afternoon I scanned the room as though a jack-in-the-box might spring from the floor.

My friends were at a table, drinks in hand, no August in sight. I breathed easier. It was also nice having space from the journal and the possibilities it might hold. "I hope this is for me." I nodded to the white wine near one of two empty chairs.

Rachel squinted at me. "Should I have ordered you a bottle?"

"Do I look that bad?"

"You don't look like you."

Even my best friend sensed I was an imposter. "Things have happened."

My mother things. Finding my father things. *August things.* Unsure where to begin, I sat in the seat beside Rachel. Ainsley was on her right, their boyfriends across from them. They all watched me, waiting. I sipped my wine, stalling. I tried to remember that I wasn't alone in the complicated-relationship department.

Owen was the strong silent type, the tiniest twang to his baritone, a rugged man who'd look at home corralling sheep and saying ma'am. Here he was, smitten with Ainsley, a blond bombshell whose closet rivaled a Bloomingdale's display. Rachel's freckled innocence was a sharp contrast to Jimmy's inked skin and biker style, but they'd fallen cupid stupid in love with each other.

I'd watched both girls the past year, falling in love, then not falling, then falling harder, then hurting before eventually zooming to cloud nine. I was thrilled for them. They deserved the world. Watching them find their *other* had also torn at me, on a fundamental level.

My dating hiatus the past year had been necessary. The only way to break a habit was by going cold turkey, and my asshole dependency had become a problem. Part of me had believed I didn't deserve more; a girl who slept with her first love's brother wasn't high on Santa's Nice List. Part of me was just plain tired of no man ever measuring up to the one who owned my heart.

I did want my *other*, though. I dreamed of it. Yearned for that and more.

A family of my own.

If it didn't happen one day, I'd toss my name in the adoption pool, find a baby who needed a loving mother, someone who would support her, rub her back when sick, celebrate the highs and commiserate for the lows. I would do it, on my own if need be. It wasn't my first choice. I wanted the whole package, but there was only one man I'd ever imagined in that role. A virtual impossibility, no matter our earlier flirtations.

I sighed into my wine.

Ainsley nudged Rachel, the two of them striking up conversation as though I wasn't there. "Is this because of the soccer guy? Her old crush?"

"Considering he showed up at her mother's house unannounced, I'd go with yes."

"I need details."

"Do you ever." Rachel looked as bewildered as when I'd confessed my WTF. "But it's not my bedtime story to tell."

I glared at the girls, who chose an inopportune time to play our Make Her Squeal game. If two of us ignored the third while hanging out, and talked about her in front of her face, the ignored friend eventually caved and spilled her stockpiled gossip. Which was what I wanted to do, break this dam holding my August and lost-luggage drama hostage.

Unfortunately, explaining it was easier in my head.

"Is he as hot up close?" Ainsley went on.

Rachel fanned her face. "Hotter."

"Damn."

"Exactly."

Jimmy lifted his wineglass, studying its garnet color through the light. A sophisticated move for such a rough guy. "If this is how you guys talk while we're at the table, what do you say when you're alone?"

"Nothing," Rachel blurted.

Ainsley tipped up her chin. "We'll never tell."

I snickered. I doubted he'd want to hear how we'd discussed his cock *in detail*, a fun topic we brought up with Rachel as often as possible. Anything to make our friend blush.

"Anyhoo." Ainsley was on a roll, intent on making me crack. "What's soccer man's name again?"

"August." Owen took a healthy pull on his beer. "We played with him, weekends and evenings in the California Regional League. Went to different schools, but we hung out plenty."

The soccer guys. The coincidence still astounded me.

Jealousy would sting me every time August would go out and have fun with his friends, while I'd break my brain over calculus and science. My mother's strict rules had also included a curfew. Another barrier to tagging along with August. I'd never ask for details about his nights, hadn't wanted to know who he'd seen, what he'd done. Hearing about his fun would only have enflamed my envy.

But I had attended his odd soccer match, would watch from the sidelines with his family. Back then, I'd only had eyes for him. Hadn't paid the other players a lick of attention.

Now we were all friends.

"Right. August." Ainsley nodded at Owen like she'd forgotten the only guy I'd ever mooned to them about. The actress was being a sneak. "Was he as hot back then?"

She also had a one-track mind.

Owen's brown eyes swirled with amusement. "Emmett asked him out once. No. Wait…" He shook his head and smiled. "Twice. It was definitely twice."

Ainsley hitched her shoulders, hands clutched together excitedly. "Does that mean August's gay? Is that why he and Gwen never hooked up?"

Owen's brother was in a relationship now, but I'd heard stories about his rampant dating prior, how much of a player Emmett had been. Learning he'd hit on August when younger wasn't a surprise. August's hot factor had been just as high back then.

What was a surprise was having August turn up right as Ainsley asked that mortifying question.

"I'm not gay," August said, sidling up to our table. His eyes were trained on me, skewering me with enough heat to spark a wildfire.

My breath stalled as I attempted to douse those rising flames, because *wow*, did he clean up well.

His worn jeans hugged his narrow hips, a few threads at the seams escaping. His plain black T-shirt accentuated his wide shoulders and sinewy arms. His dark hair was still damp, my favorite cowlick swimming against the current. A hint of minty aftershave wafted from his clean-shaven cheeks, and I ached to run my nose along that smooth jawline.

Until he answered the latter of Ainsley's questions. "Gwen and I didn't hook up because we had a misunderstanding in college, and she slept with my brother."

Owen and Jimmy froze. Rachel and Ainsley's eyes filled half their faces. My world tipped upside down, like I'd bungee jumped, my stomach remaining sky high while the rest of me plunged.

Ignoring the statue game going on around the table, August leisurely pulled out the chair opposite me. He slid *my* wineglass toward him and took a sip, licking his lips as he swallowed. He grinned at me.

Grinned.

At me.

If he were closer, I'd twist his nipple so hard, he'd see the Milky Way.

"Glad you could make it and turn my friends into stone," I told him, my voice rising in pitch and aggravation. "The girls and I are going to the bathroom now. Together. Like girls do. We might be a while."

My chair screeched on the concrete floor as I used my head and thumbs to gesture toward the back of the bar. Rachel and Ainsley picked up on my game of charades lickety-split and followed my hurried strides into the bathroom.

The space was decorated like a country porch, complete with cushioned seat, barn-style stalls, and sunflowers. "He's insane," I said as I fell onto the yellow cushion.

Rachel covered her mouth with her hand. "I can't believe he blurted that."

"He must want to torture me, slowly and painfully. It's his form of retribution." It was probably why he'd agreed to come out. To humiliate me. Make me look bad in front of my friends. *Our* friends. Whatever.

Ainsley's eyebrows finally descended from her hairline. "I can't weigh in on what went down until you fill me in."

I contemplated putting her off, not reliving my teenage stupidity *again*, but there was no point. It was easier this time. The confession still shamed me, but the more often I spoke about it—to Rachel, with August, now Ainsley—the easier it got. "Do you think that's why he aired our dirty laundry?"

Ainsley cocked her head. "What's why? I don't follow."

"When he showed up, that ambush of his seemed—"

"Technically," Rachel cut in, "it wasn't an ambush. He was answering Ainsley's question."

I glowered at Ainsley. "Remind me to thank you for that later."

She plucked a sunflower from a sink vase and offered it to me. "A token for my *peccadillo*."

I accepted her gift and spun the massive flower. "Have you been playing crosswords again?"

"Yes, but I cheated for that word, which means a small transgression. Like August's fumble now. But isn't everything better out in the open?"

"Which brings me to the point I was trying to make." This conversation was tangling as quickly as my thoughts. "I hadn't spoken with anyone about that night for nine years, and I get the impression August hadn't either. Even thinking about it before made me feel like I'd eaten one of Ainsley's vegan desserts." I mimed an upset stomach. Served her right for the accidental ambush.

She rolled her eyes. "You guys love my baking."

We did not, but we ate the horrible efforts anyway.

"What about now?" Rachel asked me, avoiding the vegan discussion like the good friend she was. "Do you feel less pukey about the whole thing?"

"If I stop and relive the fiasco, I start to spiral, but it's easier. So either August wants to torment me in front of you guys, or he's trying to lighten our history, make it less of a big deal."

Option A meant this reunion of ours would end shortly, no friendship maintained. Option B meant he might truly want to put our past to bed. He might want *me* in that bed with him.

The possibility excited and terrified me in equal measure.

Ainsley looked over my head, at the mirror behind me. Her purple wrap dress hugged her generous curves, her small stature elevated by matching stilettos. She adjusted the tie that hung at her side. "Judging by the way he looked at you, I'd say the only tormenting he wants to do involves ropes, hot wax, and silk sheets."

That visual had heat flooding my neck. "How was he looking at me?" I fanned my face with the massive flower.

"Like you're a supermodel, and he's had your picture on his wall forever, like the skimpy bikini kind, and he just realized he gets to sex you up."

I choked on air. "That was specific."

Ainsley gestured toward the door, as though August was

there. "So was his extensive eye-fucking. He wants bikini-poster sex."

Too frazzled to compute that, I stroked the sunflower's petals. "I'm in deep water here. The shark-infested kind. I mean, August is, without a doubt, the one who got away. If I had another chance with him, I'd jump at it." Pole vault, to be precise. "But there's been another development."

More drama to unload, because I was living in soap opera central. Once I finished outlining the arrival of my mother's lost luggage, the time gap between its contents and it going missing, the journal, and the first clue I'd found, the girls had sat on either side of me, scooched close in a love sandwich.

Rachel gathered my hand in hers. "Are you nervous about searching for your dad?"

Terrified. Nauseated. Overwhelmed. "Definitely." I tried dissecting the million and one thoughts boxing my brain. "I believe we get what we get in the family department. We don't choose our parents or siblings or relatives. I got short-strawed and made it through, but I spent a lot of years resenting my mother, and resenting myself in the process. It's part of the reason I pushed August away back then—my shitty self-worth. And I'm worried searching for my father now could take me back to that place, but I also see finding him as a brand new chance, my last-ditch effort to have family. I have so many questions for him."

Did he seek adrenaline rushes, too?

Had he chosen to leave me, or had Mary never told him I existed?

Did he hate mayonnaise?

Was he afraid of spiders?

When he looked out the window at the moon, did he sometimes wonder what it would be like to float through space?

I had a journal full of questions, some silly, some scary, and I wanted to ask them all. Not at once, obviously. No sense scaring the man stiff. But the questions had built up over my teen and adult years, so many it was hard to breathe at times. Like the pressure against my breastbone would rupture if I never sat face-to-face with the man and found out who he was.

Ainsley pressed her hand to my knee. "What if he's awful? You don't know anything about him. Maybe there's a good reason your mother never told you his name."

She could be right, but the more I thought about meeting him, the greater my curiosity grew. Exactly why I'd needed to talk this out. "I think I'd rather know. I'd rather meet him and see for myself he's an asshole. Without that, I'll drive myself nuts."

When families came to me, desperate to adopt, I'd warn them how long and grueling the process could be, how emotionally draining. Little good that did. Each phone call and meeting, nerves and fear would invade their voices. Wisps of hope. Nothing beat giving good news to prospective parents. I wouldn't trade those joyful tears and hugs for anything. Letting others down often led to Ben & Jerry sessions with the girls, where we'd heckle bad reality TV and commiserate.

Still, I preferred it to the limbo of the parents not knowing. Answers, good or bad, meant they could move on. Make another choice. Reevaluate their lives. Like I had after I'd tracked down my grandparents.

That shit show had involved my grandmother asking if I'd found God, then listing all the ways young girls sinned. Instead of the cookies and tea and hugs I'd dreamed of, I'd gotten a fanatic only interested in preaching at me. The confrontation had been upsetting, but it had allowed me to quit obsessing over something I'd never have. I moved on.

Exactly what I needed to do with my dad.

Until I knew unequivocally, one way or another, if my father was a good or bad man, a drunk or a saint, funny or mean, warm or cold, I'd exist in a perpetual state of uncertainty, those wisps of hope to one day meet him never letting me close that door to my past.

"I think knowing is better than limbo. If he's a dick, so be it." I rubbed my eyes, forgetting I'd applied more eyeliner than usual. Raccoon eyes weren't sexy.

Ainsley patted my thigh. "Then we're here for you, for whatever you need. But back to the August issue." She peered at me intently, getting up in my face. "You said you asked him to help find your father. Did he answer?"

I squirmed, remembering the solidness of him as he'd held me on his very *firm* lap. How I'd panicked afterward. "He flirted instead. And when I confronted him later, asked why he came by, he said he wasn't sure anymore."

"Your past is pretty intense," Ainsley said.

"Maybe he showed up wanting closure." Rachel's soft voice was more soothing than her words. "He could've been surprised how much he still felt for you."

That prospect was preferable. "But why now? My mom dying, the luggage, August—it all feels too coincidental. I'm not sure it's smart to deal with August with all this other...*stuff* going on."

Rachel rolled her bottom lip between her teeth. "You guys remember the blackout when we made our wish? Last year?"

It was impossible to forget that crazy night: the three of us with our eyes closed, holding hands as midnight struck, making our resolutions as a blackout had pitched the bar into darkness.

Crazy with a side of loop-dee-loo.

"Well," Rachel went on, "I kind of thought something larger was going on that night. Something bigger guiding our choices. It was part of the reason I worked so hard to realize my resolution. As far as I'm concerned, there's nothing wrong with believing in the impossible. In us being connected to unseen forces that impact our lives. You wished to find your father because it was important to you, and now you have your mother's diary and your first love giving you sexy eyes, all before your chosen deadline. If it were me, I'd stop trying to figure out why. I'd take the breadcrumbs offered and follow their trail. Maybe August turned up for a reason."

"Aside from embarrassing me in front of my friends?"

She pinched my side. "Aside from that. But we'll laugh about it eventually."

In her dark jeans and cream blouse, adorably freckled Rachel appeared sweet and levelheaded, not like a flake who believed in crystal balls and fairy godmothers. But she was insisting August was a sign, the lost luggage fate, the diary my destiny.

The notion was wild and impossible. Or was it?

Today's strange happenings were precisely what made it hard to dismiss her hypothesis. There was no point fighting something unexplainable, especially when the mystery brought with it a certain dark-haired musician.

I'd had it bad for August since the sweltering summer day he'd invited me to run, screaming and laughing, through his sprinklers. I'd been nine years old and struck dumb by a boy with a smile big enough to brighten my somber world.

I glanced at the exit, shaky and apprehensive, knowing he was out there. "He never answered when I asked him to help me find my father. What if he says no?"

Ainsley stood and smoothed her dress. "After the comment he made, and those fuck-me eyes, there's no way he'll say no. I guarantee he's out there right now, dishing to the guys about you. Which means I need to fix your eyeliner before we go back out."

"Oh!" Rachel clapped. "It's like you guys are performing a remake of *Grease*—us girls in here, the boys out there, gossiping about your lost love. It's so romantic."

Clearly Rachel was as delusional as me, but I pictured the silly scene and smiled as my friends fussed over my smudged face.

CHAPTER 7

6 p.m., 30 Hours…

August

"You, my man, have balls of iron." Jimmy shook his head at me, pretty much all he and Owen had done since the girls' not-so-subtle bathroom dash.

I'd gotten away with staying mum while our waitress came by and I decided on a beer, but there was no avoiding the grenade I'd launched. "My history with Gwen is complicated."

Owen shifted his chair forward. "I thought I had it rough with my ex-wife, but your situation seems sticky as hell. Actually…" He frowned at the blackboard menu above the bar. "Ainsley crushed on my brother before we met. If Emmett was straight, she would have slept with him. Hate to think where that would have left us." He rubbed his chest.

I was well acquainted with that pain. "I've been angry with her a long time."

Jimmy leaned his elbows on the table, dark eyes narrowing. He looked like a brute in this kitschy bar, daisies on the lime green tables, birds painted on the walls. "If you said that to upset her before, as nice as it's been seeing you, I'll have to ask you to leave."

Under different circumstances, his hard tone would have my shoulders bunching toward my ears, but the ultimatum meant Gwen had people who cared for her.

"I didn't." I rubbed this salty day from my eyes, unsure how much to say. I rarely spoke with Finch anymore. My bandmates were cool, but we didn't sit up at night braiding one another's hair and swapping stories. I hadn't seen these guys in twelve years, but some friendships defied the laws of time.

I shoved my right hand into my jeans pocket, finding one of my guitar picks. I spun it in circles. "I've had it bad for Gwen for as long as I can remember, and for a bunch of stupid reasons on both our parts, we never acted on how we felt. The closest we ever got was the day she turned nineteen, and she slept with my twin. But seeing her now…" My body hummed at the thought of her. "I'm tired of letting one fuck-up ruin our chances. Not sure I can let her walk away this time."

Studying her packed box filled with our memories had knocked my head clear. She hadn't let go of me, like I hadn't let go of her, even though I'd tried.

I'd driven to my hotel afterward, unable to shake thoughts of her. My bitterness had dripped into the drain as I'd showered, imagining Gwen under that hot stream with me. It had thinned into nothing as I'd dressed and hopped in my car, jumpy and nervous. Not because I dreaded seeing Gwen.

Because I couldn't wait to be with her again, anywhere near her, touching her, breathing her in.

One afternoon, and I was hooked.

Jimmy stared at me like I had carrots dangling from my nose. "So you thought you'd share your history with the group?"

I released the guitar pick and passed my hand over my

mouth, wishing I'd sewn it shut. "It kind of slipped out. I'm tired of us tiptoeing around each other."

He barked out a laugh. "*It kind of slipped out.* Have you met these girls? Ainsley will eat you for breakfast, lunch, and dinner." The asshole kept laughing.

If making our history non-taboo helped Gwen and me rediscover our footing, it was worth it. Getting over her night with Finch would still be a tough wall to scale, but we'd made huge strides earlier, and walking away now would leave me with less closure than before. Just a few hours with her had lyrics looping through my head, odd fragments I'd been jotting down since I'd left her mother's.

Time licks wounds. Touch remembers. Infinite flames.

Finch's betrayal had been more personal, complications that had stemmed from decisions made prior to that shit-storm. Gwen, I could forgive, and I meant what I'd told her earlier: I was done analyzing my actions. If I wanted to flirt with her, I would. If I wanted to touch her, tease her, kiss her, I would.

I just had to figure out what to do about her mother's letter and the news it brought.

I could come clean, explain how I'd ignored a dying woman's wishes to share Gwen's father's name. How I'd needed time to process before facing the only woman I'd ever loved. Feelings that still lingered all these years later. I could tell her I waited and delayed, procrastinating like a prick, and when I finally looked up her father the other day, to make sure he wasn't a drunk or druggie, or some skeeze who'd hurt her, the intel I discovered had punched me in the gut.

I'd sat in my car afterward, eyes squeezed to the point of pain, wishing I could turn back time.

But her father had died of a heart attack.

Eight days prior.

I'd sat on his name for two months. Because of my procrastination, Gwen would never meet her father. Because of me, she'd never talk to him and find the missing pieces of her puzzle.

The waitress set down my beer, and I grabbed it, thankful to busy my hands.

Owen reached over, knocking his bottle against mine. "Here's to finding your feet with Gwen and avoiding Ainsley's wrath."

"Of which wrath do you speak?"

Ainsley swayed her hips as she approached, more amusement than ire in the sultry pout aimed at Owen. He raised an eyebrow at her. "Doll, don't pretend like you aren't terrifying. Jimmy still needs counseling."

Ainsley sat primly opposite her boyfriend, folding her hands on the table. Rachel followed and slipped into her seat. I exhaled a long, slow breath as Gwen sauntered forward. Her dark jeans and white tank top worshipped her body, her shoulder-length hair loose and messy. Dark makeup lined her green eyes. She was the picture of cool and casual.

She was the only woman I'd ever imagined in my future.

The only one I wanted in my bed now.

Today. This minute.

My calves tightened, my toes contracting, every bone in my body tense and alive. Heat stroked my groin. I gripped my beer, hoping the cold, damp bottle would tame the fire smoking through my veins. I launched her my most charming smile. "Glad you made it back."

Before she could answer, Ainsley pinned me with her feisty blue eyes. "Ignore the counseling crack. Owen's just talking about the time I threatened to leave a candiru fish in Jimmy's toilet bowl. The ones that swim up a urine stream into a guy's penis and gnaw on its flesh?" She rolled her eyes, as though the comment didn't send my nuts running for my stomach. "Which is silly, really. It's nothing like that smallpox virus. You get that sucker, and you don't have a clue for a week or two, and then *bam*. Pus-filled blisters are everywhere. In your nose and mouth, covering your entire body. And when they rupture?" She shivered dramatically. "You'd be wishing for a fish gnawing on your junk. So like I said to Jimmy, don't hurt my friend."

She punctuated the horrifying threat with a grin.

My face felt as green as Jimmy's looked. "Your girlfriend is terrifying," I muttered to Owen.

His eyes turned hazy as he stared at her. "She's one of a kind."

I might have to reevaluate what horrors I'd walk through to reach Gwen, but the way she was laughing under her breath, a slight shake to her shoulders, it was worth the nauseating visuals.

Jimmy berated Ainsley for ruining his appetite, but he opened a menu anyway, the four of them debating which appetizers we'd share.

I barely listened, couldn't tell you what music played, or how full the bar was. All I saw was Gwen, and the amusement draining from her face. She leaned forward. "Were you trying to hurt me before, saying what you did?"

As much as I believed we needed to speak openly about what had happened, not sweep it under the rug like we'd done for nine years, I regretted the comment. "It just came out."

Her eyes widened. "It just came out?"

I stretched my legs under the table, making contact with her shin. "You're repeating me again."

"Because you're not making sense again. Comments like those don't *just come out*."

No, they didn't. "I wasn't trying to hurt you, Gwen. If I did, I'm sorry. But I'm tired of pretending it didn't happen. It did. It sucked. And I'm ready to move on. Question is, are you?"

She glanced at our friends, who were going out of their way to give us privacy. She slid her attention back at me. "Move on how?"

I could tell her I had every intention of living out my teenage fantasies: Gwen grinding on me, me thrusting into her, slow and deep, my tongue writing songs between her strong thighs. I still had a tour to finish, another album to write, a life in Europe. Gwen's life was a big unknown.

She didn't do social media anymore, my creeping of her over the years unearthing zero intel. I had no clue what she did for a living, or if she'd entertain the notion of traveling with me, but my mind was already there.

To the two of us racing down narrow cobbled streets, stopping to kiss in the rain, laughing as we mangled German translations, feeding each other baguettes and cheese in France.

Jesus. I'd seen Gwen for half a day, and I was fifty steps ahead, practically naming our kids. But that wasn't what she was asking. We were on fragile footing, late winter ice still lingering after a harsh season. "For starters," I said, nudging her leg closer with mine, "I'd be happy to make an agreement."

Her leg didn't move, but her eyebrows did, drawing close together. "You're being mighty cryptic, Cruz."

"Then I'll simplify things for you." I sat straighter, squaring my chest and heart. Hoping she'd judge my honesty. "I'm interested in you, Gwen Frances Hamilton. I miss you and feel like our potential slipped through our fingers, but it's not too late to try and get it back. So I want to move on, with you in my life. As friends, if that's all you can handle. But I'm hoping for more. I'd at least like for us to try, for you to agree to give us a shot." I knocked back a swallow of beer. "Is that clear enough?"

No more games. No more subtle flirting. The only regrets in life were the risks we didn't take, and I was done letting my past undermine my future.

Her throat bobbed, a few slow slides that had me shifting on my seat. A blush stained her nose and cheeks. Had I gone too far? Was she about to bail on me?

But her calf pressed closer to mine. Even through my jeans, awareness splintered through me. Sudden. Fiery. Biting. Like my body was designed to respond to Gwen's alone.

"That's plenty clear, August *Eugene* Cruz." She emphasized the middle name she knew I hated. Just like she hated hers. Way back when, it would have rankled me. Tonight, in the light of our new understanding, it was a gift. "Which leads me to my earlier question."

"You want help learning to pole vault?"

"You seem kind of obsessed with the sport."

"You have no idea." My voice sounded so damn thick.

Her deep inhale said she'd be keen to explore those athletics, too. And man, did I want her hand wrapped around my cock, fisting me, pumping me. Almost as much as I ached to watch her fall apart. Unfortunately, I knew which question dogged her.

The one I'd avoided.

The one I still wasn't sure how to approach.

Her calf slid against mine purposefully. "I have some idea, but the question you sidestepped is if you'd like to wear your Badass PI badge and help me find my father."

I froze, the cold bottle caught in my death grip.

Deciding to pursue her didn't ease my guilt over what I'd done, but I couldn't reverse time. My choices hadn't been malicious. Still, if Gwen learned I'd stolen her chance to meet her father, intentional or not, she'd shut me out. I could drop clues, lead her to him without admitting what I'd done, but that would hurry things along, limit our time together.

Time was already in short supply.

I'd also reread Mary's last line, before leaving my hotel. *Remember what I told you on Gwen's nineteenth birthday.*

Gwen's mother had shocked me when I'd called her nine years ago, her unexpected revelation leading me to buying Gwen her birthday ring, which had led to our epic disaster. Like this letter was more of the same—Gwen's mother more involved in her daughter's life than Gwen had ever realized. I wasn't sure what that meant. Figuring it out seemed important.

More time I needed.

"Of course I'll help you find your father," I said, buying myself more hours.

———

Gwen

Whenever I'd stand on the edge of a plane door, about to skydive, my heart would pummel my chest, exhilaration and nerves spreading as wind blasted my face. Free. It always made me feel incredibly free.

Like I was a superhero. Invincible. Immortal.

Exactly how sitting across from August felt.

"You're sure?" I asked, unwilling to believe he'd agreed to this nutty adventure. That he'd laid out his heart, asking me to take a chance on us.

"Stop questioning everything I say."

He was asking the impossible. Even after his confession, my courage faltered. He knew I'd crushed on him as a teen, but he had no clue how intense those feelings had been, or that they'd continued long after. I probably still loved him now. Words that would send most men running for the hills. I also hadn't realized how badly I wanted his help finding my father until he'd agreed.

I'd be spending the night with August Cruz, my partner in crime, who really was perusing me like my bikini-clad picture had decorated his teenage wall. I took my fill of him, too: the dark circles under his stunning eyes, his masculine jaw, the way his broad shoulders stretched his T-shirt.

He played the part of brooding singer well. Too well.

Being with him while chasing down clues would be a challenge. Already, I debated dragging him to my apartment instead of into San Francisco's Tenderloin district. August was the best and worst distraction. One I couldn't entertain. I had a birthday wish to fulfill by midnight tomorrow. No matter how slim the chances of that happening, I'd do my best. Which meant waiting out this storm cloud of sexual tension.

First and foremost, August and I had been friends. Best friends. If we were going to explore our undeniable connection, starting here made sense.

And I wanted to start now.

I faced our friends. "You guys okay if we take off? August agreed to help search for my father."

Rachel spun her wineglass restlessly. "We can come, tackle other leads. Our wine tasting event later isn't a big one. I'd be happy to cancel."

"Whatever we can do," Jimmy added, compassion in his earnest gaze.

Silent communication passed between Owen and Ainsley. "I was supposed to attend a store opening," he said. "A new place selling my furniture, but I'm cool to bail. Give you whatever help you need."

Ainsley beamed at her man, but said to me, "We'd love to come."

A wave of warmth rolled over me. I may not have blood relatives in my life, but I had this crew, people ready to drop their commitments and come to my aid. Owen's offer in particular touched me. He didn't know his father, either, and his mother had disappeared from his life. He'd been lucky enough to have a loving grandmother raise him and his brother, but understanding shone in his soft brown eyes.

My throat grew scratchy. For a woman who rarely succumbed to emotion, I was sure getting blubbery today. "You guys are the best, but you have food coming, and I only have one lead so far. More people won't help."

Rachel pursed her lips. "Fine, but call if you need us, and we're hitting the gym tomorrow. Come if you can. If Ainsley signs up for a step class, we can watch her trip and glare at the instructor."

One of my favorite pastimes, and I'd hate to miss our gym time. I saw Rachel too rarely now, her Napa Valley life making our visits precious. "I'll do my best. It just might be a shorter session than usual."

Meeting them early shouldn't derail my search, and something told me I'd need the girl time.

"Does that mean we're getting out of here?" August's leg pulled away from mine. The loss of contact was worse than if I'd found myself marooned in the tundra, cold and alone.

I nodded quickly, wondering if he'd press his hand to my lower back as we left, or walk ahead and not glance back. He did one better. He waited for me to stand and join him, then he threaded our fingers together.

My best friend, the boy I'd loved my entire life, was holding my hand.

Goose bumps erupted up my arms.

Rachel blew me a kiss. "Call if you need me."

Ainsley copied her move. "What she said."

"We're heading on a run in the morning," Owen told August. "Boys only. We'll talk about the girls behind their backs. You should come."

August grinned. "How could I turn that down?"

"I'll plant a wire on him," Ainsley fake-whispered to Rachel.

The boys joked about running naked, giving August and me a chance to leave before Ainsley unleashed more of her scary threats.

But I was gone hours ago.

So far gone for August Cruz.

He was a slight step ahead of me. I followed close on his heels until we were outside. We paused, fingers intertwined. He faced me and ran his thumb over the back of my hand. It was a simple brush, but there was nothing simple about touching August.

We both glanced at our clasped hands. My breath faltered. The past few days had been warm for April, the heatwave steaming the evenings, too. Being with August made it steamier. People passed us on the street, a blurred parade of figures. Music drifted from passing cars. Scents of gasoline and rubber permeated the air, all sensations drifting to the background.

August wound both our arms around my back, pulling me against him. "You look beautiful, Possum."

His nickname for me pinched my heart. As kids, I'd pretend to sleep sometimes while we'd watch TV, like a deceiving possum playing dead. I'd then bolt upright to scare the living shit out of him. A screeching August was supremely entertaining.

I tilted my head back to look into his eyes, every memory we'd shared reflected in those hazel pools. "I've missed that nickname."

His free hand came to my cheek, knuckles brushing it gently. "I've missed you. It was always there, under my skin, in every song, but I didn't realize how much until today. My heart is fucking racing."

God, this man. I squeezed our laced palms and unfurled my other over his sternum. Over his heart. Need bellowed in that thundering beat. "You don't smell like grass."

He wrinkled his nose. "I used to smell like weed?"

"Like *grass*, dummy. The lawn mowing business."

He smiled and shook his head lightly. "We can roll around in a park, if you want." He sucked on his bottom lip while eyeing mine.

Lord have mercy. "I can't believe this is happening."

"Oh, it's happening." He gripped my hand tighter, pulled me closer, brushed his nose against mine. Then he stepped back. "But not here. I'm not wasting our first kiss on a sidewalk, surrounded by people."

"It's not our first kiss," I blurted, pointing out the massive blemish on our history. Making out with August while Finch had dealt with his condom had been the world's worst first kiss.

Way to go, Gwen.

His attentions drifted over my shoulder, tilting up to the cloud-dotted sky. He closed his eyes. Shit. *Shit, shit, shit.* Here we were—touching, flirting, finally on the same page—and I go and mention my WTF.

But a second later, he shrugged a shoulder. "You have a point."

He leaned down and kissed me softly, a reverent touch that had me rocking on my heels. My belly dipped. We both moaned. Tingles cascaded down my spine.

August's lips were on mine, where they were meant to be.

Our hands moved and heads tilted, a natural shift that allowed us to open to each other. Open to our past. Accept it. Move on. I clutched the sides of his T-shirt, my fingers curling into the soft fabric. Mine. August was finally, maybe, almost mine.

He cradled my neck, tugged my hair. His breath filled my lungs, sweet and hoppy with the tang of beer. Deeper. Hotter. We were putting on quite the show.

When his tongue skimmed mine, I whimpered.

I'd never whimpered when kissing a man. My skin had never felt like it had shrunk, every inch taut and aware, my clothes and underwear suddenly suffocating. And wet. The damp heat between my thighs engulfed me. He pulled back too soon.

My eyes fluttered open. August came into focus, the street around us reminding me where we were, and of the task ahead of us. Still, I didn't move. "I'm scared to leave this spot."

He rested his forehead against mine. "Why?"

"This could be a dream. I could lose you again. I just...I don't think I can handle that."

He smoothed my hair and kissed the sensitive skin by my ear. "It's not a dream, Possum. And if this is one of *your* stupid pranks, I'll fill your bed with spiders."

I shivered involuntarily.

"But that was..." His breath skimmed my lips once more.

"Yeah, it was," I agreed. Everything.

He stared at me a beat longer, then scanned the street. He cleared his throat. "Your car or mine?"

I was about to say, *either as long as we get naked in the backseat.* But such extracurriculars would have to wait. This was Mission Find My Dad, and Badass PI partners didn't mix business with pleasure. "Let's meet there, in case we have to split up to chase different leads. It's an artsy center in the Tenderloin. My mother danced there or something. She referenced a guy who would watch her some days and pick her up."

Instead of agreeing, he frowned, and my stomach sank. Was he having second thoughts? Was he suddenly overwhelmed? "What is it?"

He toyed with my fingers, dragging his thumb over my cuticles in seductive half-moons. "Nothing. I'll follow you."

After pointing out our cars, we separated slowly, walking backward, our hands the last things to part. Again, a cold desolation gripped me. I almost changed my plan and dragged him to my car, but that was the crazy talking. *Daffy as a duck.* When my heel cranked into a lamppost, I finally turned and hurried to my Impreza.

CHAPTER 8

6:30 p.m., 29 ½ Hours…

Gwen

My driving skills on the way to the TASC center were an embarrassment. I cut off two cars, nearly plowed over a man, and I drove so slowly at one point, honking blared for five seconds.

All I could picture was losing August, his rental car disappearing from sight, him disappearing from my life. I could win that show: *America's Worst Driver*.

In one of America's seediest districts.

The Tenderloin had a smell about it, eau de vomit mixed with rotting garbage and a skunkiness all its own. Weed mixed with gasoline. The homeless community owned the sidewalks, sleeping and loitering twenty-four/seven. Random shouts competed with grinding brakes, and this was an improvement from decades ago.

Again, I tried picturing my mother venturing here, blouse buttoned to her chin, gray-streaked hair close cropped. Pointed nose. Thin lips. *Severe.* That was the word that best described her, in looks and personality.

Yet her younger self had spent time in the Tenderloin.

I dodged crumpled garbage on the cigarette-littered street, stopping once to drop a bill into a woman's panhandling cup. San Francisco's homeless problem was always upsetting. The number of displaced people here threatened to flood my already overwrought heart.

They were also intimidating, especially the man swerving toward me, who smelled like he'd bathed in whiskey. "Gimme some sugar, hot cakes."

August appeared at my side and wrapped a protective arm around my shoulder. "She's only serving sugar to me," he said, curt, leading me toward the rec center. His handsome profile was a granite mask.

When he escorted me safely up the stone steps and inside the front doors, I kissed his smooth cheek. I still couldn't believe I could kiss his cheek, smooth or otherwise. "My Prince Charming."

He kept me tucked into his side. "Please don't come here alone."

"Are you feeling protective?"

"I'm feeling like I want to cut out that man's tongue and feed it to him after marinating it in E. coli."

"I think Ainsley rubbed off on you."

He shivered. "I'd prefer to remain on her good side. We should also find you a parka to wear, keep leering men away."

I glanced at my white tank top, tight but not showing excessive cleavage. "This isn't exactly skimpy, and I could have handled myself on the street."

He backed me against the hallway wall and planted one hand on the plaster by my head. His pupils blew wide. "Do you know how gorgeous you are? I swear to God, Gwen—I can barely focus around you. It was always like this, like I couldn't think about anything but you when we were together. All I could do was write songs. You just exude this strength and confidence, even back when you thought you weren't worthy. More so now. And there's nothing sexier than a woman who can handle her own, but I do *not* want you handling yourself with sloppy men who have no issues taking without asking."

A piano's harmonics drifted toward us, each struck key mimicking my sharp pulse. I flattened my palms on his firm chest and almost whimpered again. "I used to distract you?"

He chuckled, a low devious sound. "Oh, honey, you have no idea."

"I want an idea." I wanted all of his ideas, every thought he'd ever had. I wanted to collect them. My secret jar of hearts. And *honey*? Sign me up for that endearment.

"We'll discuss my ideas during your pole vaulting lesson," he said.

I inched my leg between his, until my hip made contact with his groin. "Will these lessons involve show and tell?"

He rotated his hips, enough for me to appreciate the solid bulge behind his zipper. "Since you sucked at school, I thought visuals would help."

A PowerPoint presentation would be appreciated. "Says the guy who dropped out of college and made a sport out of shooting green Jell-O from his nose. And I worked hard for my degree, thank you very much. I also rock at my job."

Although I was teasing him, his faced sobered. He created space between us. "What do you do for work?"

Right. He didn't know. I may have followed (stalked) his career, but I didn't have a Facebook page. I'd avoided social media since my catastrophic WTF. He wouldn't know defining details of my life. No details at all, really.

His arms hung limp at his sides. Instinctively, I wrapped mine around my waist. "I work at an adoption agency, placing babies in homes."

"Wow." He jolted slightly, his voice low and heavy. "That's amazing. Do you love it?"

Even talking about it had me grinning. "I never expected to find a career that fulfilled me like this, but it's so rewarding. As painful as those student loans and school headaches were, it was worth it. I found my purpose." *To give kids loving families and the childhood I never had.*

He was frowning again, like my success upset him. "I'm happy for you," he said, no happiness in his flat tone.

A chill descended between us. It was easy to get carried away with this newness, kissing in the street, flirting, but this awkward interlude was a reminder how little we knew about each other. It was also easy for him to say he could forgive me and move on from our past. Actions spoke louder than words, and his body language screamed *wary.*

I should take his lead and focus on finding my father, not on pole vaulting and August Cruz. Although pole vaulting with August Cruz was a notion I could get behind. Or in front of. Or underneath.

Instead I pulled my Badass PI badge from my purse. "Tonight I'm not an adoption agent. Tonight we're private investigators hot on a trail."

He latched onto my attempt at levity and dug his badge from his jeans pocket. He held it up between two fingers. "I take my PI work seriously."

"Want me to sew it on your shirt?"

"I doubt you have a needle and thread in that tiny purse, and I've seen you sew, Gwen. You'd likely pierce my nipple."

He was referring to the stuffed monkey I'd made in eighth grade, otherwise known as Mutant Monkey.

I maneuvered my Coach shoulder bag, the compact stunner a donation from Ainsley's collection. Fancy yet functional. I pulled out a mini sewing kit. "For emergencies."

PI badge wedged between his fingers, he covered his nipples with both palms. "You're not coming near me with that."

"Jimmy has piercings. All the cool kids are doing it."

He mock-snarled. "Unless you want to wake up with a tarantula in your bed, I suggest you back away."

I gave him my best sleazy eyes. "Just one poke. It'll feel so good."

He hissed in a sharp breath, my unspoken *that's what she said* joke hitting its mark. A mark I should avoid. This addictive flirting was getting away from me again. Being with him was too intoxicating, too novel. I couldn't rein myself in.

August, however, said, "I'll pass," and averted his eyes. He shoved his badge back in his pocket and studied the hallway, newfound stiffness in his stance.

So much for my levity.

Ignoring my growing discomfort, I followed his lead and read the community posters on the scuffed-up walls. Each advertisement listed classes, from poetry tutorials to tai chi. Piano still echoed from somewhere, stopping and starting, along with a commanding female voice. Up a set of stairs was a glass case that held photos and pottery.

Pretending August's distracted state wasn't distracting me, I pushed past him, led by the sporadic music, but the glass case drew my focus. Most stored photos were yellowed, filled with legwarmer-clad girls and mullet-haired boys. Eighties and nineties styles. Some looked even older, bell bottoms and peace symbols dating them. I wondered for the millionth how teenage Mary Hamilton had hung out in a place like this.

I abruptly muted that thought. She wasn't why I was here. She was a lead and nothing more, a path that could end at my father's door.

I scanned the faces in each photo, searching for her. If she was in here, he might be as well. One showed actors in a low-budget play, another framed a handsome man playing guitar, which reminded me of the silent presence at my back. I stayed focused on the photos, assessing if any men had one eye slightly rounder than the other or a freckled lip. Not that my attributes were necessarily DNA linked, but I was working with limited resources.

Next was a picture of three girls doing a jazz lunge, arms wide, legwarmers on, hair flying as though they'd finished a wild spin. My eyes skimmed past the photo but snapped back.

Two girls looked familiar, the middle one in particular. The one with the wide smile and bright eyes. Holy shit. "That's my mother...and I think my aunt."

August moved to my side and bent forward to study the picture that had me gawking. "You sure?"

The smile—no, my mother's joyous *glow*—wasn't familiar, but her narrow features and long face were unmistakable. My aunt was less recognizable. I'd never met her, but I'd found a few photos when packing my mother's belongings. They resembled each other, my Aunt Sarah only a year younger than my mother. A recluse who'd moved to the East Coast.

Aunt Sarah used to send me a yearly birthday card. The only family member who'd gone out of her way to show she cared. One card a year for eleven years. Until my mother had gotten into a fight with her.

I'd overheard a phone conversation shortly after receiving her last card. Just the end, but it had been enough: Mary hissing into the phone, telling her sister not to call again. That as far as she was concerned she was an only child. The birthday cards had ceased after that. I hadn't realized how much they'd meant to me until they'd stopped.

It was likely another reason I hadn't felt I'd deserved August's friendship. No one had stuck around in my life, not my aunt or my grandparents. I'd believed I hadn't been worth loving.

I couldn't be sure it was Aunt Sarah in the photo, but the resemblance between the two girls was too distinct to ignore.

"I'm pretty sure it's them." I nearly plastered my face against the glass.

"Your mother looks so happy," he said quietly, as though to

himself. Then louder, "How did a woman who danced and listened to Depeche Mode become cold and rigid?"

He took the words right out of my mouth. His arm brushing mine stole the breath from my lungs. I wanted to slide my arm under his, link our elbows, but he still seemed distant. Dissecting his strange vibes was as appealing as analyzing Mary Hamilton's descent into Frost Queen.

I scanned the case for other photos of her, unsuccessfully. "This confirms she danced here, at least. Probably often. They wouldn't have immortalized her picture if it had been just a few times." I straightened and glanced down the narrow hall. The piano had stopped. Young girls filed from a room, ballet slippers on their feet. Parents waited on a couple benches. "It's time to do some recon."

I marched toward the classroom, August following. Chatter from excited girls echoed off the ceiling. A boy left the room in tights, twirling toward his father, who clapped and beamed. The warmth filling the hall was a contrast to the Tenderloin's filth and stench outside. Flowers blooming in a barren field. We waited for the kids to leave.

August stayed quiet, hands shoved in his pockets. He leaned on the wall, away from me.

I chewed my cheek.

An older woman sporting a prim bun exited last, her slender frame accentuated in her leotard, pink tights, and black skirt. She was pushing seventy with a body a thirty-year-old would covet. I glanced at August, unsure how to approach her.

As teens, he and I would perform different roles when investigating. He'd use his smarts to lead us to potential suspects, and I'd play the part of school reporter or Navy SEAL or international spy. Tonight he hung back, broody stance in place, letting me lead the way. Considering our strange reunion, it shouldn't be surprising, but I wasn't sure what role to play.

Unwilling to let the moment slip by, I stepped into the ballet instructor's path. "Sorry to bother you, but I'm trying to find information on a girl who took dance classes in the late eighties. Have you worked here long?"

She studied August, a slow perusal that had me wanting to send out a cougar alert. To me, she said, "I've been here since the center opened, but I'm in a rush. Come back next week, same time, and I can answer your questions."

Nope. No way. A week wouldn't cut it. That suitcase didn't land in my lap the day before my birthday only for my search to lose steam now. I motioned to August. "My friend here isn't feeling well. I told him not to order the refried beans, but he's stubborn as a mule and can't resist them. If he doesn't find a bathroom soon, well…it might get ugly. If you don't mind showing us the way, I can ask you a few questions as we walk?"

Her next glance at August was less cougar and more repelled. I bit my tongue to keep from cackling. He cradled his stomach and winced, playing along, but there was no missing how his lips compressed and the veins in his neck strained against his skin. He didn't like his given role. It made me enjoy it even more.

She huffed out a breath. "Follow me, then. Whoever built this space didn't have a clue how often kids need bathroom breaks."

She strutted ahead, feet slightly turned out, her perfect posture envy inducing. August shot me dirty looks, hand still pressed to his stomach. I winked and mouthed, *Suck it up*, then hurried to keep up with the ballerina.

"Do you have ledgers here?" I asked, trying to match her elegant stride. "Lists of who took classes back then?"

A prim huff escaped her. "That would imply a level of organization."

Disappointment deflated my posture, but I didn't let up. "There's a photo in the glass case, near the entrance—one of three girls doing a jazz slide or something. Do you know which one I mean?"

She took a sharp right down another hall, arms swinging, shoulders back. "Those would be the Sunshine Girls."

"Sunshine Girls?"

She stopped abruptly and pointed to two doors in an alcove. "Bathroom is there."

August, never breaking character, offered a pained smile. I muffled my laugh with a cough.

The ballerina cocked her head at him, another long perusal taking him in from head to toe. "You're August Cruz."

He froze mid-step toward the bathroom. I tried to keep my eyeballs from popping out of my head.

Still hamming up his upset-stomach performance, he winced but nodded. "I am."

She planted her hands on her slim hips and shook her head. "Well, I never… I'm a fan, of your early work in particular. 'Girl with the Black Heart' played on repeat in my home during an unpleasant divorce."

Of course August met a music fan while pretending to have the shits. *Of course* she mentioned the song that immortalized my WTF.

But the fan part was the bigger deal, his successful life coming into focus. He'd always be the boy who'd pluck on his guitar strings, his tongue poking out of his mouth in concentration, but this interaction was a reminder how far he'd come.

He was an immense talent, revered around the globe. Not a limelight-bathed superstar chased by paparazzi. More like an undercover celebrity only recognized by true fans. A musician who lived out of a suitcase while touring. I wasn't sure where'd I'd fit into that life with him. *If* I'd fit in.

The ballerina glanced at the bathroom door, and her wrinkled cheeks colored. "Look at me, keeping you from relieving yourself. Go on, then."

He shot me another glare. Hopefully she read the aggravated scowl as *pained*. "If you stay here a minute," he said through gritted teeth, "I can autograph something for you when I'm out."

Embarrassed or not, he was thinking ahead, giving me more time with our mark.

She tipped her head. "Consider it done."

He escaped into the bathroom.

She turned to me. "The Sunshine Girls were three girls who danced here a few times a week, often on their own. Two sisters and one friend. They would light up a room, hence the name. Real free spirits. They always drew a crowd."

Those visuals rocked me as much as August being recognized, but the confirmation of my aunt's identity had me frowning. I'd assumed my mother and her sister's relationship had always been tumultuous, one easy to toss away. If they'd been close enough to dance and rehearse together, how had they wound up so estranged my mother had cut her sister off? She'd even refused to contact Aunt Sarah when she'd gotten sick, and I couldn't find a number to let my aunt know her sister had passed.

If I had to guess, it was likely my mother's "sunny" personality that had led to their falling out, whatever the reason. Not that it mattered now. All that mattered was finding my father. "Mary Hamilton was the middle girl in the photo," I told the ballerina. "She was also my mother."

She clasped her hands in front of her waist. "Was?" I nodded, and she clucked her tongue. "I'm sorry, dear. I remember her being quite the clown, always laughing with her friends. She brought a lot of life to this place."

Forget being rocked. That information was like being shoved, elbowed, and kicked in the gut. My mother's dislike for me hadn't been a secret. She'd barely glance at my school work, regardless of my prodding. She'd eat her dinner early some nights and leave me at the table alone. She'd never once called me after I'd moved out. The only reason we'd ever seen each other was because I'd initiated contact.

Her lack of affection and sharp words hadn't needed deciphering. Her disdain for me and her life had been crystal clear. But if she'd been such a clown, *a bright light in this place,* it meant

I really *had* been the thing that drained the music from her world. The big change in her life.

Questions flooded my mind. "What do you mean by clown, exactly? Like what did she—" Abruptly, I censored my tongue. Asking about the Mary *before* would only result in another harsh blow. Nothing learned now would undo her harsh parenting. Best to stick to my interrogation. "Sorry. What I'm actually after is information about a boy who watched her dance."

"Many boys watched those girls. Drew them like bees to honey."

Mary Hamilton, the Male Magnet. Another impossible fact. The ballerina checked her watch and tightened her lips. A bathroom toilet flushed. Time wasn't on my side.

"This guy picked her up some days," I added quickly. "Waited for her to finish."

She studied the ceiling while pointing and flexing her foot. "Sorry, but that's all I know. You could try speaking with Mr. Hawton. He's the only other instructor left from back then. He's away for a month, but should return toward the middle of May."

August emerged, ending my interrogation. Not that it mattered. I may have learned my mother had been a silly clown who'd lightened rooms and had seduced men, but this lead had dried up.

Adorning his rock star persona, August escorted his fan to the exit. She fawned over his music and the song about him dousing me—*my shadow*—in gasoline. Always a good time. After having her purse signed and cheeks kissed by her crush, Loretta Walsh, as we'd come to know her, left the center a happy lady.

August, however, glared at me from inside the exit. "A bad stomach? I just *love* my refried beans?"

I swirled my hand in a dramatic flourish. "I was in character."

"And now rumors will spread that I get the shits."

I didn't even try to curb my snickering. "Everyone uses the

bathroom and puts their pants on one leg at a time. You're no different, Mr. Rock God."

A sweet blush highlighted his cheekbones. He dropped his gaze and rubbed the back of his neck. "I'm no rock god. I just play music."

His modesty had my heart tripping over itself. "Don't downplay what you do." When he didn't reply, I said, "I lied, by the way—at my mother's house. I listen to your music all the time. It's brilliant."

He glanced at me through his thick lashes. One beat dragged into two. "Thank you," he said softly.

Forget tripping. My heart freefell, taking my belly with it. And my IQ. It was nice to be joking with him again, talking about real things, even as my wits scattered, but his earlier reserve lingered. He hadn't moved to touch my back or hold my hand.

When with my friends, I never hesitated calling them on their bullshit. I believed in laying your cards on the table, being honest with those in your life. After my WTF, I'd realized too late how vital it was to be honest with *yourself*. Yet here I was, since August had parachuted into my life, hemming and hawing, thinking more than speaking. Keeping the depths of my thoughts on mute.

"We should take off," I said. "Before someone breaks into our cars." Not the thing I should have said. It was the easy thing. The *don't get hurt* thing. "We'll need to read more of my mother's diary, search for more clues."

He cast a dark glance at the street beyond the exit. "Best to meet somewhere else, a bar or something that doesn't come with men who want your sugar."

Heading to our separate vehicles meant another round of erratic driving. I was bound to lose my license before I officially lost my mind. "Maybe we should pare down to one car? We can meet at my apartment. Go through the diary there, then stick together after."

His eyes dropped to my chest, then skimmed up to my neck and face, lower again to my breasts and hips. The zig-zagged pattern tied me into knots. "Sure," he said.

I looked back in the direction of the glass case, where my mother's photo was tucked inside. A strange pressure cramped my lungs, as though fresh oxygen lay that way. Answers. Stones I had yet to turn. But there were no more clues leading to my father. Nothing here would help me find him.

August placed his arm around me as we pushed outside, shielding me with his body. A silly effort. Although a few panhandlers called out for cash, no one paid us much attention. Not that I minded leaning into his side. We arrived at my car too soon.

I gave him my address, and he followed me home and up the stairs to my apartment. I put my key in the lock like I had a thousand times before. I opened my door by rote, but I didn't enter the space.

Not with August behind me, ready to enter as well.

My place looked stark from this angle, my surfboard and mountain bike hidden from view. All that lay ahead were empty slate walls, an *Outside* magazine splayed on the kitchen counter, a shopping list stuck to the fridge. August was about to walk into my home, my life, and learn things about me. Discover the woman I'd become. What struck me harder, though, the blow that had me frozen in place, was that he hadn't fully known me all those years ago, either. Not really.

He'd seen what I'd let him see. He'd heard what I'd chosen to say, never fully speaking my heart. Even when tipsy and texting on my nineteenth birthday, I'd diluted the truth, hinting at an older crush, not admitting I'd still loved him irrevocably.

I had no clue how long he was in town, if our lives could converge, or if this was a wild waystation we'd been stranded on. He'd made the first step, at the restaurant, blurting our history to our friends. It was my turn to offer some blunt honesty, share the extent of my feelings for him back then: hiding from them had never served me in the past.

All he had to do was open my closet door and see the August Cruz poster tacked inside. Proof my feelings hadn't diluted much. (Note to self: remove at first opportunity.)

"Gwen?" His hesitant voice was close, just behind me.

Gathering the strength that served me when powering through an insane workout, when I was sure my lungs would give out and my legs would buckle, I turned to my former best friend, and said, "I loved you."

CHAPTER 9

7:00 p.m., 29 hours…

My abs flexed, like her words had struck my gut. Adrenaline spiked my heart rate. It took three rough breaths to compute what tense she'd used.

Loved not love. Past not present.

Even worse was the heavy disappointment that crushed me at the realization.

She clutched her mother's diary in one hand, her keys in the other. I didn't cup her cheeks the way I ached to, or pull her into my arms. I kept picturing her face when she'd spoken about her job, how much she loved it. How she'd found her life's purpose. A life that didn't include traipsing around Europe with a touring musician.

But, man, the rawness in her voice. "When?"

A sad sigh slipped past her lips. "I don't know. For as long as

I can remember. Like, as kids, being around you made it hurt to breathe. During high school it got worse, especially at the end. And that shitty, lonely year after. Not just because of the lonely part, me building it up in my head."

She tossed her keys and purse and diary on the floor behind her. Like she was angry. "I'm not talking about a teenage crush here, August. This was bone-deep love. And I was sure you didn't feel the same. I thought you pitied me. Or it was my own lame excuse to push you away. I pushed everyone away. It's what I did. Sorry. God." She covered her face with her hands. "I'm not making sense."

But she *did* make sense. Too much sense.

Hand jammed into my pocket, I flipped my guitar pick over. Her texts nine years ago had hinted at the intensity of her feelings. That *Zap* she inspired had leapt from my phone the second I'd seen her name. This morning, at her mother's, the way she'd spoken and the heat in her eyes had said all she hadn't. My instant connection to her had been just as strong.

It had never faded. Not fully.

I'd tried to make sense of this Gwen habit over the years, how I'd pull that zoo picture up on my computer, stare at her, miss her. An addiction I could never kick. Each wallow session ended in sad songs sung. So, yeah...I understood what it was to feel like the marrow had been sucked from your bones, the hollowness that lingered. Nine years of emptiness. Nearly eleven if her previous silent treatment counted.

I also recognized the way she was breathing harder now, eyes round and wide. Filled with doubt and longing—hope that this second chance would stick.

I stepped toward her, a fraction closer. She had loved me. *She loves me,* my body and soul taunted. Whatever the tense, her truth had me addled. It was why I'd backed away from her earlier. This was not a woman I could casually *fuck*. That kiss in the street had resounded through me, like a tuning fork had vibrated through my blood.

This was a woman meant to be worshipped, strummed, discovered, *possessed*.

And she had a life here she loved. Friends. A great job. Not to mention I was helping her track down a deceased man.

Letting this go any further would be irresponsible. That didn't stop my honesty from matching hers. "I loved you, too. I realized it when I started resenting Finch hanging around us. I hated him making you laugh, hated you wrestling with him or running through the sprinklers together. I wanted you to myself, but I also knew I was all you really had. That thought scared the crap out of me."

Her hand floated up to her neck. "Why?"

"If we didn't work, where would that have left you? With friends like Kayla who only ever wanted to social climb? Feed you false information, so she could make her move on me?" I shook my head. "I couldn't risk it."

"You knew Kayla did that?"

"Not until much later. The night I broke up with her, when… everything went down, she didn't walk away easily. She badgered me awhile, and when she figured out something happened with you, she told me you hated being my charity case. That what we had hadn't been real. She framed it in a catty way to make you look bad, but it was easy to read between the lines, that she'd turned those tables on you, too. At the time, it was more shit heaped onto a shit pile. But I know you, Gwen. I understand how your mother beat you down. How one word from someone like Kayla would infect you."

Her spine went rigid. "My mother never hit me. I would have told you."

"Emotional abuse is just as bad."

She winced, and it crushed me. I'd walked in once, unannounced, to overhear Mary Hamilton call her only child worthless. Stupid. The word *disgusted* had been used. Always in that acrid tone, like Gwen was lice stuck in her hair.

"Thing is," I shut the door and inched forward, walking until we were in her kitchen, her back pressed to her island counter-top, "you never cowered when she laced into you. You would lift your chin and take it. Stand taller. I never pitied you, Gwen. I was *amazed* by you."

She tilted her head to meet my eyes. Disbelief shone. "Really?"

"Oh, honey. I was in awe of you." I planted my hands on either side of her, caging her body against the counter. The space between us swelled with nine years of bridled heat.

"But you don't know me now," she said, her voice breathless. "I also wasn't fully honest with you earlier, when you asked why I slept with Finch."

My grip on the counter stiffened. "What do you mean?"

"You asked if I did it to hurt you, and I think part of me did. Aside from being sad and lonely, and wishing Finch was you, I was devastated when I saw that stupid picture of Kayla. I was angry and knew sleeping with Finch would hurt you. I knew, and I did it. I wanted you to feel my pain." She finally touched me, her hands branding my chest. "I'm sorry. It was so wrong."

My first instinct was to wrench away from her and pace an angry line, but to what end? Feed the demons that had chased me these long years? Try to surgically remove this woman who lived under my skin? I'd only cut myself. "I understand," I offered instead.

But she curved forward, her shoulders sloping in dismay.

"Look at me, Gwen." When she lifted her head, I held her chin between my fingers. "You loved me. I loved you. We should have done something about it, but we didn't. We hurt each other instead. But what I see in front of me now is a fresh start with the only person who knows I love *Gilmore Girls* and who spreads rumors I get the shits from eating beans."

That earned me a smile. "I should run your fan club."

She should be the goddamn president. I erased the inches separating us, pressed my hips into hers. My dick lengthened, got hot and heavy. She mewled at the contact, her hands snaking around my waist. She pulled me into her.

Lust blasted up my thighs. "Please tell me you want this, too. Because being with you is killing me. I've never wanted anything so badly as I want you right now. You have no idea."

She latched her leg around mine and rolled her hips. "Then stop talking and start kissing."

I slammed my mouth onto hers. There was no holding back the years I'd fought our pull, the eternity I'd dreamed of sinking into Gwen. My thrusts rocked her into the sharp counter, my lips working hers open. She let me in, sucked on my tongue, my bottom lip. I palmed her ass and pressed into her.

Her aggression rivaled mine. She pushed back so hard I lost my grip on the counter and tumbled to the floor, taking her with me. Because I wouldn't let her go. Not now. Maybe never. Fuck, I had Gwen Hamilton in my arms, under me, on her apartment floor. Abruptly, I shoved my hand up her shirt. She gasped. My knuckles skimmed her taut stomach until her breast was in my greedy grasp. Her bra was lacy, her nipples hard buds beneath. My cock throbbed with each squeeze of my palm.

Gripping my hair in unforgiving fists, she rutted against me and sucked on my neck, her jeans abrading mine so wildly sparks were sure to light. I thrust harder; she cried out. We were dry-fucking like a couple desperate teens.

"Jesus, Gwen. I can't last like this. I need you so fucking bad."

"If I don't fuck you in the next three seconds, I'll die."

"Don't you dare."

"Then get to work."

A command I'd happily follow. She pushed up my shirt and yanked at my belt buckle. I made quick work of dragging off her jeans, but mine only made it to my knees. My hand was in her underwear, the slick heat of her obliterating me. "You're so wet."

She writhed beneath me and cupped me over my briefs. "That's all for you."

A gift I'd never have dared wished for. The pressure of her hand on my cock, rubbing brazenly, had my eyes rolling to the back of my head. She pulled at my waistband, so hard she trapped my hips against hers. I eased her back. "Easy, sweetheart. I need space to get them off. And we need a condom."

"No." She stilled beneath me, both of us breathing hard. "I'm on the pill. Are you clean?"

Christ. Bare and balls deep in Gwen Hamilton? Fresh fire leapt up my thighs. "I'm careful and I get tested."

"Me too."

And I was about to lose my load.

My ass flexed as we shoved my briefs down, my cumbersome clothing hooked around my knees. Her tank top was shoved above her bra. My shirt was still on, too, hiked high enough that our abdomens touched. Warm skin on warm skin. Gwen's skin against mine. Sweet anticipation spiraled through me, and the instant her hand circled my rigid flesh, I bucked. It wasn't pretty. It was instinct. Her hot palm played me, my hard length singing in response. I'd never been burned up by desire. Not like this, riled and flushed with wanting.

The hard floor didn't matter. We could be locked in a prison cell for all I cared. All that mattered was her willing body under mine, my best friend about to become so much more.

I kissed her neck, sucked on her ear. She guided me to her entrance, a firm grip that didn't waver. I should have slowed down, eased into her, but the second I felt her cleft, the very center of her, I thrust in. "Gwen, fuck. Oh, fuck." *My Gwen.*

The words tore from my throat. Her name resonated in my chest, ringing with rightness.

She clawed my ass. "August, God. How do you feel this good?"

"I'm so hard, baby. So hard inside you."

Her inner walls clenched, sucking me deeper. I spasmed at the hot tug. I didn't slow. I couldn't. Hard, fast strokes followed. Skin slapping. My forearms and knees dug into the hardwood floor, Gwen's body caged below me. We locked eyes, our mouths open but not touching. We traded grunts and pants, but the intensity didn't allow for kissing.

There was also a hint of anger in each snap of my hips. Uncensored bitterness for what she'd done, her one senseless act stealing almost a decade from us. But it played like a dead note, a muffled guitar string that enhanced the backbeat. Made it what it was. This was our time.

Now, not then. Anger and all.

It whipped through me, coupled with the way Gwen's eyes shone with tears, our lips still brushing but not connecting, her knees drilled into my sides.

Anyone else, and what we were doing would be fucking. Not with Gwen. This was making love to the woman I'd dreamed of most of my life.

Real, raw, wild.

"August." She panted my name. "I'm so close."

We clutched each other like this was the only moment we'd ever have.

"I'm gonna explode the second you let go." I slammed harder into her, nearly winding myself.

"Oh, wow. Yeah. That. Don't stop *that*."

I growled my approval, loved her asking for what she needed. I was on a thin wire, my thighs screaming for release, my balls drawing up tight. When she called my name again, it soared with a sharp cry, her pussy clamping on me so tightly my release detonated—a fast, hot surge that blasted down my spine. It lasted an eternity, each convulsion blinding.

I kissed her then, finally, pressing my cock deeper inside her, fucking her mouth with my tongue as the waves lessened. Her tears stuck to my cheeks. I kissed her eyelids, the underside of her jaw. Worked my way back to her perfect mouth.

I couldn't get enough.

I also had to tread carefully.

Explaining I'd ruined her opportunity to meet her father

could mean this would never happen again. It could wreck our fresh start. There was nothing to be done at this point, no bringing the man back, but I could be with her on this journey, support her when she found out. Maybe we'd learn more about him during the process. If I told her the truth now, she'd stop following the clues. She'd push me away.

Both outcomes unacceptable.

I rotated my hips, still high on the heaven of her. "My knees are skinned."

She laughed and wrapped her arms and legs around me. "My ass is bruised."

"What a glorious ass it is."

"You didn't even see it."

"I squeezed it. And I plan to see it shortly."

She clasped me closer. "That just happened."

I rubbed my nose up her ear. "It did. And it better happen again."

"Don't pull out yet."

Her heart raced, a rapid percussion against my chest. Pounding with anxiety? "I'm not going anywhere, Possum."

Except that wasn't true. Another unpleasant reality. I had to get on a plane in less than two days.

———

Gwen

I trailed my nails down August's scalp, and he sighed. When I clenched my core, a delicious rumble moved through his chest. Little things. New things. Precious discoveries I wanted to hoard.

He pressed soft kisses all over my face. "Stay here. I'll get a cloth to clean you up."

I flinched as he pulled out, the emptiness instant, but when he tripped kicking off his jeans and briefs, we both laughed; the silly intimacy of it filled me back up. The way he reached behind him and yanked off his T-shirt had my laugh trembling into a moan.

He smirked over his shoulder. "Like what you see?"

"Love it." The defined muscles of his back. The divots at the base of his spine. How his toned ass flexed with each move. "Bathroom is down the hall to your left." I watched him in all his naked glory until he disappeared. I tilted my hips to keep his release from spilling farther down my thighs, and the wackiest of wacky thoughts blindsided me: *I wish I wasn't on the pill.*

I pressed my hands to my flat belly and almost keened. The urge to have a permanent reminder of what we'd shared ripped through me. A piece of August mixed with a piece of me. Forever. If he could read my mind, he'd probably bolt so fast the air would spin.

I focused instead on the tenderness between my thighs.

That had been life-altering sex. Moving with him, staring into his eyes while he pumped into me hadn't been like I'd imagined. And I'd imagined it a lot. This had been more intense than expected, deeper. Like we'd never lost our connection.

Or maybe the intensity was because we *had* lost it. The anger, the regrets—they'd fueled our flames. And what flames they'd been. Unfortunately, flames too often left scars…and unhealthy baby-making thoughts.

While waiting for him, I removed my bra and tank top. I lay on my hard floor, naked and exposed. Instinctively I knew nothing in my life would be the same. *I* wasn't the same. I closed my eyes, pressed my fingers against my breastbone, tried to tame my rattling pulse. Heat pricked my neck.

"Gwen, honey?" I opened my eyes. August knelt beside me and ran a warm washcloth up my inner thighs. "You okay?" He worked as he talked, tenderly moving the cloth over my sensitive flesh, and I melted. He was buck as naked got, on his knees, taking care of me. I was a puddle of happiness. I was petrified.

"I don't think I'm okay."

He frowned and tossed the cloth behind him. Leaning on his elbow, he pressed to my side, his legs stretched next to mine. With his free hand, he traced dizzying patterns on my abdomen and breasts. "Talk to me."

"You're going to leave. Go back to Europe, aren't you?"

His fingers faltered. He flattened his palm on my ribs, below the curve of my breast. "I am. But—"

"When?"

His answer took too long. He swallowed one too many times. "Two days. Early Monday morning."

If this was how getting punched in the gut felt, I'd leave boxing out of my workout regime. I curled away from him, stood and gathered my clothes, blinking the burn from my eyes. My throat stung. My belly churned. How would I say goodbye to him?

"Gwen."

I kept moving, kept breathing, kept blinking.

"Gwen." When I didn't answer him a second time, he wrapped his arms around me from behind, stilling my frenetic movements. "Don't you dare do that. Don't you dare cut me off again. Not after tonight."

He cocooned his naked body around mine, forced me to drop my clothes. He spun me around and locked me in his arms. "That was the best sex of my life. It's the beginning, not the end. We have another day and a half together, and I plan to spend every second of that time with you."

"Aren't you scared?"

He sputtered out a laugh. "Are you serious? I'm fucking terrified."

"How do we do this?"

"Easy." He loosened his hold on me, stroked my back. "We take this one second at a time, while I figure out the rest. I don't want you thinking about anything but each moment, because right now I have a beautiful, naked woman in my arms, but she's frowning. These are not things that should coexist."

A small smile escaped me. "One second at a time?" It seemed impossible.

"Make each one count. Leave the rest to me."

I couldn't pick up and leave my job. I didn't want to. He had no clue the life I'd created for myself here, in San Francisco. The years and determination it had taken. Yet the prospect of losing this amazing man in two days—*one and a half*—had spots clouding my vision. I wasn't sure I could compartmentalize my emotions, give him what he wanted. All I could do was try.

My rigid posture thawed slightly. I nuzzled my face into his neck. "Every second."

He wove one hand into my hair and sighed. "Every second, Possum."

When he thickened against me, I extricated myself from his hold. "But no more bikini posters now."

"Bikini posters?"

Ainsley's ridiculous comment about him staring at me like my scantily clad poster had adorned his teenage wall wormed into my mind. I motioned to his gorgeous cock, half-stiff and flushed at the tip. "Sex. No sex right now."

He squinted. "Bikini posters means sex?"

"Just go with it."

He mumbled something like "Girls are weird," but his eyelids lowered and he stroked his length once, roughly. "But there will be bikini posters later, right?"

His searing glance had tingles erupting across my skin. "Definitely later. For now we need to go through my mother's journal and search for more clues." I needed to regroup. Find my feet. Reorder my upside-down world by putting on some clothes and creating emotional armor.

———

August

After a quick snack of cheese and fruit, Gwen and I relocated to her plaid couch, her mother's diary and an awkward silence between us. It wasn't okay. I wasn't okay. My Monday morning flight meant we only had a day and a bit. The timeline was akin to torture. We hadn't mentioned my departure date again. We hadn't said much of anything. The prospect had new lyrics looping through my mind: *cruel fate, wicked ways, oceans apart.*

I had commitments in Germany and France, unbreakable contracts, weeks and months scheduled on the road. But this wasn't the beginning of the end. I wouldn't let it be. I simply had to make a plan and figure things out. Think long-term.

Still, she was freaking out, shutting down in increments.

Which meant beginning with the small stuff, here and now, was important. Making use of all our seconds. "When did you start surfing?" I needed to learn everything I could about Gwen Hamilton.

She glanced up from the worn journal. "Sorry?"

I nodded to the board taking up the opposite wall. "Surfing, I don't remember you wanting to try it." Or skydiving. Or mountain biking. Gwen had always been athletic, running track and acing gym class, but she'd never been an adrenaline junkie.

Keeping the journal open, she leaned her shoulder into the couch. "During college, my third summer off, I was bartending at night but needed as much cash as possible. A daytime job renting surfboards came up, and I got bit by the bug. The job allowed me free lessons and equipment use."

Watching her navigating a wave, water dripping down her toned body, hair slicked back would be quite the sight. "The only time I surfed involved me sucking back buckets of sea water."

Her attention darted to my mouth. Her pupils flared, as though mention of inhaling the ocean was akin to dirty talk. "Learning is rough."

"Have you ever taught?"

"I prefer the rush of riding." Her gaze dropped lower, to my groin. She nibbled her lower lip.

Was she picturing riding me? A shot of lust accompanied that visual. Although making love to her had been unreal, I hadn't explored the lean lines of her body, kissed my way up her strong thighs. I suppressed my groan. "Maybe you could teach me some time."

Although too turned on for my own good, I did mean the surfing. I wanted to enjoy a lazy Sunday walking the streets with Gwen, fall into a small lunch spot, lie in the grass while she read and I wrote music, learn to surf with her, sleep next to her, wake with her. Collect all our seconds, turning each into an eternity.

She stopped the lip nibbling. She might have stopped breathing, too. "Sure," she said. It took a moment to realize she'd answered my surfing question, but it had been a distracted sure. A *we don't have a future* sure.

I really fucking hated that sure.

She returned to analyzing the diary. I kept analyzing her: the full bottom lip I'd had between my teeth, the swell of her breasts in her fitted white tank top. She had beautiful breasts, small yet lush with tight pink nipples I hadn't gotten to feast on, since I hadn't removed her bra.

She slid her jaw to the side as she read a section carefully. I didn't remember her doing that when we'd studied together, and I would know. I'd spent most of those hours like this, watching her, picturing her hands on my body, tugging down my jeans. My mouth on her.

We were close enough that I could reach forward and run my fingers through her wavy hair. I followed my instinct. I couldn't keep away.

Air rasped through her teeth. "That's distracting."

"You're distracting."

"You know what I mean." But she didn't pull back. She leaned toward me.

My sweet Possum. "These are my seconds, honey. I need to touch you. And I'll figure out the rest with us. Please don't worry."

Already, I'd been poring over my schedule in my mind, blocking out times I'd return to San Francisco. Weeks I could fly Gwen to Europe. I'd plan it out, make it foolproof. She wouldn't have to do a thing but say yes. Instead of fighting me further, she turned her face into my hand and kissed my palm. Not an agreement, exactly, but the tender move nearly split me in two.

We stayed like that awhile: her flipping through her mother's journal, my hand in her hair, my heart playing an unsteady bass line.

Suddenly, she sat straighter. She lifted a flimsy cocktail napkin from inside the book. "She mentions a bar a few times, a place a guy used to take her. I think it's the same guy who watched her dance, but she never mentions his name."

"Considering she hid the journal in a defaced bible, I'm guessing she was worried it would be riffled through. Her parents weren't exactly lenient."

Gwen had snuck into my room the night she'd searched out her grandparents. She hadn't cried or ranted, but she'd picked her nails until they'd bled and had asked if she could sleep over. I'd watched her breathing softly the entire night.

She closed the book and held the napkin gingerly. "By the sounds of things, this guy knew the owner of the bar or a bartender, had no issues getting my mother served without her ID. Mary Hamilton liked her Long Island Iced Tea."

"I can't picture your mother drinking."

"I can't picture her smiling or laughing or dancing. Drinking is tame compared to that. And this isn't about her, anyway. I couldn't care less what she was like. None of it changes the woman I knew."

Her defensiveness said otherwise. Not that she'd listen to me. Gwen was stubborn like that. My fingers slipped through her hair in slow strokes. She clasped my wrist, stilling the movements. "I think this is our next clue, where we should go. If this guy knew the owner and he's still around, we might get answers."

Ted Mercer, I almost blurted. *That's your father's name.*

He'd lived in Oakland, only twenty minutes from his daughter. I hadn't dug deeper, no point after learning he'd passed, but I had the name she'd sought her entire life.

I nearly spoke it aloud, but I clamped my mouth shut. Not because of my guilt or knowing my deception could obliterate our fragile footing. Not fully, at least. There were too many coincidences piling up: her mother's letter to me, my choice to delay, Mary's death, her luggage. A journal offering more insight into that woman than Gwen had gleaned in twenty-eight years. Like everything was happening for a reason, including learning about Mary Hamilton.

Gwen could pretend these scraps of information meant nothing. I saw how her eyes had widened when peering at that dancing photo in the TASC center, how she'd sucked in an amazed breath when Loretta Walsh had called Mary and her sister the Sunshine Girls.

Not knowing her father had always been a thorn in Gwen's side, but living with a frigid mother had been the larger bruise on her childhood. This journey could help her understand what had stripped the light from Mary Hamilton's world, lead Gwen to accept the woman Mary had been. That type of closure was invaluable. Plus, the odds of Gwen actually learning her father's name before I left were slim to none. I'd have time to explain after.

"If that's our next clue, then we better get on it," I said.

"Badass PI partners?"

"As long as you don't go telling anyone else I get the shits."

She cackled. "I make no promises. And"—she held the napkin flat and read the writing on it—"looks like our next stop is the Blue-Eyed Raven."

I reared back, stunned into silence. Three rough swallows

later, I found my voice. "The Blue-Eyed Raven?" *Please tell me I heard her wrong.*

She nodded. "In Haight-Ashbury."

Just my twisted luck. Another coincidence, this one as pleasant as chewing rocks.

Of all the bars in all of San Francisco, Mary Hamilton had to have set up camp where my twin brother now worked.

CHAPTER 10

10 p.m., 26 Hours…

Gwen

According to August, the Blue-Eyed Raven was a Haight-Ashbury fixture, the sprawling bar once home to performing greats like Neil Young and Joni Mitchell. In its heyday, smoke had curled through the three-hundred-seat supper club, guitar licks rippling in the hazy air, weed and booze plentiful. Women had danced with women. Couples had swapped spouses.

Another of Mary Hamilton's shocking hangouts.

"Is it still popular?" I asked as I parked near the venue.

"Yes."

"Have you played there?"

"No."

"Do you *want* to play there?"

No answer.

I turned off the ignition but didn't release the key. We'd taken my car, and August had kept his hand at the back of my neck during the drive, his thumb rubbing mindless circles. As nice as the contact had been, the mindless part had been the antithesis of nice. The closer we'd gotten to the club, the quieter he'd become. The louder I wanted to scream.

I opted for confrontation. "What happened to your *let's savor our seconds* pact? Because the imposter in this car is freaking me out."

This entire situation was a giant pile of freak out. I'd shut down on him in my apartment, kept yo-yoing between the consuming desire to touch him and continuing my Popsicle routine, freezing him out. I wanted to thaw, but defrosting could end with me as a gooey, blubbery mess.

August released my neck and massaged his chest like it pained him. Streetlamps and passing cars cast buttery slices of light through the darkness. One spilled through the windshield, emphasizing the broody angles of his face. Without a word to me, he undid his seat belt, pushed open his door, and slammed it shut behind him. My seat vibrated. *I* vibrated. I wanted to be vibrating with August's hard length thrusting inside me, not because I was a defrosting Popsicle.

My mind kept replaying how he'd felt, how my body still sizzled and swelled with want. On the drive here, I'd almost slipped my hand between his thighs, over his thick denim, to cop a feel of his girth. Fear had kept me fisting the steering wheel.

I sat immobile now, the car key clutched in my hand. I debated turning the ignition and tearing off as he rounded toward my side. I could leave right now, forget this journal and August and everything that had the power to break me, but I played my Popsicle game.

He opened my door and poked his head inside. "Come out here. We need to talk."

His no-nonsense tone brooked zero argument. The dominance of it was kind of sexy, but mostly scary. *We need to talk* only ever meant heavy subjects, and I had all the heavy I could handle.

Instead of complying, I said, "Beetlejuice."

August snort-laughed. The sound calmed a fraction of my panic.

Beetlejuice had been our safe word. When he'd pinch my underarm skin to distract me from his Monopoly cheating? Beetlejuice. When I'd twist his nipple until he'd give me the remote control? Beetlejuice.

Blurting the word now was easier than facing his ominous *we need to talk.*

He straightened slightly, taking his face out of view. He leaned his forearm on the car roof. "You don't need a safe word for this conversation."

"Says you." But I could hear the smirk in his voice. I also liked the view.

The way we were situated—his crotch at face level, me strapped into my seat—I could undo his belt buckle, slip his zipper down, and take his length into my mouth. I salivated.

He backed away and crooked his finger, beckoning me. "Stop looking like you want to lick me, Possum. We need to talk. It won't be a nice talk, but we can't go into that club before it happens."

"That's quite the sales pitch." It was downright alarming. Unfortunately, I saw no other options.

I worked methodically, going through the steps of shoving the journal in my purse, leaving my car, and locking up extra slowly. *Delay, delay, delay.* A hot dog vendor was down the block, thick scents of charred meat teasing my nose. My belly rumbled. Our cheese and fruit earlier had only been a snack. I was hungry for food. I was hungry for August. I was *not* hungry to learn about the thing that wasn't nice to discuss.

I moved to the sidewalk and anchored myself against the car. "Go ahead. Rip off the Band-Aid."

His right hand was in his pocket. The fabric bulged rhythmically. He probably had a guitar pick in there. Whenever August was nervous or uneasy, he'd spin his pick restlessly. Like now. He gnawed on his bottom lip. "Finch manages the Blue-Eyed Raven."

I pitched forward slightly. "Excuse me?"

"Exactly."

Well, wasn't that just my luck? The day I made love with the brother I'd always wanted, I had to stand in a building with him and the one I should never have fucked. Good times, Gwen Hamilton. "How is that even possible?"

"How is it possible I show up at your door the same day as your mother's lost luggage?"

A slew of impossible impossibilities. I glanced toward the club, then to August, then at the inky sky. Nerves twisted my insides. I replayed Rachel's comment earlier, how she'd thought her birthday wish had been touched with magic and that believing in the unbelievable had given her the push she'd needed to fulfill her resolution. My self-imposed sink-or-swim deadline was in twenty-six hours, and fate had been dumping a pile of life preservers on my head.

August was entwined in this search, for some reason. Now his brother was, too. Trying to figure out why would drain energy and time I didn't have. The bigger issue was how seeing Finch would affect August now. The confrontation could shake the rickety suspension bridge we were navigating.

Maybe it already had.

Questions built in my throat until it burned. "Do you regret sleeping with me?"

He was on me in a heartbeat, his hands cradling my face. "No. Not for a second. Why would you think that?"

Relief flooded me, but barbs still chafed my windpipe. I hooked my thumbs through his belt loops. "The drive here—you were so…distracted? I mean, I get that seeing Finch now isn't ideal, but he's your brother. We can't avoid him forever." Which implied August and I had forever. *Seconds*, I reminded myself.

This was nothing more than seconds and *right now* and enjoying the moment. I had a life here. A job. He was leaving. The barbs dug deeper.

He loosened his hold on me, enough that the scratch of his calluses became more pronounced. "The only regret I'll ever have with you, Gwen, is taking too long to pull my head out of my ass to understand we're bigger than what went down between us. This thing with Finch—my moodiness on our way here—is partly because of that, but there's more to it. Stuff I didn't want to discuss tonight."

"What stuff?"

Spine rigid, his attention drifted over my head, to the club beyond. "You sure you want to hear this now?"

"We're about to see Finch, so I think the answer to that is obvious."

The muscles in his jaw shifted, working mercilessly. I kissed the clenched knot and he softened slightly. "I know you think Finch and I always got along, but things got tense between us during high school." He tilted his head side-to-side, brushing his cheek against my lips. "It's great having an identical twin, growing up with someone who's literally a part of you. I wouldn't trade our childhood for anything. But looking the same comes with expectations of acting the same, performing the same. It frustrated the hell out of Finch."

He leaned back slightly, his eyes shifting from distracted to piercing. Like he'd forgotten I was in front of him. "You are so goddamn beautiful."

My heart swelled three sizes. "Are you stalling?"

He stared at me until my pulse pounded in my ears. "I might need you to pinch me sporadically, because I keep thinking I'm dreaming. The fact that I can touch you, kiss you"—he planted a hard one on my lips—"floors me. So if I stop mid-sentence from time to time to tell you how gorgeous you are, that your green eyes remind me of the first breath of spring, you'll have to deal with it."

I pinched his upper arm, as requested. To lighten the mood. To shrink my heart back to its proper size. Any bigger and the effects would be irreversible. "I see where you get your lyrics from."

"Many from you, Possum."

Oh, dear Lord. "Let's not discuss 'Girl with the Black Heart.'"

He shrugged a shoulder, no apology in his open gaze. I didn't want an apology. I'd deserved every biting word. "Back to the Finch issue," I said, nudging August's hip with mine.

He turned and planted his sexy behind against my car. I wanted to worship his ass. Bite the firm globes. Suck on the length of him until he shuddered and spilled into my mouth. God, even here, minutes from facing Finch and searching for my father, I could do little more than fantasize about August.

He drew me into his chest. "Finch started acting out end of our junior year. He was pissed I was chosen to captain our soccer team. He started smoking weed regularly. His grades dropped, like really dropped, and every time our folks celebrated something I did, he'd withdraw more. Not with his friends. He'd put on his Finch smile and pretend all was roses, but at home he'd barely look at me. It got worse the start of our senior year. You and I had stopped speaking, but I knew he still spent time with you, so I..." His arm tightened around my shoulder. "I asked him for a favor."

"Am I going to like this favor?"

"Unlikely."

Not that it mattered. He'd forgiven my unforgivable WTF. There were no grudges left to hold, not now, all these years later. I squeezed his waist, telling him I'd support him. I was here for him, the way I wished I'd been for the past nine years.

He exhaled a harsh breath. "I asked him to watch out for you. Spend time with you. Being cut off from you messed me up, but I was worried. Figured something else was going on. I had to make sure you were okay."

The weight of his arm slung over my shoulder suddenly

turned crushing, and I fought the urge to shrug him off. It took every ounce of my control not to whirl on August and tell him I hadn't been his charity case. I hadn't been a helpless pet. As sweet as his gestures often had been, that was how I'd sometimes felt. That I'd been a problem for him to solve. A project he needed to ace, like everything else in his life.

Even now, I felt like I was seventeen again, shrinking smaller as Kayla Morgan told me August had pitied me. That I dragged him down. Long buried insecurities clawed to the surface, and I nearly screamed.

I wasn't that girl anymore. I jumped out of airplanes, for Christ's sake.

I was no longer a teenager who believed she was unlovable because her mother had sneered at her, called her unwanted. *Stupid.* I didn't walk through life trying to make as little noise as possible, avoiding friendships, commitments, believing myself unworthy. Yet here I was, anxiety-riddled self-doubt resurfacing.

I needed to get a grip.

I slowed my overactive lungs. I replayed his explanation, how he'd been worried about me back then. There had been no hidden agenda. He may have approached our relationship from a hero perspective, wanting to be the savior, but based on all we'd admitted to each other today, asking Finch to keep an eye on me had been out of desperation, not pity.

All because I'd cut him from my life.

I nestled deeper into August's side instead of pulling away. I was that woman now. A nestler, not a runner. "Did Finch show interest in me back then? Is that why he agreed?"

"He never said, but he knew exactly how I felt about you."

"Which made what we did even worse," I mumbled, still sick about it all.

"It did make it worse, but it wasn't the only reason." He looped a lock of my hair around his finger and twirled it. A guitar pick. My hair. Always busying his fingers. "The night I asked Finch to look out for you, he agreed…but asked for a favor in return." He twirled my hair faster. "He'd tanked his SATs and hadn't told me or our parents. I didn't know how bad his grades had gotten, either. He had one more chance to take the test in December of our senior year, and he needed that score."

"What did that have to do with you?"

"He asked me to take the test for him."

Oh.

Fuck.

Identical twins.

"And you did it?" I couldn't hide the shock in my voice. I'd once asked August to help me buy a fake ID. Everyone did it. No biggie. He'd laced into me, saying it was stupid, not worth getting caught. He never colored outside the lines.

"And I did it." He quit fiddling with my hair. His body became a block of cement. "I wore his preppy clothes and his glasses, and no one was the wiser. I nearly puked before the test. I *did* puke after. Barely slept for the next few months, sure someone would find out and I'd be expelled, lose my chance at my scholarship. Be kicked off the soccer team. I was a wreck."

Shame winded me. "So you did this insane, massive favor for Finch." For me, really. So his brother would watch out for *me*. "And Finch promised to be my shadow, knowing how you felt about me. Then…that night happened?"

"That about sums it up."

If he weren't holding me up, I'd sink to my haunches and bury my face in my hands. August's requested favor explained Finch's increased attentiveness toward the end of high school, into college. Finch would drag me out for coffee, force me to meet him at the library for study sessions. But his words to me that fateful night—*I've wanted you so long*—hadn't been the words of a brother doing a brother a favor. Especially considering what August had done for him.

"I didn't think I could feel worse about what went down, but this is definitely worse." Profoundly worse. *Shove me in a cell and toss away the key* worse.

August spun me quickly, pulled me tight against his chest. "I didn't tell you to guilt you, but Finch and I never recovered from that night. We speak as needed, but we're only civil. Not because of what you did. Because my brother betrayed me. I put my future on the line for him, and he fucked me over."

It all made sense now, how furious August had been that night. The vicious punch to Finch's face. "I'm so sorry."

"No." His tone turned vehement. "Don't apologize. I'm done playing the victim. There's no changing the past, and I don't want you spending these next couple days feeling badly. I forgave you. Not just with words. There's no anger left. We're too important. Our time together is too important."

Our seconds. This finite slice of time. "I don't know how to do this."

"Oh, honey. I'll take care of you. Of us. Don't worry. I'll make this work." He kissed me, sweet and slow.

Kissing was one solution. A mighty fine one. The rest was August taking charge, always trying to solve my problems. He didn't know my life here, what I could and couldn't do. He hadn't even asked what I *wanted* to do. But his lips were addictive, coaxing mine into action. I kissed him back harder, the two of us moving against each other with such devastating need. His lips were soft yet firm. His body was all firm.

"I plan to fuck you blind tonight," he said against my lips. "Taste every inch of you. Have you come on my tongue and fingers. You don't even know."

My body sure as hell knew. "I'm so wet. You make me so wet."

"Jesus, Gwen." His mouth was on my neck, licking and sucking. "I'll never get enough of you."

Not in two days he wouldn't. But I might lose my heart.

That sobering notion had me abruptly ending our PDA. I heard a whistle, but wasn't sure it was directed at us, not that I cared. What I did care about was not falling to pieces over this man, who had to get on an airplane in *one and a half* days.

I needed to feel him inside me again. I wouldn't deny myself that. But my feelings for him were already ten-foot swells, ready to drag me under. I had to keep an emotional distance, not do stupid things like wish I wasn't on the pill.

Following the journal's clues was the perfect distraction. The breather I needed. Which meant facing Finch. "You still okay to come in the club with me?"

"I'm not leaving your side until I get on that plane."

He wasn't making my emotional armor easy to wear. "Even when I have to pee?"

"You've peed next to me before."

I had. Our tenth-grade graduation had been a raucous affair. Someone had organized a field party, and I'd drunk my weight in peach schnapps. August had stood sentry while I'd squatted in the grass. He'd later held my hair back while I'd puked. The best friend a girl could have.

"Okay," I said, tugging him toward the club.

He tugged me back. His hooded eyes drank me in, dropping to my neck. His pupils flared. "I gave you a hickey."

I touched my feverish skin and laughed. "Are we sixteen?"

"It means you're mine," he replied, his voice thick.

My voice got stuck. I couldn't be his. Not with his itinerary. Being his meant losing myself, and the last time that happened, after my WTF, I'd tripped so far down a rabbit hole, I'd gotten lost in the bramble. "When we're inside," I said, deflecting, "holler if you need to leave."

He considered me a moment, stared so intently I looked away. "I'll use our safe word," he said.

Nothing about my feelings for him felt safe.

August

. . .

I led the way to the club, still high from kissing Gwen. From touching Gwen. From marking Gwen's skin. Unfortunately, the way she'd disconnected her lips from mine and her subject change just now hinted at her worry. She was holding herself back, keeping a piece of her heart protected. I'd quit trying to guard mine. She was everything to me, the center of my best childhood memories, the reason I wrote music. She had all of me, and I'd have all of her before my plane took off. As long as this search for her father didn't backfire.

And Finch didn't ruin things again.

A bouncer was at the club door. He had a neck thicker than a tree trunk, bald head, tattooed neck. His black suit was definitely purchased at a big and tall shop. He saluted me, as though we knew each other. "You shaved, Mr. Cruz."

I kept Gwen's hand firmly in mine and offered him a tight smile. "Wrong Mr. Cruz. I came to see my brother." No point avoiding that particular elephant.

He grinned, displaying two gold teeth. "Oh…right. Sure. Go on in. Hope to catch you on stage later."

I'd wanted to play the Blue-Eyed Raven stage for years. It drew mid-sized bands these days, and bigger acts wanting an intimate setting. The sound system was killer, the audience filled with music devotees. Finch had managed the venue the past five years, bringing it back to life after it had dropped off the radar. He'd never asked me to play. I'd never offered. Our ongoing stalemate.

I led Gwen to the semi-circular bar cradling the patron-filled tables, most enjoying some sort of dessert. Between sets, likely.

She pressed closer to my side. "It's sexy in here."

"You're sexy."

Even in the sultry lighting, her eyes sparkled. "Trouble," she mumbled.

She scanned the instrument-filled stage—piano, bass, a couple horns, and one hot-as-hell Fender. The walls and ceilings had been remodeled, the moldings giving the room an art deco vibe. Blues tunes drifted from speakers. Servers wore twenties-inspired dresses and suits. Yeah, I'd always wanted to play this club, and it would probably never happen.

Never loosening my hold on Gwen's hand, I nodded to the bartender. "Is Finch in?"

The woman did a double-take. "You're August Cruz."

"I am." Although people like that ballerina occasionally recognized me, I mostly flew under the radar when outside Europe. Not where my brother worked.

She planted her hands on her hips and shook her head. The feather in her bobbed hair caught the light. "I'd always hoped you'd play here. I love 'Girl with a Black Heart.'"

From my angle, I could see Gwen roll her eyes, and I had to muffle my laugh. What had happened between us wasn't amusing. Writing that song hadn't been, either. But man, if we couldn't laugh about it now, find some humor in the darkness, we'd never make it. "It's one of my favorites," I said, dragging Gwen closer. "I used to act it out on a voodoo doll."

"Hardy-har-har." This from a glowering Gwen.

The waitress detailed a bad breakup of hers, a painful time the song had paralleled. I winked at Gwen, who mouthed, *Not funny*. But it kind of was.

"Shoot. Sorry." The waitress waved a frazzled hand. "I've monopolized you. I'll call up to Finch, tell him you're here."

Gwen watched the servers bussing tables, the animated patrons chatting. I watched Gwen. She'd always had this effortless beauty about her, but it was amplified now. Her shorter hair was wavy and loose, like she'd been at the beach, her casual bangs falling longer at the sides, framing her stunning face. Looking at her hurt in a visceral way. Tore at pieces of me. Except the hickey. That mark made me smile.

Then I spotted Finch, and my smile nose-dived.

CHAPTER 11

10:30 p.m., 25 ½ Hours…

Finch stood at a side door, arms crossed, legs wide, scanning the room like he owned the place. Which he kind of did. Not in name or money, but he'd rebuilt the Raven's reputation, act by act, month by month. I'd watched his progress from afar, impressed with the growing praise. He deserved the accolades he'd earned. Didn't make dealing with him any easier.

The second his sights locked on me, his chin jerked upward, and a fizzy feeling snaked through me. The lighting made it tough to read his expression.

"He's coming over." I anchored my arm around Gwen. *To ground her*, I told myself. But that swirling in my gut lessened.

She held her purse against her stomach. "Are you sure this is a good idea?"

"The owner isn't around much, but he's the same guy who

ran the place when your mother came here. If anyone has answers for you, it's him. Finch is your connection."

My brother was the link to her past. Maybe her closure. Maybe mine, too. All our paths converging. Keeping tabs on my twin's life from across the globe, pretending I didn't want to call and congratulate him on his success, had gotten harder over the years. Seeing firsthand how lively and full the club was made me want to drag him in for a hug. None of it changed our past.

He strutted toward us, confidence in his long strides. His hair was longer than mine, curling at the base of his neck. His short beard was new. The changes made us look different, but only slightly. It was still like facing a mirror.

He stopped in front of us, took in my arm around Gwen. Our close proximity. The bastard grinned. "Are you two finally together?"

There were a thousand things we needed to hash out, but that grin had the snake pit in my gut calming. "We are."

But Gwen said, "No," and I jolted. She talked over herself. "I mean, we're hanging out. But we're not *together* together."

What in the actual fuck?

The hickey on her neck was from me. Her body had been mine two short hours ago. She could kid herself all she wanted, but we were as together as together got. Something we'd deal with later. For now we were on a PI mission. "We're looking for Uncle Rex."

"You have an uncle Rex?" She glanced between Finch and me.

Finch shook his head. "It's the name he goes by—the club owner. Everyone calls him Uncle Rex." His eyes cut to me, squinting like a far-sighted man trying to read small type. "But if you want to play here, I'm the guy you speak with. Not Uncle Rex."

The hurt on his face was plain as day. "This isn't about playing. We need a favor."

His squinting intensified. "And you thought you'd walk in here, ask a favor of me, when we've barely spoken in years?"

"I don't know, Finch. You're the king of asking for favors and welching on your end of the agreement."

He looked down sharply, pursed his lips. Frustrated with himself? Shutting me out? We'd yelled at each other plenty since college, me calling him a selfish bastard, him telling me to grow up and forgive him already. More recently, we'd simply turned distant, flat.

"It doesn't matter," I said, but that wasn't exactly true. I still spoke with our sister. Not weekly, or even monthly, but we kept in touch, and I'd do anything for her. Fighting with Melody would gut me. But resentment between twins was different. A part of my heart had hardened over the years. Like we'd been conjoined twins, hearts linked, arteries connected, our estrangement deadening the tissue.

His eyes flicked up, a hint of pleading lifting his brow. "It matters."

That hard place in me cracked.

Gwen stayed mute, letting us do our estranged brother thing, her purse tucked under her arms like it would shield her from our strained reunion.

I hadn't planned to unleash my anger on Finch, like I hadn't planned to lash out at Gwen at her mother's house. Our shared history brought out the worst in me, which meant it needed to be dealt with. No more pretending and running and writing my angst into songs. That journal had led us both here for a reason. It was time to find out why.

Relinquishing my possessive hold on Gwen, I dashed my hand through my hair. "Can Gwen get in touch with Uncle Rex tonight? For her, not for me. She has some questions about a man who came here in the late eighties, possibly her father. And if you have a moment, I'd like to talk."

Finch was in black slacks and a gray button-down, shiny

shoes to match. The consummate professional, who'd done a kickass job bringing this club back to life.

To me, he'd always be the kid who'd shared a tent with me in our back yard, his ghostly flashlight shining on the flimsy blue material as he'd terrorize me with horror stories. He would eat the broccoli off my plate and I'd eat his lamb, his suggestions to avoid staring at food we'd rather burn than touch. Finch would make our younger sister laugh when she'd cry about the braces she'd hated or skinning her knee. He'd made us lightsabers and had rolled me my first joint. Even helped me ride a skateboard when I'd given up.

I was older by five minutes, but he'd been the wiser of us, until he'd slid downhill at the end of high school. Until he'd asked me to do a brutal favor I still regretted.

Until he'd slept with Gwen.

But like with her, during this wild day, the earlier years seemed to outweigh the later mistakes. Gwen was unpacking her mother's lost luggage, one clue at a time. Facing her demons. I was ready to deal with mine.

Finch scrubbed a hand over his beard and nodded at a round table. "Uncle Rex is here tonight, has his niece and nephew with him. I'll ask if he can spare a minute."

After another long glance at me, he moved through the room, stopping to shake hands with people, laugh with some, flirt with others. He worked the stretch between us and Uncle Rex's table like a bona-fide celebrity. I might be the one with albums and fans, but here, in this jazzy room I'd always wanted to play, he was the more successful brother.

Pride snuck up on me in a fierce jab. Solid. Good. Nice to think of Finch without curling my hands into fists.

Gwen smoothed her hand down my back. "I'm glad you'll talk with Finch. I hate seeing you guys at odds."

I hated it, too. It was time to set things right. But the last thing I wanted to discuss with Gwen was Finch. "You told him we weren't together."

She snatched her hand from my back. "Why'd you tell him we are?"

She had to be kidding me. I leaned my forearm on the bar, dipped so our faces were level. "I'm sorry, Possum…was I the only one on the floor in your apartment earlier? Did you not feel me inside you? Did I not make you come? Did we not discuss how often I planned to do more of the same later?"

Her lips parted. If the music were quieter, I'd bet I'd hear her whimper. But she said, "Having sex isn't a relationship."

"That wasn't sex. We made love, and you know it."

"We said seconds—that we'd focus on our time now, not the future. Today's the first I've seen you in nine years. No one in their right mind would call you my boyfriend. That goes against every relationship rule."

"Then I must be certifiable, because when it comes to you and me, Gwen, there are no rules. We aren't other people. The second I had my mouth on you, *my cock in you*, you became mine, and I became yours."

"You leave in two days." Her chin wobbled. I didn't want her chin to wobble. Every minute together was valuable.

I kissed her forehead, pressed a soft one to her lips. "I'll fly you out to visit me. I'll come home when I can. We'll look at a calendar and map it all out."

"It's not that simple. I've been treading water all night, trying to savor our seconds like we agreed. Not let all these emotions drown me. I want this time with you. I want…." She shook her head as though having an internal conversation. "Honestly? I have no clue what I want. And you haven't even asked me. But you're going on like we're engaged."

A notion I could sink into. Gwen was it for me. Come hell or high water, or a swarm of locusts, she would be mine. Having her once wasn't enough. Having her for the rest of my life wouldn't be enough. She didn't see it. Because of our history, maybe. Our different lives now. None of it meant a damn thing.

I opened my mouth to say as much, put my heart in her hands, but Finch returned.

"Uncle Rex will chat with you." His gaze lingered on Gwen's taut body, every compact inch displayed in her slim jeans and tank top. The urge to punch him returned. To me, he said, "We can talk in my office."

Gwen was up before I could reply, her purse clutched to her side as she maneuvered toward Uncle Rex, not a glance at me. I wanted to pummel Finch and yell at Gwen until she saw reason. None of it would do me a lick of good.

———

Gwen

I couldn't get away from August fast enough. He didn't understand how hard this was for me, how low I'd sunk after I'd thought I'd lost him for good. If I let him in fully, opened myself to the possibility that we were more than this blip of time and we didn't work out, the fall wouldn't be pretty. It would be a free-climbing disaster, a bungee jump without a cord.

You'd have to scrape me off the ground.

I kept my focus on the boisterous round table Finch had visited. *Finch.* I still hadn't recovered from seeing him again, those two boys—no, *men*—side by side. I had never apologized to Finch after our night together, either. He'd gone backpacking. I'd disappeared inside myself. Our coffee hours and library studying had vanished the next year. We'd make eye contact across a room, and one of us would turn the other way. My avoidance skills had been top notch.

Here, all these years later, I wanted to say the things I'd never said. Explain to him how dejected I'd been, apologize for using him. But not with August around. That was a conversation for Finch and me alone.

All that concerned me now was finding my father. Funny how that had become the less stressful aspect of this night. The not-easy/easier problem.

Wigged out on zany adrenaline, I zeroed in on my target.

If a walrus took human form, it would be Uncle Rex. He was a round man with a bulbous nose, his gray eyebrows an entity of their own. His handlebar moustache was overgrown, his sparse hair pulled into a frizzy ponytail. He whispered in the man's ear at his left. The tall man vacated his seat, smiling as he passed me.

Uncle Rex patted the chair. "Finch tells me you're looking for someone." His voice was gruff and rumbly, as though he'd smoked a pack of cigarettes and had shouted for an hour.

I accepted his invitation, grateful to sit. My limbs felt heavy. My heart felt heavier after bickering with August. The urge to turn and search him out was powerful, but I gripped my purse tighter, felt the journal tucked inside. "I'm sorry to interrupt your night, but yeah—I'm looking for a man who would have frequented this place in the late eighties. I don't know his name or what he looked like."

"Sounds like quite the puzzle."

I huffed out a humorless laugh. "One I've been trying to solve for twenty years."

"Okay." He twisted one of the rings on his stubby fingers. "Lay it on me. What do ya know?"

"He came here with a woman, Mary Hamilton."

He frowned. "The name don't ring a bell, but most wouldn't."

I sifted through what else I'd learned, a clue that could trigger his memory. "She danced at the TASC center, was part of a group called the Sunshine Girls."

He slapped the table, his eyes disappearing in a happy squint. "Yeah, sure. That babe lit up a room."

Now my mother had been a *babe*. Would wonders never cease? "You knew her?"

"I wished I'd known her better, if you get my drift." He winked.

Attempting to incinerate that visual, I debated what to ask next. How best to figure out who my father was. But the question that escaped surprised the heck out of me. "What was she like?"

"Sweet as pie. Funny. Always making the servers laugh. Said if she didn't become a dancer, she wanted to be a comedian. Make the world smile. But, man, when she danced?" He whistled. "The whole room watched. Bet she wound up on Broadway, like she planned."

A comedian. A Broadway star. A girl who'd dreamed of greatness. She'd had high hopes for an exciting future. Heat pricked my eyes.

I'd never forget the day I came home to find my CD collection gone. My mother had trashed them, claimed my music was the reason my grades were poor. She'd hidden my guitar, too. My gift from August. All because my eighth-grade teacher had shown up at our house to explain I had a learning disorder. That I needed visual cues and support at home and school.

My mother's supportive reply: "She just needs to work harder."

She'd excelled in demoralizing me back then, but surprisingly, *amazingly*, for the first time in my twenty-eight years, I wanted to know Mary Hamilton. Something bigger than giving birth to me must have destroyed her spirit. Something to do with my father.

The man I was determined to find.

Doubts silenced my further questions. Turning that stone could unearth a whole whack of spiders. The scary, jumping, hairy kind. I could leave that rock alone, forget this ridiculous quest, but that choice led to more unanswered questions, more wondering, more years feeling untethered. "Did you know the man?" I asked Uncle Rex. "The one she came here with?"

He motioned to a waitress and tapped his empty tumbler.

"His name was Ted, I think. Or Tom? She never gave me the time of day, but with her fella?" He hummed a rough, gravely tune. "Those two were hot for each other, but I didn't know him well."

Another image I'd prefer to torch. "Is there anything else? Anything you can tell me about him? Where he lived? What kind of car he drove? Was he ever here with other women, or just her?"

"Sorry, doll. The Sunshine Girl drank Long Island Iced Tea. They were always together. You're lucky I remember that much. Those days tend to blur and I'm—" He stopped abruptly. His attention drifted up, toward the ceiling. "Actually, there was one thing. Forgot about it until now. Another girl looking for him once, asking around. Only remember 'cause she seemed pissed. On a mission to find him."

"What did she look like? How old was she?"

He clucked his tongue. "Got me there. Sorry I can't be more help."

Disappointment set in, but I fought it off. I'd learned a name, at least. Ted or Tom. That another woman in his life had gone looking for him. An illicit lover, maybe? That would explain how a couple falling in love had fallen apart, but it didn't shed light onto why a suitcase from 1990 had gone missing in 2001, only to turn up in 2018. Still, it was more than I had before.

I sensed someone behind me and turned, hopeful to spot August, eager to share what little I'd learned. It was the tall man whose seat I'd usurped.

Taking my cue, I thanked Uncle Rex and returned to the bar. Finch and August weren't around. They were likely having their talk privately, a heart-to-heart that hopefully didn't involve comparing their sexual encounters with yours truly. Sleeping with twin brothers was something portrayed in pornos. It was the worst kind of reality show.

It was also my life, as were these meager clues, and the upsetting conversation I'd had with August. He wouldn't let the argument go. He was stubborn like that. He'd push and push until I admitted how far gone I was for him. As though that would solve everything.

If he'd seen me after my WTF, he'd know how fragile he made me. I'd built my body since then, reveling in ripping my muscle tissue, letting it repair, grow. Feeling strong made me feel sexy. It also made me feel in control. August made me feel weak. The second I admitted as much to him, the second I claimed him as mine, there would be no repairing that torn tissue.

No protecting my heart when he left.

Ignoring that prospect, I waved down the bartender and ordered a Long Island Iced Tea. Because my mother had loved them. Because she'd sat here and enjoyed this strong drink, underage, dancing and making strangers laugh. I only managed two sips.

I wedged my nose in her journal, had to carefully separate pages that had a tendency to stick together. She wrote about a lookout spot where she and this boy would watch the stars. She'd doodled in a few corners, a simple sun wearing sunglasses, a cigarette dangling from its sunny mouth. It was childish and silly, and kind of cute.

The next page had me pressing my hand over my racing heart:

He gave me my first drink. My first cigarette. My first taste of freedom. He couldn't believe I had never tried a hotdog and dragged me to the stand outside the club. If my mother saw me bite into that processed meat, she would have lost her mind.

Well, FUCK YOU MOM.

I got ketchup on the corner of my mouth, and he wiped it off. So gently. We stared at each other forever. He must have known I had lain awake wishing for a kiss. Then he did it. He just leaned down...and wow. He kissed me! I didn't know what to do. If I should open my mouth or drop the hotdog or let him slip his tongue against mine. He was so sweet. So, so, so amazing. I never knew kissing could be every-thing. That it could fill you up. Make you float. It was better than dancing. And nothing is better than dancing. I didn't want it to end. I never want us to end.

It mirrored my feelings for August, that deep, searing need to reach for permanence. To make each kiss last. If he made me float the way this mystery man had sparked life into Mary Hamilton, it meant I could wind up broken and bitter like her, too.

CHAPTER 12

11 p.m., 25 Hours…

AUGUST

Finch led me up a set of narrow stairs, into his office. He pulled a bottle of Talisker from his desk drawer, set out two tumblers, and poured us each two fingers of the ten-year-old Scotch. "I'm guessing this conversation will go down better with a little lubrication."

I accepted my glass gratefully and took a healthy sip. The burn streaked through my chest, loosened my neck. "You guessed right."

We stared at each other. We glanced at our drinks. There were no answers in the amber liquid, no easy way to broach this conversation we'd danced around for nine years.

Finch chose avoidance. "So—you and Gwen, huh?"

"If I have anything to say about it, yes." I winced at the edge to my voice. Always challenging with him. Always waiting for him to snark back.

He kept his tone even. "She being her usual cagey self?"

"She is." Finch understood Gwen's history, how hard it was for her to trust and let go. It was nice not having to explain it, but it wasn't the reason we were standing here, making eye contact and glancing away, drinking instead of saying what mattered. I swallowed a measure of Scotch, let the heat of it mellow in my chest, and finally found my voice. "I'm tired of being pissed off at you."

His shoulders lowered as a heavy breath pushed through his nose. "I'm tired of being pissed at myself, too. I've spent a lot of time hating myself, looking for relief here." He swirled his glass. A sad, defeated movement. "But I can't change what I did. Can't give you those years back with Gwen. All I can do is apologize and hope it's enough. But it never has been, has it? Which I get, in a way. Then I see you with Gwen tonight, that you've forgiven her, and…" The pain on his face cut me down at my knees. "Why can't you forgive me?"

"But that's the thing. You and me"—I gestured aggressively between us, my voice still biting, always biting—"what you did wasn't simple. It was calculated. I was desperate back then, worried about Gwen. You saw my weakness and pounced. You used me to get into college, something I still regret to this day. You used me to get close to Gwen, knowing how I felt about her. So I guess I need to know why. If I'm going to move on, I need to understand."

Hip resting on his messy desk, he stared into his tumbler again. Dark paneled walls accentuated our tension, the expanse broken up by pictures of Finch with famous musicians. The one of him arm-and-arm with Eric Clapton caught my eye. Warmth pressed against my ribs. There was that pride again, hovering below my frustration. Subtle, but still there.

Finch swigged the rest of his Scotch and grimaced. "I'd like to tell you I had some kind of altruistic motivation. I thought I liked Gwen. I actually thought I loved her. In reality, I wanted something you couldn't have, to come first in something for once."

Drink clutched in one hand, I found my guitar pick with my other, deep in my pocket. I pressed the edge into my thumb and waited for him to go on.

"Thing is, I was always one step behind you. Not as strong on the soccer field. You aced high school without even trying. You were a freak of nature with your guitar. And there I was, always known as August's brother. The other twin. You don't know what that was like, but it's a shitty reason to do what I did. I knew how brutal taking my SATs would be for you. I knew you'd lose your mind over me and Gwen. And hurting her in the process destroyed me. It made me realize I needed to grow up and own who I was. I can't change what I did. I'm sorry it happened. I'm sorry I hurt you. I'm sorry for a thousand things, but I miss my brother and I'd like to have him back."

I couldn't deny missing him. Our innate connection couldn't be duplicated—laughing at the same jokes, trading a look without having to speak, the comfort of him being in my corner. I'd also been jerked around by promoters over the years, had had issues with my record label. Finch was in the business, knew the ropes. I'd needed someone to talk to, someone I could trust.

I'd needed him.

Still, I'd held back from reaching out, nursed my grudge instead. He was right, though. There was no going back. Only forward. What he did had sucked. Holding onto my anger sucked more. "You know what's really messed up?" I said.

"Aside from the fact that the girl you wrote hate songs about was looking at you downstairs like you were a blue jelly bean?"

Her favorite candy as kids. I rubbed my overheating neck. "She looked at me like that?"

He chuckled. "Dude, you've always been blind where Gwen's concerned."

The buzz that filled me burned hotter than my next sip of

Scotch. "Trust me, I know. What I don't get is both you and Gwen resented me on some level as teens. She felt like I made her my charity case, and you obviously had it in for me. I just don't remember being overly cocky about soccer, music. Any of it. Enough to make you guys feel like shit."

"You think the sun notices when it outshines the moon?"

"Are you writing lyrics now?"

"You can fuck off. But think about it. Life was good to you. You never struggled. It taints your perception, makes you less aware of what others are going through."

I slammed my glass on his filing cabinet, harder than necessary. "I was nothing but aware of Gwen's situation. I did everything I could to help her through it."

He swayed his head side to side, unruffled by my aggressive stance. "Yes and no."

"What's that supposed to mean?"

"You offered her *your* quick fixes—the things that made you happy, because you excelled at them. You taught her guitar, but played better than her. You let her win at soccer, and she knew it. You helped her study, because she learned slower than you. Of course she felt like your charity case."

"So I was supposed to suck at things?"

"For a smart guy, August, you're pretty dense."

I bit down on my molars. "Then dumb it down for me, Einstein."

"Gwen had to find *her* answers, the things that made her happy. Like I needed to step out of your shadow and be my own man. It's not your fault. We were kids. We had to grow up and figure out who we were."

"And that makes it okay to steal the girl I loved?"

"No, man…no." He hung his head.

I swore under my breath. We'd seesawed from strained apologies to reminiscing to tense again. We might both be ready to make amends. Didn't mean the road would be easy.

"Look," he said, "you did you back then, and I reacted in a

shitty way. Gwen drowned in her self-pity. We all had issues. And the reason you plummeted off the deep end after I slept with her, besides the obvious, was because you'd never had to deal with…well, anything. Nothing was ever hard for you."

I crossed my arms, glared at the maroon carpet between us. Going off the deep end was an understatement. For a guy who'd cruised through school and sports, dropping out of college and escaping to Europe had been beyond rebellious. Our folks had lost their minds, begged me to come home and talk to them, a counselor, anyone. I spoke with them eventually, could never erase them from my life, but everything had lost its meaning.

The easy life I'd enjoyed had lost its luster.

I guess I hadn't known disappointment back then, the setback of coming in second, third, anything but first. Fuck. Had I really been that big of a prick?

Forcing my good fortune on Gwen, like that would make her happy, probably emphasized what she didn't have. What she couldn't do. All she'd ever wanted was my heart, and I'd tried to solve her problems instead.

"I'm doing it again with her," I said, dazed and clear at the same time.

"Doing what?"

"I leave for Germany Monday morning, and she keeps freaking out about it, won't get too close to me. I'm a mess over it, but I know we can make it work. We have to make it work. So I keep telling her not to worry, that we'll figure it out. But I guess that's me taking control again. Making her—*us*—my project. I haven't even asked her what she wants to do." I tried to swallow, but my saliva thickened. "I can't lose her, Finch. She's… just…I can't go through this again, not after being with her. What do I do?"

His dark eyebrows winged upward. "You're asking *my* advice?"

His surprise almost made me laugh, something I hadn't done with Finch in an eternity. It was odd to be with him, angry one second, leaning on him the next. Searching for my twin under nine years of unyielding grudges. He was there, though. He was in front of me, asking my forgiveness. Blocking him out had only embittered me.

"You know her. You seem to know *me* better than I know myself." Even though we'd barely spoken. Finch could always see right through me. "So, yeah—I'm asking for your help. Begging for it, actually."

He assessed me, a deep stare that lingered, then he grinned. It wasn't the easy grin I'd once known, but there was hope in it, thankfulness. It breathed life into my deadened arteries, beating the hardened section of my heart back to life.

"I appreciate that," he said, "more than you'll ever realize. And I know just the thing to do."

———

Gwen

So focused on the journal, I jumped when Finch settled onto the barstool beside me. He studied the diary. "Must be a good book."

A surprising page-turner. I was only halfway through because I'd slowed down. Instead of skimming for clues, I'd read Mary Hamilton's words carefully, hanging off each one, desperate to learn how I'd been conceived, if she'd sensed betrayal from her man. Another woman in his life. I hadn't even noticed the band on stage, six guys with a country-rock vibe. Plaid shirts. Beards. Hipsters with a twang and a horn section.

I pointed to Finch's scruffy face. "You'd blend in on stage."

He massaged his beard. "Makes the talent feel comfortable. I'll be sporting a mohawk and nose ring for next week's gig."

"You'd look ridiculous with a nose ring."

"I'm insulted and offended." His cheeky smirk said otherwise.

"You can insult me back. Take your best shot." Punishment I deserved. Anything to assuage the guilt that had been chasing me since August had revealed the extent of our betrayal. Finch's fault, largely. That didn't absolve me of my part.

Finch tipped up his chin, considering me. "That frilly blouse you wore for all our grade-school class pictures? That abomination burned my retinas."

"Which is why I had it incinerated." The flowered nylon travesty haunted me to this day. "Your neon high-tops broke every fashion law imaginable."

"You took your Green Day love to loser levels."

"Your soccer jersey phase would have been fine if you'd washed it from time to time." I fanned my nose.

"That jersey was the shit."

Sitting here, joking like old times, was the shit. It was also a distraction that didn't change the past. I sighed and shook my head. "I'm sorry, Finch. For everything that went down. I used you that night. I was lonely, and I wanted to hurt August, two reasons that shouldn't have ended with us in bed."

He ran his tongue over his teeth. "No, they shouldn't have. But I was just as shallow. I didn't think so at the time, really thought I'd been in love with you, but I was in love with the idea of you. I wanted what August couldn't have."

The revelation winded me. "So we used each other? To hurt him?"

"We were quite the pair."

The band finished a song, applause and whistles filling the room. I didn't glance away from Finch. My regrets over what we'd done to August lived permanently behind my breastbone. It also irked me, what Finch had asked of August, falsifying his SATs. But moving on meant accepting our mistakes. "Does that mean I'm forgiven?"

"Only if I am, too."

I pressed my hand to his thigh. Not a sexual gesture. It was grounding, a tether to our past. Hopefully one to our future, too. "Did you guys talk? Work things out?"

"Mostly. It'll take a bit to really move on, but we took the first steps. Like you guys did."

August and I had taken more than a step. We'd taken a running leap, and I still hadn't landed. I searched the dimly lit room, no sign of him anywhere. "Where is he?"

"Taking his next step."

Before I could ask what that meant, the voice that had filled my stereo and iPod the past nine years flowed through the speakers.

August was on stage, mic at his lips as he settled on a stool and introduced himself. The other band members filed off. I held my breath. I'd watched August on YouTube, had listened to each of his albums on repeat. Never had I seen him live on stage, spotlights sharpening his cheekbones, shadows darkening his eyes.

My broody, sexy man.

"I've had kind of a wild day," he said as he plucked at the guitar strings, tuning it, learning the instrument. It had always been second nature to him. Like breathing. I'd enjoyed guitar because it was something I could do with August. He'd loved it because it was his oxygen.

"The kind of day," he went on, eyes downcast, random notes strummed, "that knocks you on your ass. Reminds you what's important in life. Teaches you you're dumber than you realize."

The crowd laughed. A nervous sound bubbled out of me.

He lifted his gaze then, his eyes black from this distance. He stared right at me. "This one's for the only girl who ever mattered."

The emotional distance I'd been struggling to maintain thinned. I wanted to be at the front of the stage, tossing my bra at his feet, slinging my underwear at his face. I wanted to be his groupie and his girlfriend.

Then he strummed the opening to "Girl with the Black Heart."

Now I wanted to light the stage on fire. "What the fuck is he doing?"

Finch looked horrified. "Not what I told him to do."

I punched his shoulder, because I couldn't punch August. "Does he think he's being funny?"

Finch rubbed his arm. "I think he's lost his mind."

Oh, he was going to lose his mind, all right. I'd shake him until he couldn't form a freaking sentence. My nails bit into my clenched palms, sweat gathering under my bangs. I was going to kill August Cruz and his not-funny sense of humor. How could he think I'd enjoy this? Or was he trying to end things before they got too complicated? Hurt me the way I'd hurt him, gloriously, publicly.

August sang the opening to his hate song, unwavering attention on my face. After the first chorus, people began glancing at me. There was no mistaking August's focus and who the lyrics described.

She turned my world black
Darkness spewed from a liar
The only way to seek light
Was to light her shadow on fire.

Shame seared my throat. Energy drained from my limbs. It hurt worse than the first time I'd heard the hateful lyrics, and regret reared its ugly head.

There was hurt in August's raspy voice, but it wasn't resentful hurt, like when he'd lit into me at my mother's. That long-overdue confrontation had been ripe with bitterness. This was different—softer, plaintive—similar to our small fight here, at the bar. Because I'd held him at a distance, like always. Scared to hold on. Scared to love and lose.

Guess I hadn't changed much since my pathetic teen years.

"I'll fucking kill him," Finch whispered.

He should have directed his aggravation at me.

I'd forced August's hand. We had less than two days together, and I fought us every step of the way, giving him my body, not my soul. If this was him ending things now, because I couldn't offer him that chance, trust him with my heart, the fallout could be catastrophic. The type of regret that led to losing the music from your world. Sucking the dance and color from your life. Even so, I wasn't sure I could give him what he wanted: all of me.

The song shifted, the chorus changing from the one I'd memorized. I frowned. Then I bit my lip.

She turned my world black
Because she owned my heart
A connection deeper than forgiveness
The kind that brings a fresh start

He'd rewritten the next stanza, too, singing of his blindness, his stupidity, *his* regrets. August's lyrics were always simple. His voice set him apart. The deep rasp crooned with such emotion the listener couldn't help but be swept away.

The final chorus threatened to shatter me.

I'm hers to break or fix
A timepiece of fragile parts
My hour always set to her
The girl who owns my heart

"Wow," Finch said.

That wasn't wow. That was everything.

August's gaze was fierce, locked on me. I couldn't look away. Maybe I could do this, be with him while apart. Climb that gnarly wall of fear, a treacherous drop below, and trust I was strong enough to make it. *Maybe.*

A roadie took his guitar. August leapt off the front of the stage, took one step toward me, but fans reached for him, wanting to shake his hand, pat his back. Two women hung at his side, too close for my comfort. One whispered in his ear. The other swished her hair from side to side, fluttering her eyelashes.

That was my man. That song had been mine, angry lyrics and all.

Who do they think they are?

Except he wasn't mine. This was his life, a startling glimpse of the tours and shows and hungry women. A life oceans apart from mine.

My saliva turned hot and sour, pooling in my mouth. I grabbed my journal and purse, but paused and faced Finch. "Can we go for coffee sometime? I'd like to catch up."

He tapped his fingers on the bar top, considering me. "Sounds great. I'm sure the past nine years could fill at least an hour of coffee time."

And then some. "Also, my birthday is tomorrow."

"You think I don't know that date?" His raised eyebrow held an air of rebuke.

"I guess it's kind of hard to forget." The anniversary of our epic bad decision would go down in history. "Anyway, as awkward as it might be, I'm going out with August and friends and would love for you to come." For us to fully move on, not agree to a coffee encounter that might never happen.

He deflated slightly. "I'd actually love to, but I have plans. Also might be too soon for August and me."

His genuine disappointment meant as much as if he'd said yes, another part of my past knitting together. I kissed his bristly cheek. The impetuous move surprised him, judging by his slight jolt, but he smiled in earnest.

I could barely see August now, flanked by bodies. He pushed up, probably on his tiptoes, and nodded at me. A move to explain his delay. I understood, but I didn't like it. Waiting for him, being a hanger-on in his outer circle, wasn't appealing. "Let him know I'm outside," I told Finch.

Without another glance, I worked my way to the door. Fresh air was needed, along with a juicy hotdog. Food. Oxygen. Space from August and his perfect hate-love song that had me wanting to tear back into the club and drag him away from his harem of admirers.

In the end, I didn't have to. Footsteps pounded behind me as I crossed the street. August's voice followed. "Where do you think you're going?"

I kept moving, didn't face him. "You were busy."

"I was trying to get to you."

It was true. He had nodded to me. He hadn't cared for those women. Not tonight, at least. I put on a brave smile, pulled up my big girl panties, and reached for his hand.

CHAPTER 13

12 a.m., 24 Hours…

Instead of leading us to her car, Gwen bee-lined for the hotdog stand opposite the club, her short steps so quick I had to jog slightly to keep up. She glanced over her shoulder, leveling me with nothing but a smile. "I don't know about you, but I'm starving."

I was about to tell her I was hungry for her lips and her body, for the soft patch of perfection between her thighs, but there was an edge to her voice, a tightness to her smile.

Because I'd royally screwed up.

Play her a love song, Finch had said. *Tell her how you feel the best way you know how.*

I'd walked on stage, intending to do just that. Pour my feelings into lyrics. Then the lights had mellowed. The venue I'd always wanted to play had come into focus, and a sense of rightness had crested me.

Destiny.

Finch and I were on our way to mending fences. The woman of my dreams had been staring at me, stars in her eyes, hesitation flickering, too. I understood then, what needed doing. There was something about coming full circle, traveling every inch of our history, rather than flying over the ragged terrain. It meant more to sing the pain, the remorse, the hope. It meant more to live each sonorous note, the deep, resonant sounds moving through me. It was the only way to show her I'd moved on. That now, finally, I was ready to put her first.

So I'd launched into my angriest hate-Gwen ballad, and I could have sworn she got it. Her brow had lifted and her eyes had turned soft, as though she'd understood my message.

Now she was distant.

I reinforced my grip on her hand. Distant wasn't okay. Not with our time limit. Instead of discussing our appetites, or whatever other diversions she had in mind, I said, "You're mad I sang that song."

Unperturbed by my statement, she sauntered toward the hotdog stand, her fingers feathering across my palm. Gwen, the coy seductress. Another distraction technique. A hint of slide guitar wove from the club, twining through the air in a provocative rhythm. I didn't recognize the song, but she swayed her hips, side-to-side, like the notes controlled her. Lived in her. A hot throb of lust gripped me.

That would be something, making love to her while this tune played, moving with her to the beat. I'd have to hunt it down. Blast it from speakers as we rocked together. She glanced back at me, and her cheeks pinked, like she was imagining the same scene. Her blush wasn't an act. Neither was how hard she'd been fighting our connection. She was struggling with our intensity, unsure how to hold on.

Fixated on reading the shifts in her expression, I didn't pay much attention as she ordered us a hotdog to share. I hadn't realized she'd picked up the mustard spoon until it was fisted in her hand. The little sneak smeared it on my shirt.

I dropped her hand and jumped back. "What the fuck, Gwen?"

Lips flattened to keep from laughing, she brandished her plastic weapon. "That's how I felt."

"How you felt about what?"

"You asked if I was mad you sang that song."

I held out my hands, afraid to touch my shirt and spread the bright yellow condiment. "And you felt..." I ran through my emotions just now: shocked, horrified, confused. "Oh," I said, all irritation fading. "I see your point."

She may have understood why I'd chosen that ballad by the end, but getting there wouldn't have been fun.

I bit back a curse, annoyed with myself for being spontaneous. Reckless with her feelings. Instead of fighting the mustard attack, I dipped my finger in a thick blob and licked it off. Tart. Tangy. Sweet. "It's not so bad after the fact, right?"

Her laugh finally exploded, a glorious cackle that had her doubling over. "I..." She tried to speak, but wound up wheezing and fanning her face. "You just...." Again, she dissolved. "You look ridiculous."

We had an audience now, one woman with her phone in the air videoing us. Fabulous. That'd hit the social media circuit in no time, along with the rumor I got the shits. I should care. But I didn't. The harder Gwen laughed, the lighter I felt. I grabbed the ketchup spoon and dashed it across her tank top. She came back at me with the mustard. I retaliated until we resembled a couple of Jackson Pollock paintings.

Gwen wailed like she'd been shot. "My boobs are bleeding."

I snorted and she hammed up her performance.

Gwen, the drama queen.

Gwen, the light in my dark.

Gwen, the girl who owned my heart.

"I'mma have to charge you fifty cents for those spoons." The hotdog vendor twitched his mustache, unimpressed with our antics.

Gwen gathered our weapons and dumped them in the trash. "He's a famous musician and sings mean songs to girls. He can cover it."

I shook my head and planted a kiss on her cheek. "Happy birthday."

It was after midnight. Her official birthday.

"I really am the luckiest girl, getting sung hate songs and covered in ketchup on my special day. And by the way, you stink." She cringed at my shirt, making light of the milestone in typical Gwen fashion. If she didn't make a big deal of her birthday, she wouldn't miss the family calls and gifts she'd never receive.

"Does this mean I'm forgiven?" I asked.

"It does." Then more quietly, "I loved the song."

Her soft words hit me square in the chest.

"Dog's up," the vendor said before I pulled her to me and mixed our ketchup and mustard stains. She had to see how perfect we were together, how there was no maybe about us, different lives or not. She at least seemed less tense.

She accepted our street meat as I paid, saucing up our snack with the works. She left off the onions, and my heart gave another twist.

This woman knew how I ate my hotdog, without even asking. She'd taken up extreme sports since we'd last hung out, had a group of amazing friends and a fulfilling career. I'd made acquaintances in new countries, had learned enough German, Italian, and French to get by. I enjoyed cooking now and walking through a market, waiting to be inspired.

We'd changed a lot the past nine years, but I knew Gwen at her core, how she loved blue jelly beans and hated mayonnaise. That she'd listened to Green Day on repeat as a teen and had to knot her shoelaces twice when tying them. A silly superstition. She knew the contents of the time capsule buried in my back yard and the origin of all my scars. She was the only person on the planet who knew I cried during *13 Going on 30*.

She'd been there for me after my mother's nasty car accident, at the hospital the entire week that followed. I'd played guitar for her daily after she'd broken her wrist.

The little stuff. The important stuff. The things that filled the gaps of our lives.

Losing her now would be like losing my voice.

We sat on the curb while we ate, streaked in ketchup and mustard, sharing bites back and forth. It tasted amazing. Being beside her was even better, and I was done letting her hide from me. "You were right," I said.

She licked her fingers after her last bite, then gave up and wiped them on her dirty shirt. "About what?"

"I was jumping ahead with us, scared I might lose you. I didn't ask what you wanted or if you wanted an *us*, or how you think it might work. I wanted to do everything so you couldn't say no."

She rested her arms on her bent knees and stared straight ahead. "You're a fixer, August. It's what you do. But this isn't a quick fix."

Exactly what Finch had said. The more I replayed it, the more it made sense. Teaching Gwen guitar hadn't replaced the chill in her childhood home. Bringing her to my house for dinner hadn't made her silent meals easier to bear. They'd probably accentuated how bad she'd had it. "You don't have to leave your job or your friends," I said, trying to find a balance between fixer and compromiser. "We can work this long distance."

"We have very different lives."

"If I can guide my career to the States, I will."

"It's not that easy."

"Tell me why. Talk to me."

She picked at her nails. "You didn't see the wreckage I was after my nineteenth birthday. I was a disaster, could barely function. It wasn't pretty."

I wanted to tug her to me, hold her against my chest. Her nail picking was a red flag that kept me away. "I wish I'd known."

"No you don't. You wouldn't have wanted to know back then, and it's fine. I deserved it. But how far down I spiraled scares me. What I feel for you now, barely a day together, it's… like, *huge*."

I nudged her knee with mine. "That's what she said."

She tipped her head back and chuckled. "It *is* what she said. You have a gorgeous cock."

There was that fire again, gripping my groin. Sex wasn't what we needed now. My lame humor probably wasn't much help, either.

Her face sobered. "Seeing you in there, with that crowd, those eager women—I don't know how to handle that. I want you, August, more than you know. More than for two days. But there will be stretches of time apart and all sorts of obstacles, and I have the potential to turn into a psycho girlfriend who gets clingy and weird when you're performing for a crowd of rangy cougars. Which means we might fail. I'm ridiculously terrified of what might happen to me if we fail."

We wouldn't. I knew it as sure as I knew the sun would rise. I still understood her fear, how hard our years apart had been. If there was an easy solution, I'd be all over it. Demand she see us as a couple, not a fling. But there was no easy answer to be found. I felt inept. Useless. Stuck. All I could do was listen to her, be here for her the way she wanted. What if it wasn't enough?

"So you're not willing to try?" I asked.

"That's not what I'm saying."

"Then what? Tell me what you need, and it's yours."

She touched her belly briefly, as though cradling something precious, then she reached over and grazed her fingertips down my cheek. "Time. Our seconds, like you said. No talk of relationships or future yet. I'm not ready for that."

I gathered her hand in mine and kissed each of her knuckles.

"Then that's what you'll get." Even though it wasn't what I wanted. "But I have one demand."

"Do you, now?"

"There will be more bikini posters." I wasn't sure where her code for sex had originated, but saying it restored her playfulness.

She shimmied her shoulders. "That, my fine sir, will not be a problem. There will be a whole *Sports Illustrated* issue of bikini posters. Before that, though"—she gripped my thigh, excitement in her wide green eyes—"we have more PI work."

She went on about Uncle Rex's clue to her father's name. *Tom or Ted.* I did my best to show surprise, but the guilt over my lie thickened my throat, mixed with all the angst broiling inside me. The urge to confess what I knew rose, but I stomped it down. It was just another thing that could sink us. Another obstacle. Another reason we might fall apart.

Because of my idiocy.

But as she spoke about her mother's favorite drink and how Mary had danced in the club and had wanted to be on Broadway and had eaten her first hotdog, my niggling remorse lessened. Gwen had wanted a hotdog because her mother had eaten one—maybe in this very spot. A day ago, she'd never have sought that connection with Mary. She actually smiled when gushing over her mother's first kiss, made me read the passage. (After we'd wiped the grease from our hands.) This was the right thing, not telling her what I knew.

It also brought me back to the first time her mother had proved she'd loved her daughter.

The day of Gwen's nineteenth birthday, I'd called Mary, desperate, asking for Gwen's address. I'd denied my feelings for Gwen too long, had needed to speak with her and figure out if I was alone in my unshakable love. I'd been worried her mother would stonewall me, brush me off. She'd never liked me hanging around her daughter.

Mary Hamilton had surprised the hell out of me with two

short sentences. "Gwen loves you, August. Don't let her push you away."

After picking my jaw up off the floor, I'd gone out that afternoon and had bought Gwen a birthday ring, to pledge my love. To fix whatever the hell I'd broken. If her mother was pushing us together, I'd figured Gwen must have told her something. Let it slip, how she'd felt.

That story may not have had a happy ending, and I was pretty sure Gwen had never opened up to her mother. Understanding what Gwen wanted had been a mother's intuition alone.

As was Mary's recent letter to me. Her final line—*Remember what I told you on Gwen's nineteenth birthday*—had been a woman still looking out for her daughter, showing love in the only abstract way she knew how. She'd sent *me* the information about Gwen's dad, not Gwen. She'd wanted us together. She'd known how unresolved our feelings had been. Without that push, I wouldn't be here now, falling in love with Gwen all over again.

Fighting for her to give us a chance.

It didn't absolve Mary of her abysmal parenting, but she'd wanted Gwen to find her father, and to find me.

I may have ruined the father part, but I owed it to Mary to let Gwen discover her mother. Learn to love a part of her, if possible.

This was the right thing to do, for Gwen, and for Mary.

———

Gwen

"Will you come to a lookout point with me?" I was too buzzed to quit following clues. I could barely sit still.

"You trying to take advantage of me, Possum?"

A tempting notion. One I would indulge in later. For now I

couldn't stop picturing a young Mary Hamilton eating hot dogs and having her first kiss. "My mother mentioned a place in her journal—a lookout called Tank Hill, which I've heard of but never visited. It just feels right, to keep following in her footsteps. It led us here, to Finch and you guys talking. And—"

"You covering me in mustard?"

"It really was tonight's highlight." Joking with August was the highlight. The lightness allowed me to live in the moment. The here and now. Keep my mind from running ten steps ahead.

He pinched his defiled black T-shirt and pulled it away from his chest. "Maybe we should change first."

The stains on my tank top had begun drying, and I smelled like a hotdog, but tonight was all about momentum. We had twenty-four hours until my birthday was over. The deadline rolled closer, taunting me. "I don't care if you don't."

He shrugged and released his shirt. "Then let's move out."

We bickered during the drive. I knew the fastest way to Twin Peaks Boulevard; he thought his way was better. Men were naïve like that, and I was verging on giddy. The hysterical kind of silly unleashed when a slew of untapped emotions engulfed you. It was an epidemic.

A bubble of happiness built along with my delirium. It rippled while we argued. Another ballooned when I elbowed August, and he elbowed me back. It grew when we laughed and fake-sneered and rolled our eyes at each other. There were a lot of floating bubbles filling my chest. I didn't try to pop them or pretend playfully arguing with August didn't fill my car with joy. These were my seconds, and I'd savor every one.

We grabbed the flashlight from my glove compartment and hiked up the steep stairs to the hilltop. Our beam of light skipped over roots and logs, skimming the few trees and bushes growing on this stretch of earth. A swing hung from a tall branch, the lights of the city beyond. We stood on the precipice, the flashlight switched off, the backs of our hands brushing.

Darkness cocooned us.

I listened for August's breath, the even in-out of his lungs. Imagined his chest rising and shrinking. I matched my inhales to his.

"It's beautiful," he whispered.

"Like an alien city. No traffic. No noise." Perfect stillness.

We exhaled slowly. My world shrank to this moment. No before or after or morning or night. Just now.

"It's because Barbie-Man lives there," he said. "Keeps the criminals in check."

I shuddered. "Barbie-Man was, and always will be, an abhorrent mutation. Way to kill my moment."

His lips found my cheek in the dark. His heartbeat found mine in the shrinking space between us. "Does this make it better?"

I tried to say yes, but only managed a sigh.

He flicked the flashlight back on and led me to the large swing. It was wide and flat, a wood plank big enough to share. We crammed together and trained the light on my mother's journal. Stars shone down, the night warm and still. He shifted against me, a squirmy move as he yanked off his shirt and tossed it on the ground. The soft glow of the flashlight draped his body in sharp relief—the ridges of his abs, the firm cut of his pecs and shoulders.

My mouth dried. "Are you about to teach me pole vaulting?"

"Say the word, and I will. But the smell was getting to me."

A valid point. The ketchup whiffs from my tank top weren't exactly pleasant. Taking his lead, I squeezed the journal between my thighs and freed my hands to whip off my top and toss it near his.

"Jesus, Gwen. We're in public." His voice sounded scratchy.

"We're in a dark place at one a.m., not a soul around. And wearing a bra isn't any different than wearing a bikini top."

He still groaned. There was no denying the sexual energy pillowing around us. It was always there, whether bickering or breathing or sharing a swing. I was in jeans and my favorite

Victoria's Secret black bra. The one that gave my girls a lift. August's hand coasted over my back, crisscrossing the silky straps. My nipples pebbled. Shivers danced along my skin. Dirt rolled under our feet as we swayed.

I wanted to tug him to the ground, lose the rest of our clothes, but I wanted this, too. To sit with him under a star-filled sky, my history unfolding as the night wore on.

I found where I'd closed my mother's diary last and read her words. "The lookout is our place. No one is ever there. We lie on a blanket and he tells me about the stars and the shapes he sees. He kisses me tenderly, like I'm a secret he's unlocking. But last night, it finally happened. I had waited so long. He had been so patient. I'm not a virgin anymore."

August inhaled sharply. I should have been horrified to read about my mother popping her cherry. Like *hum songs and cover my eyes* horrified.

Instead I hunched farther over her journal, devouring her private words. "It hurt at first, like he said it would. Then it was good. He felt so good. We moved together in the best kind of dance. I wrapped my legs around him. He told me I was beautiful, that I make him feel alive. He said it while he was inside me, moving deep and slow. I tried to say something, to tell him he was the reason the sun rose, but I couldn't find the words. They caught in my throat. The second I tried, tears threatened. I have never known this. How a person can make you so happy you want to cry. And I couldn't risk it. He would think I'm too young for crying. A baby. He may be older, but we are the same. Age doesn't matter. Not with us. Not after what we did."

My voice had thinned to a whisper, my mother's love life stealing my breath. My giddiness absconded, too. He was an older man, this Tom or Ted. He seemed to have fallen for my mother. Yet Uncle Rex had mentioned another woman on the hunt for him. A jilted girlfriend? An angry one-night stand? As unsettling as those possibilities were, this diary entry provided...peace.

I'd once asked my mother, after her cancer diagnosis, when I'd realized she could die before telling me my father's name, if she'd been assaulted. If that was why she'd refused to give me this scrap of information. It had plagued me, the possibility that I'd come from something dark, but I'd finally found the courage to ask.

Her reply had been straightforward but cryptic. "You were born of love," she'd said flatly. "But love is often blind."

That had been the most detail I'd ever learned about my father. I had pushed back, begged for more information. She had stonewalled me and played her Cancer Card. Would claim she was tired and needed to lie down when I'd go over. We'd fought on and off after that, because I couldn't let it go, to the point she'd asked me to stop visiting.

There had been no magical mending of our relationship when she'd gotten sick. My anger toward her had intensified, for what she'd withheld—affection, information. She would close her eyes when I'd enter her room.

She died suddenly, a month after our last interaction. I hadn't been by her bed, holding her hand. I hadn't cried at her funeral. Her parents hadn't shown up. With no phone number or return address on my old birthday cards, I'd had no way to reach my aunt. I organized Mary's house on my own, had packed her life into boxes, but I never mourned.

Something moved through me as I sat here, her journal in my hand, her potent love for this man seeping from her words. A sob moved up my throat. "I'm sorry," I said to no one and everyone. To her. To August. To the father I didn't know. "I'm sorry I ruined your life."

It came out as a snotty, phlegmy sound, the words running together. Giddy one second, snotty the next. This day had been nothing but a rollercoaster, and I was about ready to get off.

August removed the journal from my trembling hand, led us to a soft dirt patch. He lay on his back and cradled me against his chest. He made shushing sounds as he stroked my hair and let me cry. I clung to him, my salty tears sliding over his collarbone.

He tucked me closer. "I'm here, baby. Let it out."

And I did. It wasn't pretty. It was loud and hiccupy, and off-the-charts unattractive. My mother had been so alive before having me. Hopeful. Spirited. She'd loved this man deeply. I didn't have proof he was my father, but a sureness formed as I grieved: a strange connection to these words and this spot, maybe where I'd been conceived.

"I never said goodbye to her," I finally managed. "She died thinking I hated her."

"No, she didn't."

"But I did hate her. I was awful to her. We were awful to each other. The word love wasn't in her vocabulary."

"She loved you, Gwen. In her own twisted way, she loved you. You were always in her thoughts."

He spoke with such confidence, as though he knew something I didn't. As though she'd told him as much. It didn't matter. What was done was done. I had her journal now, a window into the girl she'd once been. I was also sure I'd find my father. The bigger piece. The more important connection.

The flashlight was still on, shining away from us. August was a warm stamp in the near darkness, a solid shape holding me together. We were both covered in earth, the dry ground smeared on our jeans, dusting our skin. I splayed my palm over his abdomen. "I made you dirty again."

It was easier to focus on dirt and the slow pulse spinning through my belly than swirling regrets.

He shifted lower, tipped up my chin. Soft lips landed on my nose, both my eyelids. He kissed my tear-streaked cheeks. The rise and fall of his chest slowed. It stopped. "Gwen, I..."

There was trepidation in his tone, his unfinished "I" dangling between us.

I love you. Is that what he was about to say? What he'd

promised he wouldn't do? *I love yous* came with expectations and a future and all the things I wasn't ready to discuss.

A girl couldn't face her Worst Terrible Fuck-up, her dead mother's diary, and a phantom father, all while fighting to maintain her sanity in the face of a possible *I love you* from the one who got away, when he'd be leaving in two short days. No. Not two days. It was one day now. My birthday was today.

August was leaving tomorrow morning, because tomorrow was today. *God.*

These seconds needed to slow the fuck down. Stop. Go in reverse.

Terrified he was about to say the three most terrifying words in the English language, I opened my ridiculous mouth, and blurted, "I stole your underwear."

Gwen Hamilton, winner of the Dumbest Confession Award.

CHAPTER 14

1 a.m., 23 Hours…

AUGUST

I wiggled my hips in my jeans, but my briefs were still on. They hadn't magically disappeared. "Explain yourself, Possum."

"Nothing. Forget I said it." Gwen dashed at her drying tears.

"Forget you said that you stole my underwear? On what planet would that happen?"

"Uranus."

I barked out a laugh. One minute ago, my lungs had ceased to function. I'd been a second from telling Gwen I had a letter from her mother, proof the woman had cared about her and wanted to see her happy, which would have led to her father's name, and that I'd lied by omission, and had been letting her chase a ghost.

Now I was laughing. "As nice as I'm sure Uranus is, we're on

Earth. And on Earth women don't get away with saying things like 'I stole your underwear' without—"

I stopped midsentence, a sudden flash of my lucky boxers, the black ones with the green four-leaf clovers, stripping my voice. The ones I'd worn to every soccer match. The ones that had mysteriously disappeared my senior year. "You stole my lucky underwear."

"No I didn't. You heard me wrong. I said I stole your honey bear."

"My honey bear?"

"The one your mom kept in the kitchen. The jar thingy with the weird fake apron, where you put your keys and stuff."

"My keys and stuff?"

"The honey bear!"

I flipped us, straddling her waist from above. The flashlight beamed across her panicked face. She was so not getting away with this. "You have five seconds before I tickle the shit out of you."

"You want me to shit on you? I'm into experimenting, August, but defecation doesn't do it for me."

I full on snorted that time. It was still her funeral.

"*Fivefourthreetwoone.*" I dug in, tickling her ribs mercilessly while she screeched and flailed and tried to toss me off her. She didn't deserve the full five-second countdown. Not if she'd stolen my treasured boxers. She was also unbelievably strong. Her toned arms and legs strained against me. My cock strained against my jeans.

Goddamn, did she have a killer body.

I was a second from losing my grip on her, when she cried, "Beetlejuice!"

Our safe word. Dammit.

Keeping her locked between my thighs, I released her ribs. We both panted. The panting made me horny(er). I circled her upper arms in a vise-like grip. "What did you do with them?"

She slackened, her limbs turning to noodles. "We hadn't

spoken in months, because I'd ghosted on you, and I kind of, *maybe*, one day snuck into your room and might have smelled your shirts and lay on your bed."

That was one hell of a visual. Gwen Hamilton in my childhood bed, tangled in my sheets. "You're worried about me being into kinky defecation sex, and you're an admitted boxer sniffer? I might need to rethink things between us."

"Your *shirts*, dummy. I said I smelled your shirts. The boxers were a spontaneous moment of criminal masterminding. I hid them in my underwear drawer."

"So our undies could mingle?"

"Something like that."

"Oh, baby," I cooed, enjoying her torment. "That's so sweet."

She mumbled something under her breath and kicked her feet like a petulant child. "I am now sufficiently embarrassed. You can let me up."

Except I had her right where I wanted her, under the night sky, tears no longer streaking her face. I hated seeing her cry, but being here for her, to hold her—it meant the world. Being with her while she uncovered her mother's history was important.

When the time was right, I'd tell Gwen about her mother's letter, *after* we'd followed more clues. Without a last name, she'd never actually find her father. There was no way for her to know I'd visited his house. Not now, at least. Down the road, when we had more time, once she'd discovered all she could about Mary Hamilton, I'd tell her the truth. Giving Gwen these hours with her mother's memory meant more.

I also knew how to keep her happy.

A thin strip of light cut across the sleek plane of her stomach. Her bra did phenomenal things for her breasts, but they'd look so much better bare and in my mouth. "There's punishment for being a pervy boxer stealer, Gwen."

———

Gwen

August was on me in seconds, his lips working their magic. My embarrassment fled. My sanity fled. My clothes needed to flee.

I pressed my fingers into the knobs of his spine. His muscles shifted, strong and coiled with each purposeful movement. He nudged my knees as we kissed, anchoring himself between my thighs. *Right there.* He rolled his hips and I rocked into him, my whole body clenching. We were at it again, dry-fucking like kids, this time at a stereotypical lookout.

He wrenched his lips away. "I had no idea you were so kinky."

"There's lots you don't know about me."

"I plan to learn it all."

The comment skimmed close to future talk, but a twig or something scratched at my back, the line of his cock pressing exactly where I ached. I couldn't do anything but *feel*. "Can we do this learning while fucking?"

"That can be arranged." Another thrust of his hips, and desire snapped through me.

I dragged my hands over the grooves of his back, circled his biceps, traced his collarbones, slipped my fingers into the dip at the base of his neck. "We should stop. Anyone could come up here."

He lowered his chest to mine, slowly, inch by inch. Warm skin. Firm muscle. He cradled my head in his hand, protecting me from the hard ground below. "You said yourself it was dark and empty. And I thought you craved adrenaline?"

"Is that what this is?"

"Oh, Possum. This is way more than adrenaline."

He was sneaky, hinting at the truth behind my bravado. He wasn't wrong. This was August and me, half-naked on a dark hilltop, enough history between us to fill an encyclopedia.

Instead of fighting the depths of my emotions or making a

joke, I stared at him through the cover of night, wondering if he could see the extent of my feelings. They burned so bright I was surprised a blast of light didn't blind us.

"Now. I want you now." I didn't recognize the desperation in my voice.

A masculine sound pushed from the back of his throat, and his lips bruised mine—a hard, hot kiss that gripped the tips of my curled toes. His tongue delved into my mouth, seeking mine, sliding roughly. Our bodies writhed, hands and lips and teeth everywhere.

Need became hunger; hunger became a frenzy. I didn't care where we were or worry about who could stumble upon us. The darkness gave me a sense of security as he stripped off my jeans. It allowed me to pretend we were in another time and place where airplanes didn't separate lovers. Where clocks could be silenced.

For tonight, we were limitless.

Removing his jeans took too long and only reached his knees again. I'd never had sex like this, the pushing, pulling, grunting kind where the need to join was such sweet agony. We were insane for each other. He rotated me on top of him, anchored my hips as he pushed into me from below. Again, there was no time for foreplay. No time to explore the landscape of his body, every valley, plain, and ridge I'd been denied. Too many years had been stolen from us.

Urgency colored his gravelly voice. "I'm gonna come in you, Gwen. So fucking hard. You're mine. You're so fucking mine."

The permanence of him in my body was undeniable, a deep imprint every time our hips slapped. The sense of belonging was overwhelming, like every hardship could be overcome as long as I had August with me, telling me I was his.

How would that work when he was oceans away?

I banished that uncertainty to the darkness around us, focused on our limitless cocoon. I rode my man, my bra still on, the night air caressing my skin, wringing every drop of pleasure

I could. Soaring. Falling. Flying. Divine thickness, hard inside me.

There was no adrenaline rush better than making love to August Cruz.

I planted my palms on his chest. "I'll need new kneecaps by the time we're done."

"I'll kiss them better," he grunted.

I ground against him, delicious circles that rubbed me just right. "Your cock is fucking fantastic."

"Being inside you is a fucking dream."

"We say fuck a lot when we fuck."

"Because it's so fucking good."

Good was an understatement. We were transcendental. I wanted to learn his body, each lick and bite that earned me a growl. Each shift of my hips that made him swear. Yet he was leaving me. *Stop*, I ordered my mind. *Stop freaking out.* I worked my body harder, held on tighter, my nails tasting his flesh as the edges of my orgasm bloomed.

"I'm close, Gwen. So damn close. I want you to come all over my dick."

His dirty words enflamed my desire as he filled me, his length dragging against me in exquisite torture. I'd normally touch myself to go the last mile, to *chase, chase, chase* the burning ball at the end of this ride. But there was no pursuing this release.

It yanked me under, a sharp tug that splintered through me. I clenched and called his name. More *fucks* fell from my lips. The stars fell around me.

August dug his thumbs into my hips, holding me slightly higher, thrusting up into me in hard, fast strokes. His mouth was open, his eyes black in the darkness. "Fuck, Gwen. Fuck, fuck, fuck. Oh, *fuck*."

He jerked and shuddered, one last drive impaling me to the point of pain, but the best kind. The thoroughly used kind. The kind that eased into bliss as I sank on top of him.

"That was five fucks. For a man who writes songs, your verbiage seems limited."

He held me to him, his length still nestled deep. Breathing hard, he pressed my face into his neck and kissed the top of my head. "Making love to you could rebuild worlds. It could part oceans. Drop the stars from the sky. Making love to you is my reason why."

This man was a triple threat. "That was cheesy"—I kissed his neck, his jaw, his lips—"and I loved it." *I love you*, I wanted to say. There was no denying it. It had always been August for me. It also didn't change what tomorrow would bring.

I tried to reel my emotions back in, but it was like rewinding a ball of yarn, the shape never quite right again, always threatening to unravel. I also couldn't ignore what I'd just experienced. "I want to stay like this all night," I said, taming my freakout.

He clamped his hands on my ass, keeping himself seated inside me. "Might be weird when people show up in the morning."

"It could be great for your career. No such thing as bad publicity, right?"

"Considering the rumors that likely got started today, I'm hoping the answer to that is yes. But"—he rocked me against his pelvis—"I'm still dying to get you on a proper bed and take my time with you. I haven't tasted you yet. I need that like I need to breathe."

Whoa, boy. I wouldn't take much convincing, but I didn't want to leave yet. We'd had sex where my mother and father had made love. Where I might have been conceived. I wasn't ready to walk away from my bone-deep connection here. The first place I'd grieved for my mother. "Can we look at the stars for a while first? I'd like to read a bit more of the journal, too."

He ran his nose through my hair, stealing a scent with each pass. "Anything, Possum."

We got dressed, the two of us ridiculous in our condiment-streaked clothing. We lay on the ground, diary and flashlight in hand, reading my mother's heart.

She'd loved her man. She'd hated her parents. It sounded all too familiar. She mentioned a vacation with her guy, a sneaky trip camouflaged to her parents as a church excursion. Hozier's "Take Me to Church" came to mind, and a whole lot of "taking." It could have been where her luggage had gone missing, but it wasn't the final entry and didn't explain the eleven-year gap between being packed and riding a Greyhound.

A few lines about trust also gave me pause. *I didn't think I would trust anyone after Marcus. I didn't think I would ever date again. But Ted is a man, not a boy. He is different. He wouldn't hurt me like that. He better not hurt me.*

Wariness bled through her words. Distrust. After August read the passage, I relayed Uncle Rex's comment to him, how some girl had come looking for Ted or Tom. "If my mother had been betrayed by this Marcus guy before, she'd be wary of it again. It would hurt worse a second time."

"It likely would."

"Right, but…if this new guy got her pregnant, and she later found out he was seeing someone, don't you think she'd flip?"

August paused, but didn't offer much insight. "That kind of betrayal would cut deep, for sure."

His lack of rebuttal annoyed me. As teens, we'd pick apart clues, him more than me, always analyzing, figuring, solving. I wanted to do the same now. He seemed distracted. With all we had on our plate, I couldn't hold it against him. But my mind whirred, questions and possibilities spinning.

I wasn't sure a cheating boyfriend was enough to embitter my mother, unplanned pregnancy or not. Flat out refusing to share my father's identity seemed too extreme, but she'd been a kid with no parental assistance. It was possible.

Without August's analytical mind to bounce ideas with, I read on. Her tone resumed its previous swooniness, especially when mentioning a bench they'd visited at Fisherman's Wharf.

"We should go tomorrow," I told August. "After I meet the girls at the gym."

The bench in question had supposedly been inscribed with my mother's name, a rebellious scratching into wood she'd done instead of doodling in a notebook margin. The kind where you wrote your boyfriend's last name as your own.

Possibly my father's last name.

If she had, it was the key to finding him. With that clue, I could narrow the possibilities and visit each man. I didn't mention the last-name detail to August. He didn't seem keen to obsess over this as much as me, and it felt too fragile: a wish only possible if kept private. I also needed to talk with Ainsley and Rachel about this insane night. Specifically how I wanted to handcuff myself to August and never let him out of my sight.

"I'll take the guys up on their run offer," August said. "We'll hook up after."

I snuggled in closer. "That means we'll be apart for a bit."

One arm latched around me, he dragged his boot heel over the loose dirt. "I'll miss you."

Raw, simple honesty.

He deserved the same in return. "I'll miss you, too." And it would only be a few hours. Not days or weeks or months.

A shiver ran through me.

He rubbed his hand down my arm. "You cold?"

I wished it were the cold. I rested the journal on my belly, needing to talk and drown the shouty voices in my head. "What's your favorite part about touring?"

He played with my hair. "Singing. Unleashing everything into song."

"And the worst?"

"It's lonely."

I ached at his desolate tone. I'd always imagined him surrounded by people, busy and smiling. I'd assumed his life was fuller and happier than mine, like when we'd been kids. The greener grass that was more AstroTurf than natural growth. "Aren't you close with your band?"

"They're good guys, but we don't stick together. I've used studio musicians for different stretches of the tour. People come and go, and outside the music scene, no one really knows me. It's not all bad. The solitude is great for writing. The venues I play are usually full, packed with music fans there to listen. I get paid doing what I love."

It was one thing watching him play that hate-love song tonight. The possibility of watching him in concert, entertaining a smoky European club, had me itching to hop on a flight with him. To be his person who filled his lonely moments. Such a tempting idea. "Do you always play 'Girl with the Black Heart'?"

A light laugh moved through his chest. "People go nuts over that song, but I'll play the newer version now."

"People are sick and twisted," I grumbled.

"Maybe I'll write a new song. Something cheesy. Just for you."

"You know I like my music loud and screamy."

He pinched my shoulder. "You also like to take the long route when we could have driven here faster, if you'd listened to me."

I pinched him back. Because he was wrong. We kept joking, sharing. He talked about the roads in Europe and how wild the driving there was. We'd for sure murder each other navigating that madness. He confessed he missed his parents, who'd moved to Chicago for his father's consulting work. His sister, Melody, was a high school music teacher there, all three Cruz kids drawn to the music industry in one way or another.

I explained the intricacies of my job, then he peppered me with questions about surfing and mountain biking and jumping from planes. I barely got one answer out before he shot out another. The night drew on, my eyes grew heavy. He hummed a soft tune.

I hadn't planned to fall asleep here, but my languid limbs

wouldn't move. He hummed some more, I pressed closer. All I'd learned about my mother and her boyfriend—*my father*, my gut told me—looped through my mind, puzzle pieces jumbling together. He'd watched her dance, had taken her to clubs and for fast-food dinners. He'd lain with her below the stars and had treated her with respect when taking her virginity. He'd loved her. I was sure of it.

Would he really have cheated on her? Unless it had been the reverse. She could have been the other woman, an escape for him, true love he didn't have in another relationship. The possibility wouldn't excuse the deceit. Or maybe the girl who'd searched him out at the Blue-Eyed Raven had been a friend or coworker, a close relative.

The only clarity was August's steadiness below me, and that this journal could lead me to my father and the answers I craved. In the light of day. Before my birthday was over. Exactly as I'd wished. No other outcome was acceptable. Not when August was leaving and the only thing that could save me from that impending heartache was finding my dad.

CHAPTER 15

6 a.m., 18 Hours…

AUGUST

Gwen covered her mouth with her hand and spoke through her fingers. "I want to kiss you, but I can taste my breath. It could kill a small country."

"You think I care? Mine's just as bad." I stalked toward her until her back was pressed against her apartment's brick exterior. Her place was a few floors up. I wasn't leaving without a kiss.

"If you don't care, there's something wrong with you."

I caged her between my hands, but was smart enough to keep my hips back. Already, I was hard. Primed for her. If my body brushed hers, I'd be dragging her upstairs and neither of us would see our friends today. Not an unpleasant prospect…. "There's something wrong with me, all right. I'm crazy for the girl who stole my boxers."

"They look better on me." Still with her hand over her mouth.

"Stop being so adorable and kiss me. We both drank water. It dilutes the morning breath. Or we can stand like this for the rest of our lives, like those street mimes who never move. I'll paint you red and me yellow."

Like our shirts.

We'd woken up with the sun, tangled together, smelling like ass (aka ketchup, mustard, dirt, and sex). My body had ached from sleeping on the hard ground. My heart ached every time Gwen glanced at me. My flight was at 8:10 a.m. tomorrow, which meant I had to be at the airport by 5:30. Not enough hours from now. I needed every kiss I could get. "Give in, Possum. You know I never back down."

She rolled her eyes, and I pressed a soft kiss to her hand, as though it weren't covering her lips. I gave it a lick and she squealed. Fast as lightning, she jerked her palm away, planted a close-lipped kiss to my mouth, then darted under my arm. I'd take what I could get.

The street was quiet, the few morning devotees either jogging or zombie-walking toward the nearest coffee joint. When she reached her building's entrance, she paused and faced me. She smoothed her hands down the sides of her slim jeans.

As though on a spring, she hopped forward, back toward me, dodging a zombie along the way. She kept enough distance between us that she didn't cover her mouth. "I just wanted to say, because I don't think I did, that I couldn't have done this without you. If you hadn't shown up at my mother's, I wouldn't have known Finch was at that club. I probably wouldn't have spoken with Uncle Rex. The ballet teacher wouldn't have given me the time of day."

She was all fizz and bubbles, but the air in my lungs turned flat. It was one thing to keep Mary's letter and what I'd learned from Gwen. I didn't need her thanking me.

She twisted her fingers together. My insides corkscrewed into a violent knot.

"You're part of the reason I'm going to meet my father," she went on. "I want you with me when I knock on his door. If he's amazing or awful, I want you there. Which means we need to find him today, before my birthday and your flight. And I didn't mention it, but my mom wrote that she'd scratched her name into a bench at Fisherman's Wharf. The one by the Alcatraz booth? A romantic etching, you know, using his last name instead of her own—cute teenage hopes of marriage or whatever. If it's still there, and the bench hasn't been cleaned up or replaced, it's all we need. I'll be able to find him."

She took one step back, then two. Her cheeks glowed brighter. "But not before I brush my teeth and tell the girls about our night together."

Her departing wink was equal parts fun and naughty, exactly what I wanted for our last day, but my heartbeat became sluggish. My posture sank. I watched her slip into her building, disappear down the corridor.

I stood. I stared. I nearly retched.

If Gwen's mom had scratched *Mary Mercer* into that bench and Gwen traced it to her father's house, I couldn't return there and continue this lie, pretend I hadn't talked with his widow. That would be relationship suicide, and I never believed Gwen would get there. Not in two days. But the possibility of her discovering that last name, the coincidences that had led us here…

This had the potential to go very south, very fast.

I could derail her search, beat her to that bench and scratch out his last name if it was there. It wouldn't be hard.

It would also be active sabotage. No way was that happening. That left telling Gwen the truth, confessing I was the reason she'd never meet Ted Mercer.

Another impossible option.

———

"August!" Jimmy growled from behind me. "Slow the fuck down before I have a heart attack."

My thighs screamed with each long stride, my pounding feet reverberating in my skull. I'd hoped my run with the guys would give me clarity, an option beyond my two excruciating choices. All I had was a side cramp and smarting shins. Sweat dripped off my forehead.

I slowed to a jog, my lungs working harder as I lost momentum. My chest felt ready to rupture. A session with my guitar would have been better than trying to chase away my guilt.

After I'd walked in on Gwen and Finch nine years ago, I'd played guitar until my fingers had bled, literally. I couldn't get the visual of him in his boxers out of my head, kept picturing them in bed together. I'd felt so stupid. Angry at Gwen's mom for suggesting I had a chance with her, furious at Finch for abusing my trust. Sickened that I still yearned for Gwen. Even with my hardened calluses, I worked the fretboard so harshly, my skin broke.

I itched for that same pain now, but my favorite Gibson was in Germany. Where my life was. Where I'd end up alone and scratching my heartbreak into lyrics if I botched this.

The boys and I had run a circuit through Owen's neighborhood, ending in a park. Owen planted his hands on his hips, head tipped back as he caught his breath. Jimmy walked in circles, cursing me for setting the frantic pace. I yanked off my drenched shirt, could practically squeeze out the sodden fabric. I squeezed my fists instead.

It was a Sunday. Families were playing on a jungle gym, balls and Frisbees tossed. Dogs kept time with their owners. Everyone with normal lives. I didn't envy their nine-to-fives and daily routines, assuming most of them walked that treadmill, but I envied how they lounged and laughed like they had forever. Living their lives with their loved ones. With their kids.

Another stitch cramped my side.

"Mind telling me what you were chasing out there?" Jimmy stopped pacing. He sat his ass on the grass, under the shade of a large oak, arms dangling over his bent knees. "This was supposed to be a leisurely morning run. Not a sprint."

"I have stuff going on."

"Yeah, I figured that out. You've been scowling so hard *my* teeth ache."

I loosened my always working jaw, dragged my hand through my sweaty hair.

Owen sucked back a large breath, exhaled as he studied the blue sky. More blue. So much blue in San Francisco compared to Europe. I had missed this. I'd missed being able to run with friends, even though we hadn't said a word while pounding the pavement, the type of comfortable silence that allowed you to brood or think or not feel so alone.

Silence that settled the soul.

It wasn't helping much today.

Owen's shirt joined mine in a heap. He stretched his long body out next to Jimmy, hands behind his head like he was lounging at a pool. "I'm guessing the mood is because of Gwen."

I couldn't sit on the grass. My blood still rushed from our run, my mind as busy. I jammed my toe into the ground. "Because of her and something shitty I did."

"Isn't she the one who slept with your brother?" A shaft of sunlight cut through the leaves, slashing across Jimmy's tattooed arms.

I appreciated his candor. It was why I'd blurted our sordid history when we'd met for drinks. No point pretending that shit show hadn't happened. But this was worse than Gwen drowning her sorrows in Finch, and Finch using her to get to me.

This was unforgivable.

"What Gwen did sucked, but it was years ago. We've changed since then. We've talked it out, and I've forgiven her. The real kind of forgiveness, like I know I can really let it go."

"So you guys had a good night together?"

My queasiness persisted. That didn't keep me from smiling. "We had a great night. Most of it, at least." The frantic sex on her living room floor. The frantic sex on a patch of dirt in the middle of the night. Talking to her until we both fell asleep, her warm body tucked into mine. A great fucking night. "Unfortunately, this is about a letter I got from her mother before Mary passed away. Something I haven't told Gwen."

One big, massive thing.

Owen squinted at me through the sun. "Lay it on us. We've both been through rough times with Ainsley and Rachel. We know what it's like to screw up and almost lose the one. Assuming that's how you feel about Gwen."

The ebbing of my adrenaline had me dizzy. Or maybe it was thoughts of Gwen. "She's it for me. She's freaking out because I go back to Germany tomorrow. I'm losing it, too. Hate the idea of being apart for a second." Even now, my senses felt dulled. The way a shorted guitar pickup deadened the ringing notes. Without her, everything was muted and worries invaded my mind. Was she talking to the girls, telling them she couldn't keep seeing me? Talking herself out of us?

Fresh sweat beaded. The cold, clammy kind. "I'm not willing to lose her, but I did something stupid. If she finds out, she'll probably cut me off."

"You'd be preaching to the choir," Owen said. "I mean, Jimmy screwed up way worse than me. Not even sure Rachel should have forgiven him."

Jimmy kicked Owen's shin. "Asshole."

"She's way out of your league."

"Tell me something I don't know. And I'll warn you upfront," Jimmy told me, "Ainsley gets scarier when you hurt her friends. I'd hire a bodyguard."

An adoring grin swept across Owen's face. "Love my girl."

And I loved mine. A smack-down, hook-line-and-sinker, irreversible love. She didn't want to hear it, though, had asked me to keep things light. Our blasted seconds—my stupid suggestion when I'd been high from making love to her our first time.

It didn't change how I felt. Or what I did. "If Ainsley finds out what I've kept from Gwen, I might have to join the Witness Protection Program."

Jimmy yanked grass from the ground and peeled the blades. "Sit down, already. Your pacing's making me nervous."

I hadn't realized I'd been on the move. I couldn't run from what I'd done or play it away in a song. I sat in a sunny spot, hoping the heat would ease the chill slipping down my spine. "You guys know how Gwen never knew her father?" They nodded, and I forged on. "Gwen's mother sent me a letter a month before she died, two months ago now. In it, she wrote Gwen's father's name. For some reason she wanted me to tell Gwen, asked me to be there for her when she found him."

I didn't mention Mary's subtle reminder to recall our conversation on Gwen's nineteenth birthday. *Gwen loves you. Don't let her push you away.* I wasn't sure it was in my control anymore.

Owen sat up slightly, leaned on his forearms. "But Gwen said you guys were going to look for him, like she didn't know who he was."

"Gwen doesn't know about the letter."

Both guys winced. Jimmy opened his mouth, probably to tell me I was a jackass.

I talked over him. "My past with Gwen was intense for me, and getting that letter brought it all back. I didn't think I could handle facing her. I was away, touring. Figured twenty-eight years had gone by, what difference would another month or two make? Then her mother died. I missed the funeral. Made some excuses to myself about concerts I'd booked, but I was dazed at that point, unsure I could deal with seeing Gwen, facing everything that had been stirred up."

"Why not tell her now?" Jimmy quit peeling grass. He had an intensity about him, like at the bar last night, when he'd asked me to leave if I'd shown up to provoke Gwen. "Why search out a man when you already know his name?"

However things unfolded with Gwen and me—if we wound up together but I was away, or if she cut me from her life—I was happy she had her girlfriends and these guys. People who supported her.

Hopefully they knew her well enough to tell me the smart thing to do. "I decided to look him up before telling Gwen, to make sure he wasn't some deadbeat who'd hurt her or use her for cash. I realized I couldn't keep stalling and booked a flight a week ago. I found the man's house, knocked on the door. And..."

I dug the heels of my hands into my eyes until they burned. "I found out he had a heart attack. The week prior. I sat on that information for *seven weeks*. If I told Gwen right away, like her mother had asked, she'd have had seven weeks to get to know the man, ask all the questions she's built up. You have no idea how big of a gap that's been in her life. We used to spend days searching for him as kids, hours on the internet. I knew it was massive for her, and I waited because I was too big of a pussy to face her, and now she'll never meet her father."

"Jesus." The intensity in Jimmy's face turned contemplative. The idiot smirked. "That's way worse than my fuck-up with Rachel."

"And that's supposed to help me how?" I picked at my calluses.

He returned to playing with the grass. "So you're afraid she'll cut you loose when she finds out."

It was a statement. The obvious fact. But not the only one. "Partly. I wasn't prepared for what I felt when I saw her after so long. And the way she looked at me?"

My overheated blood pumped faster than when on our run. "None of it went how I planned. Her mother's luggage turned up, and she was overwhelmed. It felt like we'd been brought together for something bigger, and the journal's been insane.

Gwen's mother was a piece of work, but we've seen new sides of her through her words, and it's like Gwen's finally discovering a woman she can understand. She's grieving for her for the first time, and if I tell her, she'll stop searching for her dad. Stop learning about her mother. So, no, it's not just about me. She needs this closure in her life."

Owen hadn't said a word, his brown eyes hazy, as though he'd tuned us out.

Jimmy was back to glaring. "Bullshit."

"Excuse me?"

"That's bullshit and you know it. You love her, man. You love her and you're scared you'll lose her when she finds out."

"I'm terrified, but—"

"No buts about it. I get why you delayed telling her initially. I probably would have done the same. But now? You're traipsing around the city, searching for a dead man, and you think it's because you want her to have closure? You are seriously delusional. And forget smallpox. If Ainsley gets a whiff of this, she'll castrate you."

A soccer ball bounced toward us. Jimmy shook his head at me, his damp black hair a ratty tangle. In one move, he palmed the stray ball and hopped to his feet, jogging toward a few kids messing around.

Owen stirred and sat up cross-legged. "You know I was raised by my nana, right?" I nodded. His eyes still looked glazed, his mind elsewhere. "I didn't talk about it much when we played soccer and hung out, but I never knew my father, and my mother left us when we were kids."

"Sounds rough."

"It was, at times. But I'm acquainted with feeling adrift, not understanding who you are or where you come from. It drove a lot of my choices growing up—sticking with a marriage too long as an adult, pushing Ainsley away when I should have held on tighter. I get why this has been a big void in Gwen's life, but Jimmy's only partly right."

"The part about me being delusional?"

He huffed out a laugh. "We all are when we're falling in love. No two ways about it. The emotion gets too big to see right. But you're not wrong about the closure part for Gwen. My brother held onto more anger than I did after our mother took off. It beat him down. Understanding why she left would have gone a long way to helping him live a fuller life sooner. Maybe I wouldn't have married the wrong woman. So I get it, why you've waited. But everything has a way of getting out eventually. If you don't control that information, the fallout is way worse." The stuttering of his Adam's apple suggested he was speaking from experience.

"If I burn the letter, she'd never know."

"True. But you would."

As teens we'd drink beers under the bleachers after practice, hit on girls, talk shit about the other soccer teams, but we never discussed feelings. I had no clue Owen had been through so much. I was impressed with how together he was now.

I was far from together.

Jimmy was teaching soccer drills to a few kids. I dragged my hand through the grass, plucked at it like he'd done. It reminded me of my lawn cutting days and Gwen chasing after me, shoving clippings down my shirt. I'd never tossed out the T-shirt she'd bought for me. *Lawn Enforcement Officer*. No matter my anger surrounding our history, I couldn't part with the threadbare memory or delete her photo from my computer. She'd always been a part of me.

"I have to tell her," I said quietly.

"You do."

"I'm going to lose her."

"You might."

The air around me thickened. The April heatwave threatened to box me in. "I love her. In one day, my world's tipped sideways. There's never been anyone else for me. Doubt there ever will be."

Owen hunched forward, hands clasped in front of his crossed legs. "If you're honest about why, she'll hopefully understand. Wish I had better advice."

"It's my mess to sleep in."

My lungs felt blistered, charred and inflamed. Gwen had looked so hopeful at her apartment this morning, positive she'd meet her father and get the answers she sought. I'd be the one to torch that dream. She wouldn't forgive me. Not for this.

I pressed my clenched fist to my stomach, but the jagged twisting didn't lessen.

Helping her discover her mother had played a part in my choices. Gwen had needed to grieve, glimpse the woman who'd asked me not to let her daughter get away. But Jimmy was right, too: stalling now was selfish. Telling her meant losing her, which was the last thing I wanted.

There was no option in the end. I was her best friend. All these years later, that was my most important title. Best friends didn't follow each other on false scavenger hunts. They forgave the unforgivable, which I'd already done. They also shared the tough stuff, truths that stung.

First thing I'd have to say when I met Gwen this morning was her father's name.

CHAPTER 16

7:30 a.m., 16 ½ Hours…

Gwen

I sank into my squat, then launched upward, limbs braced for impact. A sharp grunt drove from my lungs. I landed on my box, and the shock vibrated up my spine. I hopped down, shot my legs behind me into a burpee—my thirty-ninth. Another pushup. Another box jump. Oxygen raked through my lungs. Everything burned, the kind of pain that had me pushing harder.

Just one more jump. One more rep. To better my personal record.

Win against myself.

The only battle I could control these days.

"I'll never understand the box jumping thing." Ainsley stood in her usual spot, perfect ponytail, trendy Lululemon ensemble, not a bead of sweat marring her forehead. "Why would anyone put themselves through that?"

"Because it's challenging," I managed between reps.

"Doing the thigh machine is challenging, and I don't risk smacking my face on the edge of a freaking box and losing my teeth. Plus, the thigh machine works my sex muscles. It's practical."

"The thigh machine doesn't work sex muscles." Rachel replaced her ten-pound weights. At least she exerted effort at the gym. "You should do those Kegel exercises."

"I've tried those." Emmett was to my right, giving the whole gym a show, men and women gawking as he curled his biceps. Owen's brother was sex on a stick.

I landed one more jump, my legs nearly giving out. *Forty.* It was a solid number for this morning. For each of those burpee box jumps, I hadn't stressed over August's looming departure or the possibility of finding my father today. For forty jumps all that had mattered was launching, landing, and breathing. It was everything I loved about exercise and extreme sports, how rushing adrenaline silenced my mind.

Today, however, I also needed to talk with my friends.

Unfortunately, they were more interested in Emmett. "Kegel exercises are for women," Rachel told him.

"That's where you're wrong," he replied.

Ainsley's ponytail bounced as she gave a little jump. Not a burpee box jump. More of a gossip-junkie jump. "Oh, do tell."

Emmett, in all his muscly glory, stretched one arm across his chest. His tank top gave us a nice view. "Studies show that Kegels increase the size and intensity of erections. They also reduce premature ejaculation—which isn't an issue for me," he added quickly.

"But size is?" I asked, unable to resist. "I'm surprised and disappointed."

"What? No. Of course not."

Blinking innocently, Ainsley jumped on my Tease Emmett Train. "You just said it helps with size."

"*Intensity.* They make orgasms better, for fuck's sake."

I shrugged at Ainsley. "That's not what I heard."

She zeroed in on Emmett's groin. "There's definitely a size issue."

Rachel, who often shied away from our more graphic conversations, released a sharp cackle. Her laugh was a ridiculous sound. Part wheeze, part high-pitched bray. It was one of my favorite things about her.

Every head turned our way at the sound, the perfect opportunity for me to raise my voice, and say, "I'll buy you a penis pump for your birthday."

Men lifting their weights snickered. A couple women covered their mouths.

"You're all assholes," Emmett mumbled as he shot us a scowl and stomped toward the treadmills.

Ainsley beamed at me. "That was good fun. A perfect birthday treat."

I couldn't believe today was April 12th. A full year after we'd made our important resolutions. I could be mere hours from fulfilling mine.

"I'm really buying him one," I said. "Imagine Cameron's face when Emmett opens it."

Messing with Emmett was always enjoyable, especially since he went out of his way to taunt Ainsley. She had, after all, crushed on him before we'd found out he was gay and she started dating his brother. A priceless story, one August didn't know. I made a mental note to share it with him. My thoughts stuttered on him in the process, a skipping record that crooned: *mine, mine, mine.*

The brooding lines of his handsome face filled my mind, the intensity as he'd sung in the Blue-Eyed Raven, his devastating smile during our condiment war, the heat in his eyes as we'd made love.

An imagined snapshot of him followed, one of him sitting in an airplane.

My body tensed, every muscle flexing. I was standing still,

not jumping or lifting weights, but I felt lightheaded. My heart hammered my breastbone. I pressed my hand to my chest.

"Gwen?" Rachel rubbed my back. "Are you okay?"

"No."

The girls exchanged worried glances.

"This calls for a smoothie session," Ainsley said. "We're cutting this workout short."

"That implies you actually worked out," I said, fighting to breathe through my quasi panic attack.

She looped her arm around my waist and led me toward the juice bar. "I fixed my ponytail fifty times. That counts as exercise. My biceps ache."

I snorted, her intended goal, and she squeezed my side.

Ten minutes later, we'd gathered around one of the small tables by the juice bar. Gym members walked across the hallway in front of us, the cardio room just beyond. Emmett jogged his heart out on one of the treadmills, other machines used by older and younger members following their morning routines.

This was *our* routine, when Rachel was in town. We'd exercise for an hour, then sip our smoothies and catch up and tease one another, but the royal blue walls seemed to vibrate, the florescent lighting too bright. I rubbed my eyes. "August leaves tomorrow."

"Oh." Rachel's word dropped like a rock in my gut.

Ainsley released the straw from her mouth. "Like *back to Germany* leaves?"

I slumped into my chair and drew sad lines on my smoothie cup. The cool condensation dripped downward. "He has concerts booked, things he can't change. So, yeah, he's hopping on a plane tomorrow and flying across the world."

Away from San Francisco. Away from me.

Ainsley cocked her head. "Has sex happened?"

My post-workout flush probably didn't hide the heat scalding my cheeks. "Sex has definitely happened."

"Was it good?" Ainsley dropped her voice. "I mean, there's

build-up with wanting someone that long. I'd worry about disappointment."

It was hard to explain how both times we'd had sex had been on the floor or the ground, August and I both partly clothed, him with his jeans around his knees. The urgency to join had taken over, obliterating all other senses. *Together. Faster. More. More. More.* That was all that had mattered, moving with him as quickly and deeply as possible. Waiting for a bed and trading languid kisses hadn't been an option.

And disappointment? I'd never come so easily, no manual manipulation required. Our connection had been absolute.

"It was perfect," I said. Our perfect—a little messy and a lot wild. There were no rules for August and me, like he'd said.

Rachel dipped her head to catch my downturned eyes. "Will you do long distance?"

"I don't know." I hated how my voice cracked. I prided myself on surviving my mother's indifference with my chin up. Living without a father or extended family. Being strong on my own.

Ainsley slammed her smoothie down, the green liquid sloshing. "So that's it? He screws you and leaves, doesn't want to bother trying?" So much for her lowered voice. "What a typical musician. Chasing women, not caring about the carnage left in his wake. If he thinks he'll—"

"It's not him," I said quietly, interrupting her tirade.

"What's not him?" She still sounded ready to shave his eyebrows.

"The screwing and leaving. I'm the screwer and leaver."

"Ex-squeeze me?" She leaned toward me, and I leaned away.

I bounced my foot restlessly. No matter how much I swallowed, my strawberry banana smoothie felt stuck in my throat. "I can't do it. I have my life here, my adoption work, and he has his music and groupies, and he's in new cities every week." *And he has groupies.* "I don't fit in that life. Not the way I'd want to. I love my job and you guys. I don't want to pick up and leave.

Plus, my scuba and surf stuff are here, my mountain bike and rock climbing gear. I can't travel with it."

"Your surfboard and scuba gear? These are your priorities?" Now it sounded like she wanted to shave *my* eyebrows.

I waved a flustered hand. "It's expensive."

"You can store it."

"What would I use in Europe?"

"You'd rent equipment."

"It's not the same as having my stuff." My voice shrunk with each feeble excuse. I didn't even believe me.

"Gwen," Rachel cut in, no nonsense in her tone, "since you're the one who usually forces us to face hard truths, we're at a disadvantage. I can't read between the lines as well as you, but you're being a tad irrational. What's going on? The truth this time."

This was why I'd met the girls this morning. I could have canceled, gone for a run instead, but I'd wanted their advice, which meant quitting my vague routine. I stilled my bouncing leg and met their concerned gazes. "I'm scared."

Rachel moved aside her half-finished smoothie, turning all her focus on me. "Scared he'll cheat on you?"

I pictured him at last night's club, the women vying for his attention. He'd spent that time looking for me, trying to extricate himself politely. He wasn't the issue here. "No. Not really. I'm worried *I* can't handle it. That I'll freak myself out until I'm convinced he *will* do something to ruin us, when I'm pretty sure he won't, and then I'll act like those stalkerish women in the reality shows we heckle. I can't be those women. Those women are the worst.

"And look at our history—we've both admitted we loved each other as teens, and all we did was screw it up. Me more than him, obviously, but our timing was always off. This feels the same. Like we know we'd be amazing together, but our lives simply don't line up. Maybe we aren't meant to be."

"Does he need a penis pump, too?" Ainsley asked, straight-faced. "Is that the problem?"

I kicked her lightly under the table, but my favorite fashionista had me smiling. "There are no penis concerns." I'd happily bronze his gorgeous cock, place it on a mantel. Come to think of it, I could bronze it, add some wiring and batteries...

I fanned my face, but I needed to stay on target and explain to the girls how rough I'd been the last time August had disappeared from my life.

"Imagine being so sad you could only drink boxed wine," I told Rachel, who mimed a puke-a-thon. "Or wearing white after Labor Day and tossing your Coach purse collection because you're having an epic pity party." Ainsley clutched her chest, horrified. "That's how I was after losing August, but more of the *emo drown myself in screamer music and ramen noodles* depressed. I never went out, barely attended my classes. I hit rock bottom, and we'd only ever kissed *one time*. We've been together less than twenty-four hours now, and I can barely go two minutes without aching for him. I won't survive losing him this time. It's easier to end things when he leaves."

My friends stared at me. The vinyl seat under my bare thighs got sweaty.

"I'll take it from here," Rachel told Ainsley.

She wore a similar black tank top to mine, but hers said *Save Water Drink Wine*. I focused on the writing, which meant I was staring at her boobs. Easier than facing her impending confrontation.

"Who did you lean on when you were nineteen?" Rachel asked, all business, like we were on an episode of *Law & Order*. "After the incident we aren't supposed to mention."

"No one." Finch and I had quit our friendship cold turkey. Clean Your Damn Area Claire had been nothing more than a roommate. I'd had no caring family to call.

"Did you like school?" She crossed her arms, covering the writing on her boobs.

I forced my attention to her stern face. "I hated school."

Which she already knew.

"Were you part of CrossFit?"

"No."

"Had you started surfing or rock climbing or jumping out of planes?"

I narrowed my eyes at her, gradually following her breadcrumb trail. "No."

"And now, nine years later, do you love your job and adore your *amazing* best friends, and have a crew of CrossFit buddies who jump on boxes? And when that isn't enough, do you do insane activities like toss yourself out of airplanes?"

When I stood on the precipice of a skydive, I'd look down and study the broad strokes of a town or city, the roads and forests and lakes in their expanse. Hikers below could enjoy the wild flowers and sprouting mushrooms. Fishermen could inhale the briny air and listen to yodeling loons.

Different perspectives of the same place.

Exactly how Rachel was reordering my history in a new way, forcing me to study it from a different angle, and acknowledge that the woman I was now could handle more because I *had* more.

"Yes," I said quietly.

She looked at Ainsley and fanned a hand toward me. "I'd like the record to show that teenage Gwen had no support network, and present-day Gwen has an incredible amount going for her." She placed her palm face-up on the table, waiting until I put my hesitant hand in hers. She gathered my fingers. "Losing him would be awful, but not giving him a shot, when you're clearly swoony over the man, would be worse."

"I'm still scared."

"Does bungee jumping, which you've done more than once, still scare you?"

"It does." No matter how many times I stepped into that void, adrenaline would send my blood rushing, fear and excitement mixing.

"Think of dating August like that. We're your rope—us and all this other amazing stuff in your life. If your leap takes a turn for the worse, we'll keep you tethered."

"I'll take you shopping," Ainsley added. "And we'll get Rachel drunk and watch her embarrass herself."

A guaranteed pick-me-up, and I exhaled a slow breath.

I'd assumed my downward spiral after my WTF had been because of losing August, that he'd been the eye of that storm. He had been, to some degree. But I'd never considered my situation at the time, how it had played a large part. A *bigger* part. Without coping skills and people to commiserate with, I'd wallowed. No one had tossed my unwashed laundry at my face and told me to get a grip. No one had hugged me when it all became too much. No one had acted out *Law & Order* or told me penis jokes.

Sitting alone in a dank apartment had been a one-way ticket to Self-Pity City.

A wave of emotion rocked me. "I love you bitches."

Ainsley covered her heart with her hand. "Nicest thing anyone's ever said to me. And meeting you two was the luckiest day of my life. I'm honored to share our birthdays, and I can't wait to celebrate tonight." She raised her smoothie for a toast. "To being radical bitches and scaring ourselves...and buying Emmett a penis pump."

Rachel's cackle erupted. "To us and fear and penis pumps."

We clinked our smoothies and chatted about tonight's birthday outing. The plan was to meet for casual drinks, us with our men. Emmett and Cameron would join us.

And August.

I still couldn't believe he was my man, but he was. It didn't matter that yesterday had been our first day together in an eternity. Crying on his chest last night, letting him see me vulnerable and weak, had made me feel strong, not alone. Not as a charity case. He was my other, and your other was supposed to support you and protect you. Exactly how I felt about him. I wanted to protect him, understand the man he'd become.

There was no use fighting our pull, and the girls were right: I'd survive no matter the outcome. Which meant it was time to jump in with both feet. I had unused vacation days, enough to string together a few weeks of travel. I'd check my calendar this morning, figure out when I could meet him in Germany. Although anxious to open up fully and put my heart and future on the line, I had to try. I'd loved August as long as I'd known him.

Even still. Even now. All this time later.

The girls kept chatting, but I could barely sit still. I couldn't wait to share my decision with August. I'd tell him the second we met at Fisherman's Wharf. But my restlessness was more than that. Realizing I'd interpreted my depression after my WTF wrong, that I'd been too entrenched in the intensity of my sadness to understand more than August had knocked me sideways, left me unsettled.

I'd also been sure finding my father was the right thing to do. That knowing him, even if he was an asshole, was better than living with the ten million unanswered questions I'd amassed. Was this the wrong perspective, too? If he was horrible, would I truly be happier knowing?

There was a reason my mother had never told me his name. It could have been personal—her fears and issues driving her. Or it could have been to protect me from something awful. If I gave up this search and forgot about my birthday resolution, I could spend the next day with August, in a bed, a shower, against a wall, on the floor again. We could make excellent use of our seconds. I suddenly wasn't sure on the smart move.

My attention drifted toward Emmett, who was running on his treadmill. His mother had left him and Owen when they'd been young. They had different fathers, men they'd never known or met. He would understand my situation more than most people, another new support in my life.

I drained the last of my smoothie. "I need to chat with Emmett, then I'm heading out."

Ainsley launched an air kiss my way. "Ask him if he needs the small or extra-small penis pump."

I snickered.

Rachel shushed our friend. "More important is that you're going to pledge your undying love to August before you meet us later, right?"

I drew an X over my heart. "I'll offer to have his babies."

Not such a farfetched concept, considering my reaction after our sweaty session on my floor, how I'd wished I hadn't been on the pill. I almost touched my belly now, willing it to be so.

I dodged the weight machines and stopped at the side of Emmett's treadmill. "Can we chat a second?"

He glowered at me. "I'm not talking to you."

"This isn't about your penis size." But I said it loud enough for the girl at his left to gawk and stumble as she ran. No point missing an opportunity.

Muttering under his breath, Emmett slowed his treadmill until it stopped. He grabbed his towel and joined me by the water fountain, a quieter alcove to the side. "This better be good."

It certainly wasn't a light penis-pump talk. "Do you wish you knew your father?"

He reared back at my sharp conversation turn. "What's this about?"

I leaned my shoulder into the wall, the cold, hard plaster steadying. "I never knew mine either and it's always plagued me, the kind of void in your life that consumes you. And I have this chance to maybe find him, something I've dreamed of forever. But, I don't know…all of a sudden, I'm wondering if I should let it go."

"That's definitely not penis talk."

I snorted. "Yeah, no. Sorry to be so heavy this early in the morning."

He mopped his forehead with his towel, taking his time. "It's a tough one to answer. Part of me would like to know the man responsible for half my DNA, and part of me doesn't care. He had his chance to know me and didn't take it, or maybe he never knew I existed. To be honest, I stopped letting either possibility affect my life a while back. Dating Cameron had something to do with it—accepting my past doesn't dictate my future. I have a great brother and grandmother. A hot boyfriend who knows I don't need *a fucking penis pump*." His glare was adorable. "Not sure that helped much."

It echoed what Rachel had said, how my current life was full, no matter what curveballs were tossed my way. Still, I felt unmoored. "I want to find him, I'm just worried it'll send me for a loop when I have a lot going on right now."

A lot being the understatement of the millennia.

He fisted his towel and folded his arms. "All I can suggest is this: you have to do you. Owen and I coped differently with our past, but we both made it through. There's no wrong or right. So if this is something you need, for closure or whatever, then putting it off will stress you more. If you think you're ready to let it go, then"—he shrugged—"let it go."

Shrugged. Like it was that simple. You know, just uncover my father's name, meet the man who might have chosen to ostracize me from his life, or like, whatever…*let it go.*

But when it came down to it, I guess it was kind of simple.

When the clock had chimed midnight last year, there'd been a reason I'd chosen this resolution. Ainsley, Rachel, and I had promised to make our wishes big ones, things we'd believed were essential to our lives.

Finding my father was essential.

I guess that was my answer, in the end. I would meet August at my mother's park bench and tell him I was ready to look ahead and plan for our future. Then we'd see, together, if my father's last name had been memorialized in that very spot. Whatever happened from there, at least I'd have August.

CHAPTER 17

9 a.m., 15 Hours…

I loitered by the Alcatraz ticket booth for so long parents side-eyed me and tucked their kids to their sides. My unrelenting frown wasn't helping. Gwen hadn't arrived yet. My lockjaw had returned. I stared at the park bench mentioned in Mary's journal, half a second from rushing over and searching for Ted's name possibly scratched into the wood.

So I can scratch it out, a dark part of me whispered.

But I wouldn't stoop that low.

The day was sunny but brisk. The sweat from my punishing run had been washed off in a blistering shower, but a feverish chill still descended.

I was about to lose the love of my life after I'd just found her.

Gwen's tousled hair snagged my attention first. Across the street and waiting for a gap in traffic, she bounced on her toes.

She wore ankle boots, a fitted T-shirt—blue with something written on it. Her tight jeans made my mouth water. They had a rip in the thigh, the perfect place for me to ease my fingers in, tease her with soft strokes.

I hadn't tasted her yet, licked and sucked and mapped her body. When she learned what I'd done, that fantasy would be shot to shit.

She made it to the bench and touched its edge, but snatched her hand back as though she'd been hit with an electric shock. She bit her lip and searched the area. Throngs of tourists walked the strip. One kid clung to her parents' hands as they swung her between steps. Carefree. Happy. The briny air expanded with chatter and squawking seagulls and laughs. My endless regrets lodged in my throat.

I should have contacted Gwen the second I'd received that letter.

Or the next day. The next week. The next month. So many days I could have given her with her father. Days she'd never get back.

I kept out of view, sick to my stomach.

She refused to talk about our future, I reminded myself. I may have been all in, but Gwen was still living our seconds. Even without this massive obstacle, she might not have given us a chance. She might be relieved when faced with my deception. It would make ending things with me easier, freeing her from the burden of pushing me away.

Yes. That was how this would go. My confession would give Gwen the out she wanted. She could keep her friends and life and not have to risk it all on me. This would be better for her.

She paced, clenching and unclenching her hands, her face equal parts excited, scared, and determined. Exactly how she'd looked at her first regional track meet. I'd been there for her that day. Not her mother. No close friends or siblings attended, only me to cheer her on. I'd screamed myself hoarse as she'd torn past the finish line.

Today, I wasn't the one in her corner. Today, I'd be the one letting her down.

When she took her lip chewing up a notch, looking ready to break skin, I scrubbed a hand down my face and trudged forward.

The second she spotted me, she waved and smiled, beaming with open affection. It was too much. Having those gorgeous eyes brimming with joy, having seen them ignite at my touch—how was I supposed to let that go?

She'll be relieved in the long run. Her life will be better.

I clipped a man's elbow as I approached her and tried to offer an apology, but my saliva was all gummed up. A break in pedestrians finally gave us a clear path to each other, and I forced myself forward. Gwen still seemed nervous and excited, shifting on her feet, hands now tight little fists. I should ask her how she was doing, hug her and offer support. That would only make this harder.

"We need to talk," I said quickly. "I should have—"

"I bought a plane ticket," she blurted before I could finish. There was a small distance between us. Mere inches. She seemed hesitant to close the space.

I froze. "You did what?"

It sounded like she'd said she'd bought a ticket, which could mean a thousand things, one of which had my heart pounding a near-deafening beat.

"I booked a flight."

"Where?"

"To Germany."

"Germany?" Yep, deafening.

"Ger-ma-ny," she said, emphasizing each syllable. "You should Q-tip after you shower. Helps with hearing." She mimed cleaning her ear.

I'd laugh if I weren't stunned. Sick. Devastated. What happened to the woman only willing to live our seconds? "You booked a flight to Germany?"

The notion wasn't sinking in. She'd imposed our no-future-talk rule. Changing the game now wasn't okay, not with what I had to say, but she was turning it all upside down.

"Well, let me see." She tapped her chin and squinted at the sky, then she grinned at me, sweet yet tentative. "I believe that's what I did."

"You're coming to Germany." A statement this time. I couldn't sound like a bigger idiot.

"Wow, so…now I'm worried you have a head injury or something. Did you fall on your run? And if this is you freaking out because I took this step and you're having second thoughts, then I'll need you to back away before I embarrass myself by puking on your shoes." She pressed a hand to her belly. "August? You're kind of scaring me."

"No, babe." My limbs finally woke up, and I gripped her shoulders. I shouldn't kiss her or pull her against me. I should keep my distance and say what needed saying. My body wouldn't obey. I pressed a kiss to her forehead, another to her perfect lips, then I crushed her against my chest. Tighter than tight. She'd for sure feel the thrashing of my heart. "I'm not having second thoughts. I want you and this more than I want to breathe. There's just…"

I inhaled her feminine scent. She smelled clean and sweet with a hint vanilla, freshly showered, which had me picturing us under a hot spray as I licked a path along her toned flesh. Dammit. This was not the time to be thickening behind my zipper. She'd feel that, too. And it was wrong.

She slipped her hands down my back, cresting them alongside my spine, over the waistband of my jeans. "I want all of you more than I want to breathe, too," she whispered.

I held her harder against me. It could be my last time. "What changed?"

"I can't lose you, August. Not again. I can only come for three weeks, and there's a chance we won't work. Long distance will be beyond painful, but I'll survive regardless. I have Rachel and

Ainsley, their guys and Emmett and Cameron, and other outlets in my life. No matter what happens, I'll pick myself up. Not giving us a shot would be worse than trying and failing. You're worth the risk."

She was worth everything. She deserved everything, including the truth.

Pulse revving into overdrive, I forced myself to create space between us. I ran my hands through her hair, skimmed my thumbs over her cheeks. "I want you with me in Germany, wherever I am for as long as you can swing it. I'll fly home often. I'll reassess my career, see about building my audience in the States. We have options. We'll make this work, and you trying means more than you know."

My mouth was desert-level dry. Licking my lips didn't help.

She fisted the back of my shirt and leaned away, tension in the guarded movement. "So why are you looking at me like we're saying goodbye?"

I dropped my head forward, focused on a crack in the sidewalk between our feet. A mini fault line that could open up and swallow me whole. "This isn't goodbye, Gwen. Not if I have anything to say about it."

I forced myself to meet her eyes. Her pupils had blown wide, darkness taking over shades of green. "Why do I sense a but?"

"There's something I have to tell you."

———

Gwen

Indiana Jones and the Temple of Doom. Doomed to Die. The Doom Generation.

I mentally listed every movie or show I knew with the word *doom* (spoiler alert: *The Doom Generation* was a hardcore film with a questionable three-way and a penchant for grotesque violence), unable to process the shift in August's demeanor. Not that processing was required. Doom was the real takeaway here.

Doom in his flitting eyes. Doom in his blotchy skin.

A couple times, before skydiving, I had nightmares prior. They'd consisted of me reaching for my ripcord, only to find it missing. I'd pummel to earth, spinning, unable to scream, the ground racing toward me at death-defying speeds. Startling awake had always been a sweaty, panting affair. Like right now.

I'd expected my flight news to come with hugs and making out, an awkward victory dance, maybe. I'd paid for a non-refundable flight, had been more honest with August than I'd ever dreamed. The words *I love you* had almost passed my lips. Present day love. Not past love. Not just because of our history. I'd leapt from a plane for August Cruz.

And the ripcord was slipping through my grasp.

A sheen of moisture clung to his upper lip, because he had something to tell me.

Doomsday. Mansion of the Doomed. The Sword of Doom.

I hadn't done this in ages, listing movie titles with key words, a nervous habit I'd thought I'd kicked. As a kid, I'd go through this obsessive exercise, a way to keep it together when my mother was hurtful or I'd flunked a test. Teenaged August would snicker at me, and say, "You're doing it again."

"Doing what?" I'd reply, royally embarrassed.

"That weird movie title thing."

"No, I'm not."

"Yes, you are."

"Am not."

"Your lips are moving, Possum."

I'd hated how well he'd known me.

Today I made sure to keep my lips stiff, but my focus was fading fast. Traffic sped behind me. The tourists in my peripheral vision blurred. Noises swirled with the scents of car exhaust and ocean air, spinning around me at a dizzying rate.

I broke free of August's arms and blinked away my sudden vertigo. "Say it."

"What?"

"Whatever it is that has you sweating on a non-sweaty day." It wasn't warm enough for him to be flushing like that.

His next swallow lasted an eternity. He didn't reply.

"Spit it out, August." I hugged myself, tried to breathe through the cumulating dread. "Is there a woman in Europe you didn't mention? Did you get someone pregnant or something?"

Which had me wishing again for my belly to swell with our baby. Not a healthy sentiment when the guy at the core of that wish looked ready to faint.

"I know your father's name," he said.

Arms locked around my waist, I squinted at the park bench, trying to piece together his statement. That bench was the reason we were here. I'd almost searched it when I'd arrived, desperate to learn if my father's last name had been scratched into the wood, but I hadn't wanted to do it alone. Telling August I'd booked my flight had been the larger thing in the moment, my need to tell him what I'd done.

Now it felt like a swarm of wasps had invaded my belly. "You searched the bench already?"

"No." Again with the swallowing. "I knew before. I wanted to tell you yesterday, when I came by the house. It's why I was there, then that suitcase showed up and the energy between us…" He tugged at the back of his hair, eyes pleading with me to understand.

I didn't understand. Not by a long shot.

He knew my father's name? Pre-crazy scavenger hunt? "Are you saying you knew before I found the journal? Before we traipsed around the city looking for clues?" Before I'd made love to him on my apartment floor.

My knees weakened, and I landed hard on the bench. The wasps in my stomach turned vicious, stinging at will.

He crouched in front of me, hands on my knees. "I knew, and

I had every intention of telling you, but then there was that spark between us, which I never expected, and I delayed. Just… to be with you, Gwen, like that, like old times but better—I couldn't give that up. Then you started learning things about your mother. You were seeing her in a different light. Right or wrong, stupid or smart, I didn't want to steal that from you. If I told you, you'd have stopped reading her diary. I know you. I know you'd have tossed it aside, and you needed the closure. You *still* need it. It's why you cried last night, why you finally let it out. I couldn't tell you yet."

I was in no state to unpack his comments about my mother, but the desperation in his voice tamed the angry wasps. He *had* shown up at my mother's to tell me something. It had gotten brushed aside with everything else: the suitcase, the journal, our intense attraction. He couldn't have planned for any of that.

It still explained nothing.

"How long have you known? How'd you even find out?"

"I know this'll sound bad, and I feel like shit about it…." He was still in his uncomfortable squat, clutching my knees. He inched closer. "I got a letter from your mother. She gave me his name and wanted me to be the one to tell you."

"My mother told you? Why the hell would she tell you and not me?" I'd only asked her a million and one times.

"I don't know why. I can only guess it was to bring us together."

My confusion amplified. My mother had actively distanced herself from me. Choosing this stealthy way to finally show she cared made no sense. How had she even known I'd had feelings for August? Unless she hadn't been as oblivious about me and my life as I'd believed. I tried piecing through her possible motivations, but stopped abruptly. "She died thirty days ago, August. When did you get this letter?"

His brow crumpled. "A couple months ago. February."

"Excuse me?" I flinched, the ripcord tethering me to him shredding apart.

Two months. He'd known two months, and he'd said *nothing*. No. Scratch that. He'd said plenty, lying to my face, pretending he didn't know this one, crucial fact.

I pushed him away, and he nearly fell on his ass. I needed space. More air. The city sounds around me muted, like I was under water. I hunched forward and dropped my head to my hands.

Breathe in, breathe out. It should be a simple action, second nature, but each inhale serrated my throat.

The past twenty-four hours he'd let me follow that stupid diary, never letting on what he knew. Wasting my time. All because he thought I should discover my mother? I lifted my head. The thing weighed a thousand pounds. "You had no right to keep that from me."

"I know."

"You stole that time, and I feel like a fool. I dragged you around the city, for Christ's sake, chasing after someone whose name you already knew. All because you thought I needed to know my mother fucked my father at a fucking lookout point?"

I recoiled at my own harshness. It wasn't the truth. Not based on the diary. My mother had lost her virginity to a caring man, and I'd just turned it into something ugly. "You should have told me." My fight drained, leaving my voice weak and shaky.

"I should have, but that letter hit me like a stack of bricks, brought a lot of hurt and issues back. It took me a while to gather the courage to see you, then this craziness happened. But we found each other during that time, Gwen, like your mother must have wanted. If I told you first thing at her house, where would we be now?"

His question depleted my reserves. My breath shuddered. Where *would* we be? Not planning a future together, buying nonrefundable plane tickets, and booking vacation time. I wouldn't have seen him play my revised hate song. We wouldn't have had a ketchup and mustard fight. Sex might not have happened.

The possibility was unthinkable.

His issues and hurt—the reason for his delay—had been my doing, not his. My WTF was why he'd waited to tell me, and he had intended to tell me yesterday, at my mother's. He was telling me *now*, twenty-four hours after barreling back into my life. Not days or weeks. The omission still stung, but there was no denying how overwhelming our reunion had been for both of us.

I curled my toes in my boots, tried to unsnarl the clutter in my head. All I was doing was wasting more time. "What's his name?"

"Ted Mercer." He searched my eyes, the way a lost sailor searched for land, unsure he'd find his way home.

I wanted to be that for him. Home. A haven. The center of his world. There was too much to absorb. "Ted Mercer," I repeated. That I could focus on. The name I'd longed to find.

He was the Tom or Ted Uncle Rex had mentioned. The man who'd wooed my mother with hot dogs and Long Island Iced Teas and romantic gestures under the stars. "Do you know his address? Is he still in San Francisco?" As the reality of the news sank in, hope replaced my shock. "I'd like to go now. Look him up first, obviously. But we should go."

No matter August's deceit, I still used the word *we*. I didn't want to do this alone.

"Gwen."

I stood and waved him off, antsy to get moving. "Save the apologizing. I'm still upset with you and not sure where we go from here, but I need someone with me for this, and I'd like that someone to be you. We'll sort through the rest later. I just need to find him, before—"

"Gwen." He stepped in front of me, blocking my path.

"Honestly, August, I don't want to deal with this now. My birthday wish is up at midnight. As much as we need to talk this out, finding my father is more important. I want to meet him today. With you. It's supposed to happen today." I shook out my hands, one rushed-out sentence away from hyperventilating.

August gripped my hips. "He's dead, honey."

I jerked backward. Thickness clawed at my throat. "What?" The syllable barely choked out.

Devastation rang clear in his pained eyes. "I went to see him when I arrived in San Francisco, to make sure he wasn't someone who'd hurt you. The woman who answered told me he'd passed away."

"What?" I'd heard him. The words had registered, but their meaning hadn't. I was supposed to meet my father. Today. It was going to happen today. "I don't understand."

I didn't want to.

"He had a heart attack."

I sank back to the bench. I was surprised it didn't cave under the weight of this crushing news. I'd wondered when I was younger, had considered that he might be dead, but it didn't jive with my mother's vehemence to keep the information from me. There would have been no harm sharing a deceased man's name.

I pressed my hand to my breastbone. The pressure didn't ease the pain.

"Gwen, honey?"

I didn't glance up at August. My father was gone. I'd never meet him and ask if he was an adrenaline junkie, like me. Find out if he hated mayonnaise. Ask why he'd left my mother. Why he'd never wanted to meet me.

If he'd even known I existed.

"I was sure I'd meet him today," I whispered. August crouched again, held my knees tight. His face blurred through my watery gaze. "When did he die, did she say?"

He didn't reply.

I wiped my building tears, needing to see August clearly, the security in his tender gaze. It was the wrong move. Tension tugged a sharp line between his brows. A muscle in his temple bunched. "There's more I need to say. I'm sick about it, wish I could go back, do things differently, but…"

He trailed off, and I shrank smaller.

I didn't ask him to spit it out this time. I sat immobile, my legs too numb to stand. Instinctively, I leaned away from him.

He gripped my knees like they were a lifeline. "He died two weeks ago."

"Sorry, what?" The same question I'd asked this entire conversation. The only one that came easily.

"It was a couple weeks ago. A heart attack, she said."

"Two *weeks*?"

He nodded.

"But you said you've had the letter two months?" The fragments of information slotted together in appalling clarity. Two months. Two weeks. The time in between I'd lost. If August had told me first thing, when he should have, I'd have met my father.

"The letter came as a shock," he repeated, desperation roughening his tone. "I was touring. It brought a lot of tough stuff back for me, like I said. And it had been years already. I figured it wasn't a rush. I delayed, Gwen. I was so stuck on how it was messing me up, that I put it off. So the fact that you won't meet him is my fault. I could have told you two months ago, but I didn't. I've been in town a week, since I knocked on his door. It took me that long to work up the guts to tell you yesterday, then everything…"

He dropped his head, and I stared over him, seeing nothing yet everything. Everything I missed out on because of what he'd done: meeting my father, learning about the man, discovering my history, my genealogy.

I also really heard August, clearer this time. Louder, his words pounding in my head. He hadn't told me because he'd been messed up. Because I'd hurt him nine years ago and hadn't apologized, and we'd spent that time nursing our wounds. He hadn't told me because I'd broken his heart.

I did this. *Me.* Not him.

I ruined my chance to meet my father.

"I'm so sorry, Gwen. I wish I could change the past. Make different choices."

A sharp laugh rattled my seizing lungs. I was the reigning queen of shitty choices. I'd pushed August away before college, had destroyed him after by sleeping with his brother. I was responsible for this twisting in my gut now, a fierce knot of failure.

I deserved the pain. Every agonizing twinge.

What I didn't deserve was August. Booking that plane ticket had been a mistake, a futile attempt to cling to what could have been. That's all we'd been doing, really, pretending we could forget. I'd never forget now. Not when my actions led to this.

Slowly, I stood, aware of passing crowds, but feeling separate. Alone. "I'd like you to give me my father's address and go." My voice sounded flat, detached.

Panic widened his eyes. "What? No. I'm not leaving."

"You don't have a choice. I need to go there, and I'm going alone."

"No way. You said you wanted me there and I want to be there for you."

I wanted him with me as much as I wanted to rewrite our past. An impossibility. I couldn't even look at August. I wasn't sure I'd ever be able to look at myself again.

Fortifying my strength, I blinked away snapshots of the past two days: August strumming my guitar, the sexy curve of his lips, his laugh, his voice, how his body had possessed mine. I blinked away imagined images of us in Germany, our rose-colored future. I poured gasoline on it all and watched it burn, like in his hate song. "Please give me his address and go," I repeated.

He gripped the sides of my head, forced my focus on him. "I know you're angry with me. I deserve it. But this is bigger than us. Please let me come."

"There's no us, August."

He flinched. "Excuse me?"

"This thing we've been doing…" I motioned aggressively between us, but he wouldn't release his hold on me. "We've been playing make-believe, pretending we can forgive and forget. It's not realistic. Too much has happened." Tears slipped down my cheeks, countless emotions pushing them free. I wanted to hate him for his actions, but I was the only person who deserved blame. I also loved him. Irrevocably. Crushingly. Embroiled in this tangle was the loss of a father I'd never met, and a stewing self-hatred flooding my veins. My choices. My actions. My fuck-ups.

"That's where you're wrong, Gwen. I've forgiven you. I'm done with grudges and self-pity. I want to move on. I *have* moved on. And I'm not letting you go."

"You don't have a choice."

The dark slash of his eyebrows softened, his hands gentling on my face. "I love you, Possum. I love you and I've forgiven you. So, yeah, I think we have lots of choices."

No, no, no, no, no. He couldn't. It wasn't fair. I tried to shake my head, but his hands tightened. I squeezed my eyes shut. "You can't love me."

"I can and I do. I've loved you since you ran through my sprinklers and stuck your tongue out at me. I loved you every time you scared me when pretending to sleep, when you shoved grass down my shirt, and fought me for my comic books. The past nine years, even. I loved you when I hated you, Gwen. So I need you to tell me what you need, how I can earn your forgiveness."

What *he* could do? After all the ways I'd failed him, he was pleading with *me*, wanting to shoulder my burden. As though I wasn't the root of this disease. I gripped his wrists and removed his possessive hold of my cheeks. "You're forgiven."

He exhaled roughly. "Yeah?"

God, his hope was palpable, a warmth I'd kill to sink into. Live in. Never leave. But he had never really been mine to keep. "You're forgiven," I repeated, stepping back, creating space. "This isn't your fault. It's mine. I don't forgive myself for what I did to you and for never apologizing. I don't forgive myself for hurting you so badly you couldn't reach out when you got my mother's letter. Not meeting my father is my doing, not yours."

"No." He shook his head, moved toward me.

I held up my hand. "Just give me the letter. Dragging this out will only hurt more."

"Dragging what out?"

"This charade. We're over. It's over. We both need to move on."

"We're not over, Gwen."

"Do I need to spell it for you? We're done." My harsh tone tasted like shame.

His posture stiffened, an imperceptible hardening of his stance. His lips compressed. "Such bullshit."

It was my turn to flinch. I dashed at my drying tears. "What?"

"This is your thing, Gwen. This is what you do. You push people away when it gets too real, when they start to care too much."

"I'm not nineteen anymore. This isn't like then. Everything's too intertwined."

"You're telling me you can walk away from us? Just like that? Like the past twenty-four hours never happened?"

If it were only that easy. "When I look at you, all I'll ever see are the mistakes I've made. All I've lost. So, no...there's no *us*. We're done."

"We're done?" He stood statue still, back to repeating me.

Nothing about me was still. Not the addled thoughts spiraling through my head, or the frantic pounding of my heart. Done. August and me. *Done. Finished.* I choked down the sob threatening to rise. This was the right move. It had to be. It was the only one I could compute right now. He'd write more hate songs and meet a woman who wasn't a train wreck waiting to happen. He'd find peace. "Yes, August. We're done."

He moved so close his hot breath brushed my cheek. "Tell me you don't love me, too. Say it and I'll go."

I couldn't. He knew it. Problem was, I didn't love myself. "Don't make this harder than it needs to be. Please. I just need the letter."

He scrutinized me.

I bit down on my cheek, willing the burn in my throat to cease. I would go to my father's house on my own, ask to see photo albums. Find out who the man had been. Learn if he'd had kids. *That* thought winded me anew.

I'd daydreamed about the possibility when younger, wondered if I might have siblings, a sister or brother to commiserate with when my mother had berated me. Someone to tease and have in my corner. The prospect had taken a backseat to the more pressing issue of finding my father, but not now.

Now they could be all I had.

I wiped my nose with my forearm. Far from attractive. "Did my father have kids?"

"I..." August's brows drew together. "Shit, I didn't ask. I was upset and took off."

I nodded and inhaled deeply. "Can I have the address, please?"

He reached for me. "Gwen..."

I angled my shoulder away from him. "I need the address and letter. I'm going there alone. We're just not meant to be, August."

A boulder lodged in my throat at the brush-off. It felt like a lie. I couldn't see the truth any longer.

His hazel eyes were glassy. That muscle in his temple jumped incessantly. I wanted to burrow into his chest, wrap myself in his arms and scent and pretend I hadn't ruined us.

Neither of us moved.

Eventually, he licked his lips and pulled a piece of paper

from his pocket. He held it out for me. "I love you, Gwen. I'll always love you, and this isn't over."

Trembling, I snatched the paper from him and spun on my heels. I waited for a break in traffic and bolted across the street, locking myself in my car the second I reached it. The paper was folded into a small square. The edges were soft, ripped slightly like it had been read often.

Before I opened it, I chanced a glance back toward the bench.

August was still standing there, his hands shoved in his front pockets, staring at me. He mouthed something I couldn't decipher. I tore my gaze away.

CHAPTER 18

11:30 a.m., 12 ½ hours…

Gwen

When I first learned August was leaving tomorrow afternoon, I'd willed our seconds to slow down. I'd wanted to stretch our breaths, elongate our words, extend our kisses into forever. Hold his hand and argue with him during the pauses in between. Stare at him to stamp his handsome profile on my brain.

Now everything moved too slowly: my fingers as they traced my mother's cursive writing, my breaths nearing a catatonic state, my eyelids that couldn't remember how to blink.

I'd read about this before, how anxiety and stress could produce numbness. I'd researched the effects for my job, to better cope with prospective adoptive parents. The insight allowed me to choose better words when preparing them for the grueling process, had helped me find ways to ease the sting when applications were denied. I'd never experienced this kind of deadening shock firsthand.

I was experiencing it now.

Nine years ago, I crushed August. Because of it, he kept information from me. My father had died. I'd never meet him. I could have siblings. I pushed August away.

Now I was underwater again, my body moving in languid frames.

Blink.

Blink.

Exhale.

Lift head.

Blink…blink.

I'd driven here on autopilot, wasn't sure how long I'd been parked on this suburban street. It was pleasant enough, trees shading the lawns, some manicured with colorful gardens, others overgrown. One had a basketball net in the driveway; another was littered with Tonka trucks.

The home to my right was nondescript. Gray siding. Red door. Purple potted flowers sat on the concrete step just outside. I didn't have plants in my apartment. I'd bought one after signing my lease. Then I killed it, over or under watering the darn thing. I had a hopeless black thumb.

I didn't know the name of the purple flowers taunting me with their prettiness. Whoever had tended them wasn't a plant killer like me. That person had a green thumb. That person had lived in that house with my father, had maybe given birth to my half-siblings.

Or maybe my father had coaxed those blooms into beauty.

Or his kid had.

Or a stupid gardener unrelated to me had, and the fact that I was still sitting here in this car rereading my mother's letter as if it would give me the courage to knock on that red door and meet the people who could alter my life had absolutely zero to do with plant growing aptitude.

Inhale.
Blink.
Exhale.
Blink.
Repeat.

I looked down and reread my mother's letter for the umpteenth time.

Dear August,

I am dying. As a dying woman, I have a request. Below is the name of Gwen's father. She has always wanted to know who he is. I ask that you be the one to tell her, be there for her when she finds him.

Remember what I told you on Gwen's nineteenth birthday.

I couldn't imagine what she'd told him the night of my WTF, but it was the words "be there for her" that snagged my attention. They were an indecipherable code, because my mother had written as though she'd cared what happened to me. As though my mental state had concerned her.

Yet this was the same woman who'd looked me in the eye, and had said, "I never wanted kids."

That nugget had been offered when I'd caught her staring at a blank TV screen. I'd asked if I could watch *Friends*, and she'd spat those hateful words. No provocation. She hadn't been drinking. Pure hatred aimed at me…because I'd come from a man she'd despised, or because he hadn't wanted me, or I'd stolen her freedom. Having a child at seventeen wasn't anyone's life goal.

Whatever the reason, that cutting comment had drawn blood, a wound that hadn't cauterized. She'd gotten up from the sofa afterward, had walked to the door and left. Hadn't even closed it behind her. Like she'd been in a trance, locked in her past.

But here, in this letter, she'd asked August to *be there for me.*

Her diary was on the passenger seat, printed in her youthful lettering, ripe with the memories of a Sunshine Girl who had loved to dance and listen to music and had dreamed of performing on Broadway. A girl who'd fallen in love. Had she wanted kids back then? Had she dreamed of carrying her lover's child?

I lifted the journal carefully, thumbed through the pages slowly. My limbs were too heavy to move at a normal speed. I stopped on her first kiss again, reread the reverence and excitement in her words. I felt for this girl. I ached to read her happily ever after. I wanted her to find true love.

I cared about teenage Mary Hamilton.

If I weren't strapped into my seat, the revelation would have knocked me over. A full stone-cold faint. Regret followed, for what she'd stolen from me. If she'd talked to me, had explained about her past, shared what had beaten her down into the shell of a person she'd become, maybe we could have connected, had some form of relationship. All I'd been left with was a shadow of her past.

Still, a hint of hope lightened the heaviness. I didn't hate my mother. I'd grown to pity her through her words. Not an ideal sentiment, but better. My pulse tapped a faster tune, and my haziness cleared. I should leave this car, knock on that red door, discover if I had a brother or sister, but the diary was on my lap, drawing me in. My mother was drawing me in.

I flipped to where I'd last read the journal, the page about the park bench. The next few entries were typical teenage drama: grumbles about a girl at school who'd ditched her at lunch, choice words about her zealot parents. She mooned over the man she loved. And dance. Always dance.

Then I caught my breath.

Cliff jumping. My mother had gone cliff jumping.

I want to fly, she'd written. *I want to be a bird and feel sunshine in my hair and the wind rushing my face. I want to jump off something higher and defy the laws of gravity. It makes me feel alive. Cliff jumping made me forget.*

It was the same reason I skydived and bungee jumped and

rock climbed, to forget when stressed. Feel alive and fly. But my mother had sneered when I'd share my daredevil stunts. I'd assumed it was judgment, her turning her nose up at my choices. That my love of adrenaline rushes had come from my father.

Maybe Mary Hamilton had been jealous, not disapproving. Seeing me and my life could have turned her hate inward, resentment toward herself for giving up on her dreams. There was no way to know, but my mind drifted to August, the man who'd given me this insight. The man I'd left standing in the street.

I wouldn't have read these pages if I'd known my father had died. He'd been right about that. My animosity would have kept me from delving into them. There would have been no point.

But I had, and everything was different now. I was clearer. Calmer. Too calm, like an ocean so flat you could see how stranded you truly were.

August had forgiven me my failings. Sincerity had bled through his declaration of love. His criticism had also been honest. *You push people away when they start to care too much.*

As a teen, I'd let Kayla's claims infect me. She'd preyed on my insecurities, telling me I dragged August down, and I'd been a willing victim. Belief I wasn't good enough for him had propelled me to cut him from my life. And I'd just done the same again, had deemed myself unworthy of his love. My self-loathing may have seemed deeper than that, rooted in our sordid history, his presence in my life destined to be a reminder of my faults. My failures.

Those had just been excuses.

I was hurting him before he could hurt me. Protecting myself. Still believing true happiness was beyond my reach.

My gym session with the girls should have taught me otherwise. Rachel's *Law & Order* performance had pointed out the fullness of my life. My friends. My physical pursuits. My job. So many good things. I'd earned them all, had nurtured my friendships, had worked hard at CrossFit and placing children in loving homes. If I didn't deserve August, that would mean I didn't deserve this goodness, either.

Which was bullshit. Like August had accused.

The childish insecurities I'd thought I'd banished still had power over me, and it wasn't cool.

I would never meet my father because of the hurt I'd inflicted on August, but pushing him away now was more pain he didn't deserve. Pain *I* didn't deserve. Like I hadn't deserved a cold mother and challenging childhood. I was better than that. I'd built myself up since then, physically, emotionally. Yet I'd boomeranged back to those insecurities and had brushed August off.

What had I been thinking?

Except the truth was painfully obvious: I hadn't been thinking. That had been reaction. Knee-jerk. Irrational. Possibly unforgivable.

Desperate to apologize, *again*, I scrambled for my cell phone, only to find the screen blank. *Fuck.*

We'd been out all night. I'd rushed to meet the girls, had then booked a flight and met August. I'd loaned my stupid car-charger to a coworker and had forgotten to get it back. Now I was stuck in my Impreza, outside my late father's house, hesitant to knock on the door or leave.

I could walk up those front steps alone, summon my courage and face whatever greeted me in that house, but all the decisions and outcomes that had led to narrowly missing Ted Mercer's death seemed unbelievably coincidental. As though the confrontation wasn't supposed to happen. Maybe that man's secrets weren't meant to be dredged up, unknown siblings, or not.

That large uncertainty kept me glued to my seat. I needed to talk to my best friend and Badass PI partner, decide on the smart thing to do, but I couldn't reach him. Even worse, he might not answer if I called.

Dead phone clutched in my hand, I plunked my forehead onto my steering wheel.

———

August

Goddamn Gwen for walking away from me. Goddamn me for letting her.

She loved me. That much I knew. When I'd asked her to deny it, her expression had been unmistakable. Her nose hadn't twitched. Her body had leaned toward me. Her lips had parted in longing…and she hadn't uttered the words.

Gwen loved me as much as I loved her, but she was stuck in one of her self-loathing spirals, hating on herself, choosing solitude over connection. Thinking herself unworthy.

Resentment toward her mother surged. Mary may have brought us together through her cryptic letter, but she was the reason Gwen was treading water now, shutting down on me. I'd been worried Gwen wouldn't forgive me for never meeting her father, stealing that precious time from her. In the end, she blamed herself. Typical Gwen. Stubborn Gwen.

And stubborn Gwen was a force to be reckoned with.

This was the girl who'd cut me out of her life with the precision of a neurosurgeon.

Twice.

Still, I should have chased after her. Followed her discreetly, at least. Only an idiot would let his best friend walk into a potentially devastating situation alone. It wasn't right. I should be with her, not leaning on the park bench from her mother's journal.

Gwen's car was long gone. I stood like an idiot, feeling chilled. Lost.

A never-ending line of tourists paid for their Alcatraz tours. I could join them, distract myself for a few hours touring the prison. Instead I searched the bench, as we'd planned. It was fruitless. Mary's name was nowhere to be found, which meant I could have lied to Gwen. I could have continued my ruse and burned the letter. I could be with her now.

Except Owen was right: I'd always know.

I stood and paced. I checked my phone. The screen was blank.

Fuck.

With all the running around we'd been doing, I hadn't charged it. Gwen couldn't reach me. I couldn't call her. What if she got to the house and panicked? What if the woman who lived there lashed out at her?

When I'd visited last week, the woman had seemed nice enough: in her forties or fifties, brown curly hair, glasses, wearing a T-shirt that read *I'd rather be gardening.* I'd donned my PI skills and had claimed a client offered Ted Mercer's name to have his driveway repaved. The woman's chin had wobbled when informing me of Ted's passing.

If Gwen told her who she was, that sweet demeanor could shift to sour. Things could get nasty fast. I gripped my phone and cursed under my breath. Screw it. She may not want me with her, but I couldn't let her do this alone.

———

The street looked the same as it had a week ago. All except for Gwen's gray Impreza parked at the curb. I pulled up behind her. She was in the driver seat, her head bent forward. Was she crying? Had she already been in the house?

I tried to unclick my seat belt and pocket my keys while opening the door. All I managed was to jam my elbow. Gritting my teeth, I made it out and reached the side of her car in six long strides.

Her tousled hair hung forward, shielding her face. The

journal was on her lap, her head firmly planted on her steering wheel. She didn't seem to be breathing.

Worried, I knocked on the driver's window. She jumped so suddenly she whacked *her* elbow on the door. She rubbed her skin and squinted at me. There was a crease on her brow from the steering wheel, moisture in her eyes. She said something I couldn't hear.

I rushed to the passenger side and let myself in, yanking the door shut behind me.

She looked like a sad puppy. "I'm so sorry."

"No, baby. I'm the one who's sorry."

"But you were right. I pushed you away again, for the same stupid reasons I did as a kid, thinking you'd be better off without me. That I didn't deserve you."

"You deserve everything. And you heard my albums—those hate songs? The sad ones? That's what happens when I'm without you. That's not better, Gwen. *You* make me better."

Her chin trembled. "I shouldn't have lashed out at you."

"I kind of deserved it." Remorse still emanated from her. Only one thing would erase it. I reached over and ran my thumb down the sweet dent in her brow line. "If you're at fault here, then you need my forgiveness, which I can offer, under one condition."

She bit her lip, waiting.

"You forgive yourself first."

Tears pooled in her eyes. Not enough to spill, but her strife was potent. An internal battle waging. Like Gwen, I was my worst critic at times, hating songs that fans loved, kicking myself for concert blunders. Reliving arguments where I should have said this or done that on an angry loop in my head. Accepting ourselves, fuck-ups and all, was no easy feat. Particularly tough when no one taught you how.

I waited.

She sniffled, soft words following. "I have a great life and great friends. A job I adore. Then you came roaring back into my life, and I was that teenager again, feeling damaged and just... not good enough. Not because of you, but when things got complicated, it was so easy to fall back into that role. Hate myself for choices I couldn't change. Like those insecurities were there, waiting for me."

I stroked the length of her hair. "They'll never fully go away. It's who you are. Like I'll always be a fixer, wanting to take over and do before asking. My job is to try and hit pause before I act. Yours is to remember how fulfilling your life is, because you're that woman, too." Strong. Determined. Sexy as hell.

"Yeah." She nodded, the movement gaining strength with each lift of her chin. "I am. And I forgive myself."

A rough sigh pushed from my chest, warmth incinerating my chill from earlier. Thank God my cell had died. If it hadn't, I could be touring Alcatraz right now, wishing for solitary confinement. I released her cheek and glanced at her father's home. "Did you go in?"

She shook her head.

"You nervous?" She shook her head again, but her lips moved imperceptibly. I'd forgotten about her silly nervous tic. "I think you are. You're doing your thing."

"What thing?"

"That weird movie title thing."

"No, I'm not."

"Yes, you are."

Color pinked her cheeks.

"Your lips were moving, Possum. What word did you use?"

She rolled her eyes and let her head fall onto the headrest. "Sex."

Now was not the time to laugh. I couldn't muffle the sound. "You're nervous about introducing yourself to your father's family, and you're reciting movie titles with the word *sex*?"

"I can't even believe I'm doing that stupid game again, but then you show up with your stupid hair and stupid face and stupid body." She gestured absently toward me. "It's the first word that came up. But don't get any ideas. There will be no more sex."

I couldn't have heard her right. "Like *ever*?"

She deflated, sprawling as much as she could on her seat. "I don't know. I'm a walking disaster. We've been dating less than a day, and I just broke up with you. I might have siblings. My father is dead. Everything in my life is changing too fast."

"So just, like, not this minute? In the car?"

She punched me lightly in the stomach. "You know what I mean, August. I need my best friend right now."

I caught her hand and held it. I did know. She needed a breather. Time to process. Our remaining seconds wouldn't be spent tangled in bed. There was no curbing my disappointment, but being her best friend meant the world. I kissed her hand. "Whatever you need, honey."

She brushed her knuckles against my lips, back and forth. The soft touch slipped through my bloodstream, heating my skin. She may have said no sex, but my body had its own agenda. I tensed my thighs. It didn't help. If I had to choose one word Gwen inspired it would be *fever*.

Heat from one look. Fire from one touch. Warmth from one word.

My next song would be titled, "Fever Junkie."

She glanced past me, toward the house. "I get why you waited to tell me, how hard it was to face me after all those years. I also can't stop thinking about how defining that was, like everything the past day: the journal, us reuniting, learning about my mom. So I've been sitting here, stewing over impossible things like fate and destiny, wondering if I wasn't meant to meet my father."

The center console kept me from pulling her into my arms. I wasn't sure she'd want that anyway. I settled on weaving our fingers together. "I've never put much stock in the idea of ghosts or the unexplainable, but I do believe in fate, and there's no denying the events the past couple months have felt…preordained?"

"So it's not just me?"

"It's not just you. It still doesn't excuse what I did. I'm sick about not telling you your dad's name sooner."

"I know you are." She fiddled with my fingers, ran her thumb over my sparse knuckle hair. "It happened, though. Your fault, my fault, *my mother's fault*—the reason doesn't matter. This is the fallout, which brings us back to reality."

I studied the red door that had her gnawing her lip. "The woman I met was nice, if that helps. She seemed sweet."

Gwen released a half-groan, half-sigh. "I want to knock on that door eventually, but maybe not now. I want to follow the journal today, learn what I'm dealing with first. Try and discover what happened between my parents. I think I'm supposed to follow those clues."

I inched closer to her. "Can I come on this journey?"

I didn't ask where we stood. The no-sex rule could mean she was pulling away, compartmentalizing our relationship into friendship. Best friends. Just friends. Friends who eventually drifted. There was a chance we'd say goodbye tomorrow and never see each other again. If that happened, I'd write a lifetime of sad songs. It wasn't an option.

She focused on me, and love glimmered in her eyes, giving me hope. "I think you're supposed to come," she whispered.

I traced her cheekbone, the smooth slope of her jaw. History and hurt and hope rippled between us. Then I said, "And you're sure there won't be any sex?"

A guy had to try. Plus the best way to keep Gwen from anxiously repeating movie titles was to flirt with her, or annoy her. Both had worked as teens.

That (sort of) joke earned me a smile. "Keep your smolder on lockdown, Cruz."

"Anything for you, Frances."

Her expression morphed from amused to livid. "No, you did not."

"Oh, yes, I did." This was the annoy tactic. Her hated middle name had never let me down before.

Her breathing slowed. Her focus dropped to my chest. "Say it again."

"Frances."

She pinched my nipple and twisted. "Jesus fuck, Gwen." Wincing, I batted her hand away. "What the hell?"

"You know I hate that name."

"It's a fine name."

"It's the worst name."

It was also the main character's given name in her favorite movie. "But then I'm allowed to say, 'Nobody puts Baby in the corner.'"

Her lips twitched. "You are such a child."

And she was distracted. Too bad my nipple had taken a hit for the team. I'd do it again, though. Anything for this woman, except walk away from her. There was no way I was leaving tomorrow without knowing we were good. Together. A couple. More lyrics looped through my mind, lines filled with words like *passion* and *addiction* and *forever*, those "Fever Junkie" verses building into a ballad.

Yet there was still a chance I'd lose her.

For now, I'd play by her rules. Shielding my chest, I pulled the diary from her lap. "Where'd you leave off?"

CHAPTER 19

12:30 p.m., 11 ½ hours…

Gwen

I dove back into my mother's diary, still sluggish, but the underwater fog had lifted. Thanks to my Badass PI partner.

I wasn't sure I could continue at our frantic pace: twenty-four hours of passionate sex, talks, jokes, and promises, pretending our uncertain future and messy past didn't affect our seconds. Too many conflicting emotions had been set loose. But having him here was a start.

Forgiving myself was a milestone.

The loss of my father still lingered like a nasty sliver, the kind you struggled to remove. Having never known Ted Mercer meant it couldn't burrow deeper.

I had, however, known my mother. I was *getting to know her*.

Learning what had happened between them was top priority.

My new birthday wish. To understand her, prove I hadn't been the root of her despair. Which meant this search would provide me closure, like August had said.

With him beside me, I read more pages, each one teeming with teenage angst. Nothing hinted at an unplanned pregnancy or painful breakup, but she had written an entry about babysitting and shitty diapers and not understanding why people had kids. It was a glimpse of the mother I'd known, the one who'd never wanted children. Not new information, but reading it still stung.

Then the writing changed.

The entries weren't dated, but a page had been skipped and a different pen was used. These lines had been jotted down one at a time, across the page on a diagonal, as though written frantically. My anxiety mounted with each word.

I never really knew him.

He'll never know about the baby.

In one night, they stole it all from me.

I didn't know who "they" was, but dread clawed up my neck. He'd truly never known about me, the choice stolen from him because he'd hurt my mother. He'd done something bad with someone, my affair theory gaining steam. I flipped the page but found it blank. I flipped back and forth faster, the stuck ones almost ripping until I discovered one more written entry.

Secrets kill the soul. Both are now buried with my heart, on a hill, at the red rock where our baby was conceived.

That was it. Nothing else was written, but the words *secrets* and *kill* escalated my worry. The pages fluttered under my rapid breaths.

I'd known a major event had split my parents apart. Growing up, discovering the source had never been my priority. I'd been focused on finding my father, then the possibility of meeting a sibling. Whatever dramatic event had altered the course of my life had only been a background whisper.

It was screaming now.

August eased the book from my grasp and read the two passages. "It sounds like she's talking about the lookout point, Tank Hill—I'm guessing that's where you were conceived."

Where August and I had slept last night. Where sex had happened. "Do you think she actually buried something there?"

"It's cryptic, but possible." He studied the diary, leaned so close his nose was practically in the book. "Pages are missing, a few cut out after her last note."

I ran my fingers along the seams. The cuts were so clean they were barely noticeable. "If she removed these, believed she had to hide something, she could have buried them."

She'd obviously enjoyed keeping a diary, had found the process cathartic. She would likely have detailed the events that had destroyed her heart. She might have buried them as a symbolic way to move on.

Secrets.

Kill.

My chill worsened.

"A time capsule," August murmured, probably recalling the two of us digging up his back yard to bury ours. "You think Barbie-Man is in hers, too?"

I elbowed him, thankful for his humor. "Barbie-Man isn't there, but I have a feeling my answers are."

He moved to close the journal, but he stopped and squinted. "I think there's..." Using both hands, he pried apart two corners I hadn't realized had been stuck. "Something's written here."

I pulled his hands and the diary toward me. A small block of text was on the page:

I hope eleven years isn't too late.

Below that vague line was contact information: one of those random email addresses that could belong to anyone (fancyfeathers123@hotmail.com), a phone number, and a Denver address.

"It's like she wrote that to a specific person," August said. "The other entries are more personal."

I didn't reply. Eleven years—something about the number rang a bell. I closed my eyes, ran through all I'd learned the past two days, fragments spinning, blurring. They rolled and rolled, until...

"The Greyhound employee." I clutched August's thigh. "He said the suitcase went missing in 2001. The diary and contents were from 1990. That's eleven years."

Like two synchronized swimmers, we turned our heads in time, slowly lowered our eyes to reread the new page. August tapped the journal's edge. "Not sure what it means, but I think you're right. The two timelines have to be connected."

"More questions," I mumbled, but the answers felt closer.

"We could call the number and see who picks up."

I shook my head. "If that number was my mother's, a secret cell or something, she won't be picking up. If it belongs to someone else, I'd rather be prepared for whoever might answer. We should follow the other clue first, the one that mentions the hill." Continue on the journal's path.

We closed the book, the weight of its final clues thickening the air between us. Air already heavy with our personal tension. August was allowing me to set our pace, determine our course. Problem was, I vacillated between wanting to slow things down and fast-forward to jumping his bones, his impending departure hovering above it all.

Freaks and Geeks. Freak Show. Freaky Friday.

Dammit, I was doing it again.

He snickered at me. "I'll meet you there. Actually, I'll beat you there because my way is faster."

"You're delusional."

"I'm right. I also plan to kiss you before I leave this car."

"August..."

"Just a small one, Possum. There will be no sex."

He invaded my space, ran his nose up my cheek. My belly

swooped in a shivery rush. He was doing his best to distract me, like he'd done as kids. It was him being the fixer, but I didn't sense the pity I'd witnessed back then—him making me his project. There was sadness behind his playful banter, empathy in his soft gaze.

As always with him, my mind quieted. All freaking out ceased.

Closing my eyes, I turned my head toward him. It was the only direction it could go. His lips brushed my cheek, by the corner of my mouth. His nose fitted alongside mine. Our lips lined up, and so, so softly he kissed me, a slight opening of his lips to capture mine. Our eyelashes fluttered together. His breath tickled my tongue. Heaven was built on kisses like this.

He pulled back, and I barely refrained from reaching for him and demanding more. I had firsthand experience with August's kissing mastery, and the man was holding out, teasing me by rationing his skill. It wasn't fair. He knew it would break my resolve. But we had a time capsule to unearth. A secret to discover. And we were losing time.

———

Although we were still alone, the lookout was less romantic during the day. San Francisco sprawled in all its glory below, but no stars lit the sky. The sleepy quiet of night had been replaced with movement. Cars. Birds. City sounds.

August and I stood side-by-side like we had not long ago, the backs of our hands touching. "I hit traffic," he said, still moaning that I'd beaten him here.

"Don't be a sore loser."

"My way's faster. In a scientific study, I'd win."

"But you didn't. And you're wrong."

"We'll do it again tonight."

"We have birthday drinks tonight."

Our last night together. I wasn't sure I wanted to spend it

with my friends this year. A daunting decision. If I ditched them on our shared birthday, Ainsley would mix Tabasco sauce in my toothpaste, but I kept spinning things with August in my mind, fear overtaking my hurt. The idea of him leaving with us in limbo, our status unclear, was worse than getting a mouthful of hot sauce.

If I asked him to spend the night with me alone, take the time to work things out, he'd say yes. He might tell me he loved me again.

Would I find the courage to say it back?

He stood beside me now, taking in the view. His arm wasn't around my shoulder. He wasn't bathing me in his sultry voice. The inches between us stretched into miles, because I'd imposed another rule: the no sex rule. Like my seconds rule. Weak attempts to control the uncontrollable while my life unraveled.

The harder I tried to slow things down, the faster my imagination rolled forward. It tripped ahead, painting a picture of our imagined future, *my future* and the babies I wanted to have one day, how I ached for a kid with his unruly cowlicks and my determination. Our shared sense of humor. I was ready before, to try long distance with August. Then life threw me another curve ball.

Here I was again, placing my hand on my belly, wishing for a second heartbeat inside me. A child created by us.

"If you keep looking at me like that, Possum, sex will happen." August's husky voice broke my trance.

I swallowed and stepped back, unaware I'd been staring. "Like what?"

He stalked closer and dipped his head to my level. "Like you love me."

I sucked in a strangled breath. That was a sneak attack. A low blow.

I couldn't deny the claim.

He shook his head, hands held in surrender. "Forget I said

that. We're here for your mother's time capsule. Not us. Let's get searching."

He smiled, as though unruffled by my brush-off, but he couldn't fool me. Not with the tightness around his hazel eyes, the sharp angle of his jaw. Keeping him at a distance was supposed to help me cope with today's troubling events. It had seemed the safer option. In truth, it was making everything harder.

He was ahead of me, circling the large tree crowning the hill. Last night's swing, the one we'd sat on while covered in ketchup and mustard, dangled from a branch. My mother's diary had mentioned a red rock, a landmark for our treasure hunt. August searched the area, then dropped into a squat and brushed at the earth.

He licked his thumb and rubbed a rock. "If she buried something, this could be the spot."

I approached slowly, dread clutching at my ankles. As sure as I was destiny had played a part in recent events, I was equally as positive she *had* buried something, and whatever it was would change my life. This wasn't meeting my father, who may or may not have been an asshole. This was discovering a secret buried for twenty-eight years.

I made it to August's side and peered over his shoulders. "It looks like a red rock."

He picked up a hefty stick, examined its tip. "You helping me dig?"

I nodded and found a flat rock. The effort distracted me from August and all I wanted to tell him, and from the entombed truths I wasn't sure I was ready to learn.

The earth was dry and flinty, hard packed. Digging was an effort. I dropped to my knees, put more muscle into it. August copied my pose, the two of us sweating in minutes. I dug harder, faster. The rock tore at my hands. I ignored the cuts, didn't bother swatting the couple flies circling my head. Sweat dripped into my eyes. August was as disheveled.

Then I hit something.

We froze and traded nervous looks. Just as quickly, we dug a wider ring, like a couple of archeologists unearthing fossils. A black box had been buried, my history captured in time. By the time we'd loosened it, dirt was caked under my nails, and I was messy again. A pattern with August and me. He took over, gently raising the keepsake.

We sat on the nearby grass, the box placed between us. I shoved my hands under my thighs. "I guess this is it."

He wiped his forehead, smearing dirt across his brow. He nudged the box toward me. "It's yours to open."

I didn't budge. All I could see was August, this man who was dirty and sweaty, all to help me. He'd forgiven my unforgivable WTF, had confessed his love. He made me feel more alive than surfing waves or scaling rocks. Whatever was in the box would change me, a twenty-eight-year-old secret that could rattle my world. But August steadied me. I'd wanted his support today. Not Rachel or Ainsley's. His. He'd been a part of me forever.

"August?" I couldn't touch that box without knowing we were okay.

He tilted his head, an ocean of affection swimming in his eyes. "Yeah?"

"Thank you." I didn't get into his choice to withhold my father's name or my blame in that decision, or explain my statement. He was here, with me. Supporting me. Relationships were hard. There was good and bad, plummets and exhilaration—a roller coaster without a safety bar. We were proof of that, as was the love blazing inside me, still fierce after our screw-ups.

His warm gaze swept over my face and his brow crumpled. "I love you, Gwen. I know you don't want to hear this now, but I can't keep it in. Not with all that box represents. Not for a million reasons. But you need to know and believe that I love you. I'm here for you, no matter what happens."

He'd said the words before, but they meant more now, after our turbulent reunion: we were strong enough to move past our painful mistakes. He was my best friend, the only man or boy I'd ever loved. He'd made my childhood bearable and had given me more joy the past two days than I'd experienced in years. Not because I hadn't been happy. I loved my life and my friends. This was more than happy, though, bigger and brighter.

He was the reason my sun would rise tomorrow.

It was how my mother had mooned about my father, before he'd hurt her. And like her, I couldn't form the words. The fire in my throat burned them up.

Instead, I said the worst thing. The crazy Gwen thing.

I looked at the love of my life, and said, "I hate that I'm on the pill."

August became a statue. "What did you say?"

I tried to rewind and eat my words. *I hate that I'm on the pill.* Only an idiot would blurt that raw truth. An absolute moron. I closed my eyes, hoping I'd disappear.

"I can still see you, Gwen. What did you say?"

"I hate that I'm on this hill?" The lie came out like a question.

He crawled toward me, forcing me to lie back. The intense lines of his face could cut glass. "No. No. That's not what you said."

I tried to shove him off, but his hands and knees caged me. I shimmied, but he didn't budge. "Finding the box got to my head, made me dizzy. Being up here feels too high."

"You jump out of airplanes and off bridges. You're trying to tell me lying safely on the ground is suddenly giving you a fear of heights? Try again."

He might love me. That didn't mean he wanted to hear about my ticking biological clock. Talk of babies was a fast track to losing the guy, but there was no escaping him or what I'd blurted. I quit wriggling and groaned. "After we had sex in my apartment, the first thing I thought was that I wished I wasn't on the pill. I wanted you to come inside me. I wanted us to join in every way possible. Make a baby. So I could have a piece of you forever. I'm sorry. I know how it sounds, and we've—"

His lips descended on mine, swallowing my embarrassed babbling. Our desperate moans mingled. I tugged his hair. He sucked on my bottom lip, each taste deeper than the last. Our tongues licked and slid restlessly.

Once. Again. *More, more, more.*

This wasn't the sweet kiss that built heaven. This was the kiss that sent well-meaning people to hell.

His lips moved in a carnal rhythm, erotic and panty-melting. A rock dug into my back. I didn't care. We were at it again, dry-fucking like kids in a lookout spot. This time in broad daylight.

He came up for air, panting. "Yes."

"Yes, what?"

"Yes, I want us to have a baby."

"You can't be serious."

"You have no idea how serious I am." He pressed his erection into me, right where I ached.

I liked his serious a whole lot. "You want a baby?"

"No. Not a baby. I want *our* baby. I want us. A family. God, I love you. I've loved you forever. I've never wanted anything this much, Gwen."

A baby. Our baby. "Seriously?"

"Ask me again, I'll tell you again."

I pressed my knees into his hips, keeping him close, wanting him closer. "We haven't even been on a proper date. Baby talk goes against all pre-first-date rules."

"There are no rules with us, Possum. How many times do I have to tell you that? And I don't want a baby tomorrow, but you're it for me. The possibility of having a future with you? A family? That's all I need."

"I love you." My harshly whispered promise caught me off-guard.

"My girl," he crooned. We breathed in sync, and I inhaled his soapy man scent, a hint of spice mixing with the dirt below us. I didn't want to move from this spot—under him, with him, safe in his arms. He lifted up suddenly, intent in his stunning eyes. "I'm going to marry you one day, Gwen Hamilton."

I bit my lip as my eyes filled. My pulse pounded in my ears. This beat the rush of flying alongside an eagle or conquering my CrossFit goals. It was adrenaline on steroids. I was so far gone for this man…still and always.

I slipped my hands up the back of his shirt, splayed my palms on his heated skin. The planes of his muscles tightened. It was the wrong move. Our heavy petting accelerated to groping, neither of us able to hit the brakes. He fitted his hand under my ass, tilted me up while thrusting, the thick denim between us infuriating. We should stop. We should breathe. I reached for his belt buckle.

And a childish screech sliced through the air.

We flew apart, breathing hard. A blond boy with a model airplane crested the hill, pumping his pudgy legs while flying his toy. I licked my lips, tasting August and his promise to marry me one day. *God.* His eyes were as dark as I'd ever seen them. My body burned, sensitive and swollen.

The boy's parents followed shortly, casting wary glances our way. Not that I blamed them. We looked homeless again, covered in dirt, clothes askew.

August straightened his T-shirt and motioned to the box. "We should probably focus on this." Still, he eyed me hungrily and adjusted himself in his jeans.

That move ruined me. We should open the box, but I only had one night left with him. Whatever was in there would change everything. I kept picturing *Raiders of the Lost Ark* and ghosts ripping through the air, sucking the life out of all who dared lay eyes on the ark of the covenant. I was pretty sure I wouldn't turn into a liquefied skeleton, but the contents we unearthed could devastate me, ruin my last moments with August. As desperately as I wanted answers, the box would be here tomorrow. Unfortunately, he wouldn't.

I needed one night with him, an afternoon even, before I

unleashed my mother's secrets. "Will you meet me?" I asked, suddenly tentative. "At my place."

"You'd rather open it there?"

"I'd rather shower with you there. I'll deal with the box later."

His Adam's apple bobbed down his tanned throat. "I'll drive your way," he said. "I think it's faster."

CHAPTER 20

2:30 p.m., 9 ½ hours…

Gwen

We didn't kiss the second we entered my apartment. Our clothes didn't fly off. We didn't hit the floor and dry-fuck like horny teens.

Soft brushes had replaced our frantic fumbling: his hand on my hip as I opened my door, my fingers gliding along his forearm when he hung back to close it, his lips on my hair as I placed the box on my kitchen counter. We moved in slow motion, stretching our seconds to make them last. A shower was still in order.

He followed me into my bathroom and started poking through my stuff.

"What do you think you're doing?" I asked.

"Investigating."

"Why?"

He shrugged a shoulder and kept nosing through my drawers. *Creeper.* His PI skills led him to my stash of condoms, lube, and the waterproof vibrator I'd purchased the night drunk Rachel had dragged Ainsley and me into a sex shop. The videoed Dildo Incident was saved on my phone.

Smirking, he held up my pink pleasure toy. "This could be fun."

"You have no idea."

He hummed appreciatively and placed it on the counter. My birth control was in the same drawer. He picked it up and spun it in his hand. "I was serious before, about wanting a family with you one day. But there's no going back from that. We both have to be all in, no matter what happens." His attention drifted to his right, as though scrutinizing my glassed-in shower.

His true focus was on my kitchen, connected to the other side of that white tile wall. Where my mother's secret box lay. He wanted assurances its contents wouldn't turn us into liquefied skeletons.

All I could offer was my honesty. "Having a child with you would be…everything. Thinking about it, even theoretically, makes my heart feel like it might explode. So sign me up for that future, August. I'm all in. For now, I want you before I detonate that bomb in there. I want to touch you and make love to you, no other drama between us." I flattened my palm on his firm chest, connecting us. "I have this feeling everything will change after I open that box, which means I'll need you more than ever."

And you can't hurt me, I refrained from adding.

"I may be leaving the country, but I'm not leaving you. Never again."

"So we're really doing this? You and me, long distance?"

Still holding my pills, his arm came around my back, the heavy pressure of his palm burning through my tank top. "It's just us now, Gwen. We come before everything. That's how we'll make it work."

"I can do that."

"Don't freak out on me."

"Don't flirt with groupies."

"Don't sleep with my brother."

I gasped, and his lips quirked to the side. "Too soon?"

My sputtering laugh was answer enough. "Definitely too soon."

Gaze locked on mine, he returned my birth control to my drawer, eyes burning with intent. To one day have a child. To build a future together. A home.

All I'd ever wanted.

I threaded my fingers through his thick, black hair, pressed to my tiptoes, and kissed him slow and deep. He trailed his knuckles along my cheek, my jaw, my neck, never disconnecting his lips from mine. I traced the hard lines of his ribs, slipped his T-shirt over his head. Mine fell next to his in the same unhurried rhythm. We were on cruise control, taking our time, enjoying every curve along the ride.

His callused fingers drew tender lines around my bra, over my lace-covered nipples, coaxing them into stiff peaks. My hips moved, rocking automatically. His mirrored mine, an erotic dance to a tune only we could hear. Actually, no. There was a tune, a soft hum coming from August, so delicate I barely heard it.

"Are you singing to me?" I dropped to my knees, helped him out of his jeans. I removed his briefs. My mouth watered as his erection sprang free. His shaft was thick, flushed, the strong vein on the underside begging to be licked.

I peered up. The desire in his heavy-lidded gaze hit me between my thighs as he ran his strong hand through my hair. "You've always inspired my music. Can't help but compose when I'm with you."

I palmed his erection, brought it to my cheek, brushed it back and forth. The silk-hard feel of him was irresistible. A glorious groan hit my ears.

"I know the words to all your songs," I said.

"I want to know the words to all of yours." Grit laced his deepening voice.

It was an odd thing to say, considering my song-writing skills were up there with my whistling ability, but I understood what he meant. We were composing a symphony of short sharp breaths and longer sighs, guttural pants and dirty grunts as I took his gorgeous cock into my mouth. Our own love album.

"Fuck, Gwen." He moved with me, gliding in out of my mouth. Not fast and rough. A slow slide, each one hitting the back of my throat, so deep I almost gagged. I wanted to take him deeper, though, give him more pleasure. The most. Drown him in it. My own desire pooled between my thighs.

I dragged one hand around his tense thigh, dug my fingers into his clenched ass. A strangled breath hissed from deep in his chest. "Fuck, fuck, *fuck*. Stop."

His slick cock fell from my mouth, and I licked my swollen lips, loving the taste of August Cruz. "You're saying fuck a lot again."

"You inspire profanity, and you're about to make me come too soon."

He yanked me up and tugged my jeans down. I reached to undo my bra, but he slapped my ass. "This goes slow." A statement. A command.

I'd never been so wet.

He dragged my thong over my legs, dropping kisses in its wake. He attended to my bra next, lavishing my breasts with the same reverent attention before sliding lower. My knees weakened in the best way. I gripped the meaty parts of his shoulders, smiled at the cowlick in his hair. The one I'd tug when watching TV, to annoy him, to get his attention, to pretend I didn't love my best friend.

"Spread your legs, baby." Words I'd never thought I'd hear him say.

He pushed me against my shower, kneeled, then hooked one of my legs over his shoulder. He trailed his tongue in a mind-numbing slide. The move was excruciatingly slow. He did it again, and again. I whimpered. I tried to move my hips, desperate for him to lick faster, press harder.

He chuckled against me. "So impatient."

I was about to tell him where to shove his impatience, but he clamped his lips on me and sucked while moving his head. "*Fuck, fuck, fuck,*" was all I managed.

Our limited sex vocabulary.

My hands were somewhere in his hair, my heart was somewhere in the clouds. We were somewhere in the world, but I had no clue where.

This. Just this. "That fucking spot."

A purely male sound rumbled from him. He took my cue, concentrating his efforts where I needed him. His fingers joined the party, pleasure building. He was everywhere: inside my body, promising me a future, reminding me of my past.

Regardless of our mistakes or what lay ahead, we'd cope. We'd always return to each other. That security had my body relaxing, enough to shape my orgasm, fuzzy edges that sharpened. *Good. This. Yes. More.*

"Don't you dare stop."

He pumped his fingers and held me steady against his face. The next lick sent me bucking. I let go in a rush, nearly yanked out his hair as I came. The aftershocks ravaged me.

Gently, he lowered my leg, kissed the curls between my thighs. "You're amazing."

"I think I'm supposed to say that to you."

"You can say it after we make love in the shower."

He worked his way up my body, stopping to knead my breasts, suck on my nipples. I was even wetter than before, uncharacteristic for me. Some women could go for rounds, rack up orgasms faster than a credit card bill. I was happy to have sex after a guy went down on me, but more so he could get off. A thank you for his hard work. Not with August.

I wanted him inside me, moving with me. Filling me. Over and over.

He turned the shower on while rubbing his erection against my belly. He nestled his thigh between my legs, the two of us grinding on each other. Then we were under the hot spray, kissing, stroking, but savoring, too. Not rushing to join. I followed the water that sluiced over the lean planes of his chest, each crevice of his abdomen, the defined bones of his hips. I sucked his length again and bit his thigh.

He moved behind me, exploring my spine while I splayed my hands on the cold wet tile. Hot water plastered my hair to my neck. August squeezed my ass and moved lower, tongued my crease. A tease before dipping farther south and kissing the backs of my thighs and knees.

Knees shouldn't be erotic. Neither should elbows or ribs. August's devout attention turned every inch of flesh into a G-spot. An E-spot. An R-spot.

New spots, each with the power to blind me.

"Now," I murmured, dizzy with desire. "I need you now."

"Now," he agreed, pulling my legs back slightly.

Still behind me, his thickness brushed my ass. I sensed him bend his knees to line up with my entrance. It wasn't low enough. I lifted to my tiptoes, but one of my feet slipped. His knee hit the shower wall.

"Shit."

"Fuck."

"Ow."

"Oof."

I fell backward into him, laughing. "Shower sex is not our forté."

He caught me around the waist. "Everything with you is perfect."

We wound up on the floor again, half in the shower, half out, still grinning, the water still running. I straddled his hips, couldn't believe August Cruz was smiling up at me, laughter and love in his eyes. "Perfect," he said again.

I lifted up, guided him below me, and lowered myself down. We both sighed, but my exhale was louder. It was full of this moment and all I wanted: to be with August, make a baby one day, a girl or boy who we'd raise in a loving home, here or abroad. Even if we had to spend time apart, we'd make it work. I wouldn't let my insecurities rule me. I'd give that child everything I never had. With August.

I circled my hips and went to lift up and show him my heart with tender loving, our bodies meant to be joined, but he gripped my hips. "Wait."

I squirmed. "Why?"

"I've never felt this." His pupils had blown wide with intensity.

I traced his wet nose. "Felt what?"

———

August

Gwen was straddling me, surrounding me, all her wet heat fisting my cock, and I struggled to explain my need to hit pause. I'd experienced this base pleasure with women before, the burn before the release. But I was still amused by mine and Gwen's fumbled shower sex attempt, how I'd loved tripping over her and winding up on the floor—again. There was no awkward moment. No hesitancy or embarrassment.

And I was bare in her. We wouldn't try for a baby until we were solid, but being nestled in her, balls deep, at peace yet rock hard, imagining our future and coming inside her soon: I just couldn't find the words.

I gathered my breath and did the best I could. "I didn't know what love was until you."

Laughter. Fumbles. Fuck-ups. Forgiveness. And this fever. This hot, thick lust waiting to explode because of the woman who'd taught me the meaning of life.

"Then love me," she said, rocking on me as much as I'd let her.

We lived in the pause, the shower making a mess of her bathroom, Gwen making a mess of my heart. I wouldn't have it any other way. Then I let her move. I palmed her breasts, watched greedily as her head tipped back and lips dropped open. I slid my hands down her body, supported her hips, met her each time she lowered. Still slow, still drawing out our pleasure.

The longest seconds in history.

I flipped her on her back, inching us farther out of the shower. On my knees, I canted her hips and thrust into her again, deeper than before. I watched each slow drag of my cock pulling out and pushing in. Fire shot up my thighs. "Wish you could see how beautiful you are." Her tight, glistening pussy swallowing my length.

"We'll video it next time."

Possessiveness surged through me at the notion. My girl, on camera for me. Something to enjoy when we're apart. "Damn right, we will."

I pumped into her harder, faster, deeper. I fell forward, ground my pelvis where she needed me. She caught her breath each time we connected, dug her fingers into my back. I sucked on her neck, wanted to leave a mark. A tattoo. A permanent reminder of who loved her, no matter what that box brought.

She may have said we'd work through anything, that she'd put us first, but that box was a wild card. It could alter everything.

We had now, at least. This incomprehensible perfection on a wet floor, her nearby birth control a reminder of our pledge. Just us. We'd always come first.

My orgasm threatened to rip down my spine, building, building.

Her knees dug into my sides. "I'm so…"

"Me, too."

"You feel…"

"So fucking good."

Her first contraction squeezed me so hard, I spasmed. She cried out—the sexiest song I'd ever heard. My grunts followed, her name mixing with the sounds as I pumped harder and spilled into her, blinding bursts that never seemed to end. We both shuddered.

"We're on the floor again," she said into my neck and held me closer.

"A very wet floor." Which meant we couldn't linger. "Cuddling will have to wait." I kissed her deeply, then lifted up.

She touched where we were joined as I pulled out, an erotic move that had me wanting to plunge back into her. "I'm not done with you yet," I said. "I'll shut off the shower. Meet me in the bedroom."

Round two had her ass in the air, my chest pressed to her back, a soft mattress finally below us. I couldn't drag out my pleasure long enough, loved learning every rhythm and angle that made her moan. It was a rougher affair. Skin slapping. More *fucks* shouted as my orgasm winded me. She claimed I'd turned her into jelly.

I kissed the back of her neck afterward, stayed in her as long as possible. "Not sure how I'll live without this." I shouldn't mention my impending departure, but there was no point denying the inevitable.

She pushed her hips back into me. "Our reunion will be so sweet."

The comment was lighthearted, but there was no disguising the break in her voice.

Needing to see her face, I pulled out and cleaned us up with a towel. Gwen's bedroom was simple and neat. Blue-gray walls, a gym bag on the floor, laundry basket, fitness and outdoor magazines on her dresser. There was one photo, a candid of her with Rachel and Ainsley. Her friends, not her family. I wanted my picture here, too, to be her family. She was already that for me, but Gwen had always searched for more. Pined for it.

More reason the box in the kitchen could hurt her, and us.

I wanted to lounge under the sheets together, forget the world for the rest of the day, but I needed to know what I was dealing with. It was her birthday, too. We had plans with her friends. Last thing I wanted was to upend Gwen's life more than I already had, especially when I was taking off tomorrow. She'd need her friends more than ever.

I crawled onto the bed, grabbed her hand, and lifted her to sitting. I kissed her nose. "I think it's time."

"To have sex again?"

Sneaky little vixen. "If I was twenty, maybe, but this old man needs a break. And we have a box to open."

"Old-schmold," she mumbled. Her silliness drained as she picked her nails. "Will you bring it in here? Actually"—she gripped my wrist as though I'd slip away—"what did my mother mean in her note, when she wrote: *Remember what I told you on Gwen's birthday?*"

With all we'd been through, I'd forgotten about that detail. "I called her, to get your address, and she said the wildest thing."

"What did she say?" Gwen looked like she was holding her breath.

"She said that you loved me. Told me not to let you push me away."

"My *mother* said that?"

"Shocked the hell out of me."

It was also one of the reasons I'd caught Gwen with Finch. A couple times that fateful night, I'd questioned if I should let things lie with Gwen, not get in any deeper. Then I'd replay Mary's words and had eventually followed my gut. Walking in on Gwen and my brother had been the shittiest day of my life, but I'd believed it was supposed to happen. Like finding this journal, following the clues. That brutal event had given me my career. It gave me this time with Gwen. If we'd gotten together back then, we might not have lasted.

I snuck another kiss while she absorbed that confession, then pulled on my briefs and retrieved the keepsake. I cleaned the dirt from it before returning to Gwen.

She sat cross-legged on the bed, still picking her nails, wearing nothing but a thin tank top...and four-leaf-clover boxers. My lucky boxers. The ones she'd stolen. They looked fucking amazing on her.

I settled across from her, placed the keepsake beside me. "I see my boxers survived your sniffing."

A sweet blush highlighted her cheeks. "They're comfy."

They were downright sexy. I blinked, wishing my eyes were a camera, capable of capturing the simplicity of a blushing Gwen, on her bed, bare legs folded, wearing my boxers.

"You can steal my underwear any time." She could have my whole damn wardrobe, as long as she was mine. I moved her mother's time capsule between us. A possible live grenade. "Whatever's in here, we'll get through it."

She quit picking her nails and switched to chewing her lip. She nodded noncommittally. Whatever her mother had buried would hit Gwen hard. There was no shouldering that burden for her. All I could do was love her hard and be her rock. That didn't keep my heart from racing.

CHAPTER 21

4 p.m., 8 Hours…

Gwen

Still shaken up over my mother's words to August, I didn't reach for the box right away. How had a woman who'd barely paid me a lick of attention known I'd loved my best friend? Why would she have shown *him* a hint of her affection toward me, when all I'd ever received was a cold shoulder?

She'd pushed us together on my nineteenth birthday, and again while she'd been dying. She had known me well enough to predict I'd push August away. Yet during her illness, we couldn't talk without fighting.

It didn't make sense, but I didn't have the energy to unwind that aggravating knot.

Unable to delay any longer, I snuck my fingers under the box's fitted lid. It took three tries to loosen it. August had obviously cleaned the exterior, but trapped dirt—*twenty-eight-year-old dirt*—spilled out as I shimmied it up. The mess went unnoticed. I couldn't focus on much besides the mysterious contents.

A gold locket was wedged in a corner. Papers that matched the diary were folded at one side, a tiny stuffed bear lodged between them.

Three things. All this stress over three little things.

I lifted the bear first, the least worrisome object. Who didn't love stuffed animals? This cutie was purple with a white muzzle and black nose, a darker purple ribbon tied around its neck. It smelled of stale, musty dirt, but the fur was still soft. I petted it, then set it aside.

August's attention was glued on me, his stare unwavering. I kept my focus on the box and reached for the papers, but at the last second I chose the locket. Again, it seemed the easier selection. The one with the least ramifications.

Dirt had lodged into its seam as well. It tumbled out when I pried it open, joining the debris on my bed. I frowned at the picture inside. "I don't get it." I rubbed my thumb over the faded image.

August leaned closer and the bed shifted. "Get what?"

Scrunching my face, I turned the locket over. There was nothing of interest except this one photo. "It's of my aunt Sarah. Why would my mother have buried a picture of my aunt?"

My affair theory darkened. I'd overheard that phone call so many years ago, Mary hissing at her sister, telling her never to call again. Could Sarah have been the other woman? Had Mary's own sister stolen her man, leaving her to raise her child alone? My body tensed at the possibility.

August eased the locket from my grip and studied it. "Seems odd, but I bet those pages explain it."

Item number three. The scariest of them all.

Sucking back a massive breath, I pulled them out. They were more fragile than the bound diary, dirt and dust unkind over the years. I spread them out gingerly. Three pages. My mother must have had a thing for threes. I lifted them and began to read.

Dearest Gwen,

You will never read this. No one ever will. It makes it easier to tell you how much I love you. I loved you the moment you were conceived. I loved you for the nine months you filled my womb. I loved you more than I have ever loved anyone or anything, and giving you up is the hardest thing I will ever have to do. But having Mary raise you will keep you safe. My sister will take better care of you.

I gasped and clutched at my chest, as though that would ease the pain squeezing my heart. Tears burned my eyes.

"Baby, what is it?"

Oh God, oh God, oh God. I couldn't answer. I couldn't read more.

August slipped the trembling papers from my hand. When he said, "Holy shit," I knew he'd read it.

As though detached, I observed my shaking hands, watched as my tears hit the gathered dirt on my blue duvet. A few spots turned muddy. I blinked and more tears fell. They felt like someone else's tears. This felt like someone else's room. That letter must belong to someone else.

"My mother wasn't my mother," I whispered.

August moved until he was alongside me, drawing me down to rest my head on his chest. He stroked my hair, kissed my head. I cried some more. I'd cried more the past two days than I had the past ten years. His soft shushing helped me gather myself. Gathering my thoughts proved more difficult.

"If Aunt Sarah was my mother, why did she stop calling and sending cards? Why did she cut me off?"

Harsh words from her sister shouldn't have triggered her to disappear. Not when I'd been clueless to her identity. And why hadn't it been safe to raise me herself? Why would Mom—*Mary* —have agreed to this?

A million questions swarmed my mind, along with a hint of relief...and a sting of guilt. Mary Hamilton hadn't been my mother. The diary had belonged to Sarah, who had loved to dance and perform and cliff jump. Not Mary, who'd cheated me out of basic affection. The fact made me happy, which made me feel incredibly awful.

Mary had put her life on hold to raise me. She'd never wanted kids, as she'd once admitted. A burden like that could harden someone, embitter them. Keep them from dancing and laughing and living fully. I had in fact ruined her life.

No. *Not me*, I reminded myself. Her sister had.

August held me close. I burrowed closer, wanting to disappear, but I wanted answers more. I wiped my snotty nose before it dripped on his bare chest, then I kissed the center of his breastbone, nosed the dark curls dusting his skin. "I'm ready to read more."

I gathered the pages and joined him at my headboard, cuddling into the crook of his arm as we read the rest together.

I didn't think I wanted kids, but the second I knew you existed, everything changed. I couldn't wait to share the news with your father. Ted Mercer was nothing but sweet with me, gentle and kind. You were created by two people very much in love. Unfortunately, I didn't know him as well as I thought.

When I went to tell him we were going to have a baby, I found him in an alley by my dance center. He and another man were harassing a third person, who was begging for his life, something about money owed. There was a gunshot. The begging man died. It wasn't your father who did the killing, but the man with him turned the gun on me.

Ted stalled the gunman while I got away. We met later, and he told me I would have to leave town, that the people he worked for were bad. I was a witness and I wasn't safe. He didn't have to tell me twice. Not with you growing inside me. I also never told him about you. I couldn't risk the information falling into the wrong hands.

I would have run as far as possible, but I didn't have money. I went to my parents for help, but they called me a sinner and turned me away. With nothing but the clothes on my back, I sought refuge with a dance teacher. Aside from the teacher and my unsupportive parents,

Mary was the only other person who knew about my pregnancy. She also intercepted a threat directed toward me, a promise to end my life if I ever turned up.

You don't know what it's like, living like you could die at any moment. I dropped out of school and wouldn't leave the house, wouldn't even open the curtains. You were born there, in the basement, and I have never loved anyone as much as you. I have also never been so terrified.

I'm in no shape to skip town with a newborn. I can't stay in San Francisco. But Mary showed up, days after your birth, with a suitcase stuffed with her own clothes because our parents had donated mine. She told me to leave town and plant roots somewhere safe. That you needed to be raised away from here. She said she would care for you until I got on my feet.

I cried for a week straight, then prepared to do as Mary asked. She put money in my wallet along with a bus ticket. She instructed me to send her suitcase back to her when I found a job and a home, explained that I should write my address at the back of my hidden journal. Somewhere discreet, in case it was intercepted. Then she would deliver you to me.

She organized everything, while I existed in a daze. She took charge, the way Mary always did. The good daughter. The strong daughter.

Today is the day I will be leaving you, Gwen, and the daze has cleared. I am not fit to raise a human being as perfect as you. I brought dangerous people into your life, before you were even born. I have no skills, no parents of my own to show me what to do.

Mary has an apartment. A job. A network of friends. I have nothing.

You deserve better than me.

I will not be sending that suitcase back. I will not be seeing you again. You will be better for it. You will lead a happy life, with my sister.

I'm sitting under a tree on Tank Hill now, about to bury this secret and my heart forever, but I don't see another way.

Please know that I love you, Gwen. So incredibly much.
Sarah

Sarah. My mother. I no longer understood what those words meant. My life had become a novel. The twisty, crime kind with mafia and wise guys and bodies dumped into rivers, but under it all was a desperate teenager, drowning in despair. "She seemed so sad and alone."

August's expanding chest pressed against my body, making us both rise. He blew out a slow breath. "I can't imagine what she went through."

"And to leave me with her sister? Never come back for me? No wonder my mom or Mary, or whatever I'm supposed to call her, resented me."

"She did come back, though, in a way. That's why the luggage went missing. Eleven years late, but she sent for you."

Eleven years. That number again. I picked apart my limited knowledge of my aunt-turned-mother. One fact rang clearer than the rest: she'd sent me birthday cards, one a year for eleven years, then they'd stopped. After a fight with her sister, because of me. There had never been a return address. I'd checked when the cards had stopped, thinking I'd reach out to her. My mother had likely been in the dark about her sister's whereabouts. Had no way to deliver me to her.

If Sarah had called her to check on me, while refusing to reveal her location, it could have provoked Mary to lash out at her, tell her not to call again.

I filled August in on those details, my words tumbling out faster as I spoke. "Sarah must have sent the suitcase the next year, after that call, before my twelfth birthday. Assumed I got it and chose not to contact her. Do you think that's why she cut our ties? Because I never reached out?"

His callused fingers grazed my arm, up and down as he stroked me. "This has to be an intensely sensitive issue for her. There's major insecurity with that. She must have assumed you didn't want contact. I'd choose to suffer over barging in on your life after that."

"But why not call? So many years later, why send the case?"

"Maybe the same reason people text and email. It's less personal. Rejection wouldn't sting as much. And the diary and note allowed you to know Sarah better than a shocking call."

I shut my eyes, listened to the *gegong-gegong* of August's steady heart. My aunt was my mother. My mother was my aunt. Mary could have been the girl who'd tracked my father to the Blue-Eyed Raven, desperate to find him. Hoping for a clue to her sister's location. There was no way to know. Mary and Ted were both gone. Still, I'd learned more today than I had in twenty-eight years.

Too much and not enough.

Here, tucked safely against August, the weight of it all felt bearable. Inconceivable, but bearable.

"Sarah gave me up to keep me safe and give me a better life," I said, as though speaking it aloud would make the choice clearer. It did, slightly.

"Sounds to me like she felt cornered, unable to care for you."

I couldn't imagine that kind of terror and impotence, but I remembered how depressed I'd been in college, how alone. No supports in my life. Add a madman trying to kill me and a surprise baby, and I might have cracked as epically as her. I also wasn't sure how to unpack this glimpse of my father, a man who'd threatened and had possibly killed people.

Thankfully, I hadn't knocked on that red door earlier. Who knows what would have greeted me? In time, I'd go. I'd ask questions and learn all I could, find out if I had siblings. For now…

I wasn't sure what I'd do for now.

"Are you angry with her?"

August's question caught me off-guard. There were too many emotions to name. "I'm feeling kind of numb."

Again, I replayed the steps that had led me here, a twisted

chess game of calculated moves and countermoves. Each bit of information learned the past two days, each second, minute, hour had contributed to discovering this secret. Without every choice made, good or bad, this box would have stayed buried, this truth forever lost.

Another possibility struck, so hard, I nearly bit my tongue. "We wouldn't be here."

August unlatched my hand from his ribs. I hadn't realized I'd dug my fingers in. He slinked down until we were eye to eye. "We wouldn't be where?"

"If Mary got the suitcase when she was supposed to, seventeen years ago, she would have given me the diary and address. I wouldn't have hesitated to move across the country." I pressed closer to him, wound our legs together. I soaked in his handsome face. "I wouldn't have driven you nuts as teens."

There would have been no WTF.

No painful years without him.

No making up and falling in love.

No Ainsley and Rachel.

August kissed me and rolled me on top of him. He secured his arms around my waist. "I hate that you missed growing up with your mother, but I'd be lying if I said I'm sorry you never got that diary. I don't know how I lived without you the past nine years, but I can promise you you'll be the first and last person I speak with every day for the next ninety-nine, no matter what countries we're living in."

I'd rather make it nine hundred and nine. "Time zones might make that tough."

"We'll send each other timed recordings."

"Of the dirty variety?"

He slapped my bottom. "Fuck yeah." He closed his eyes and brushed our noses together. A sweet, butterfly kiss.

At first, when the letter had sunk in, all I'd lost had burned my throat. I'd lived with a woman who I'd burdened instead of one who could have loved me. But if the reverse had led to a life without August, I wouldn't want it. He was my family. My life. My future. I rubbed my belly against his, imaging it swollen with our child. He would always come first.

I rested my full weight on him. He hugged me tighter. Our breaths slowed and thinned. I drifted off slightly, in and out of a foggy sort-of sleep, eventually waking half-on and half-off him. My room was dark, only a hallway light illuminating the space. I briefly wondered if I'd dreamed the letter and details I'd learned. I wasn't sure if I wanted this revelation to be real or imagined.

Real, I thought to myself. As real as the man who'd gathered me close to his thudding heart.

"I bet today is hard for her," I said, my voice thick from napping.

August stirred and hummed his agreement. "But it's your birthday, and it's already been rough. It's up to you how we spend it. You can call Sarah, if that number still works. We can hang out with your friends." He slipped his hands up my shirt and tickled my back. "We can spend it in bed."

As nice as that sounded, I was too overwrought to have sex. I kept glancing at the diary, the unearthed note. Couldn't stop picturing Sarah struggling today, hating herself for the choice she'd made. A deeper self-loathing than I'd ever experienced.

"I'd like to call her," I said, unsure it was the smart move, yet unable to put it off. "And I'd like to see the girls tonight." My support network. The women I'd be leaning on after August left. "Is that okay?"

"Only if I can kiss you all night long." He planted several soft ones on my lips.

"I'll need as many as you can give. They'll have to last me awhile."

We kissed some more, slow and deep. He hardened against my thigh but didn't roll his hips or increase his groping. He knew exactly what I needed.

He grunted eventually and nudged me fully off him—a man

could only take so much. I fell into the dirt pile smearing my bed.

He grimaced. "We need to shower again. A no-sex shower," he added, his voice gruff. "Then you can call Sarah, and *then* I'll take you out for your birthday. After, we'll talk about when I'm coming back to San Francisco and how excited I am for you to meet me in Germany. I'm gonna spoil you rotten. That cool with you, Possum?"

As nervous as I was about my impending phone call, as devastated as I was for him to drive to the airport at 5:30 a.m., my smile couldn't be faked. After all these years, August Cruz was my boyfriend. "It sounds perfect."

———

I sat on my couch, legs tucked under me, the phone heavy in my hand. My pulse feathered rapidly. I tried dialing Sarah's number several times, only to hit End each time. Part of me hoped the number was a dud, that I wouldn't be able to reach her yet. An excuse to pretend my life was normal*ish* for one more night. A foolish wish.

August was in the bedroom, giving me privacy. I couldn't see him, but his proximity boosted my courage. I dialed again. The phone rang. I didn't hang up.

Pound, pound, pound went my thundering heart. I pressed the phone harder to my ear. The ringing persisted. No one picked up. My reluctance shifted to desperation. A full one-eighty of mood swings. She *had* to answer. It had to be her number. Learning I'd never meet my father had been a harsh blow. This suddenly seemed essential, to hear Sarah's voice, connect with a parent. Tonight. Now.

The tendons in my neck felt ready to snap.

"Hello?" A voice answered. Her voice. My mother.

I opened my mouth to reply. Nothing came out.

"Hello?" Louder this time. There was a sweetness to her tone, modulated and pleasant. She didn't sound like me or her sister. She didn't sound like anyone I knew. She was a stranger, who was anything but. Another mother I wanted to know.

"Hi…" I cleared my scratchy throat. "I'm sorry to call like this. I'm just… This is…" I'd never been less eloquent in my life, the alphabet jumbling in my head.

"Who is this?" An edge crept into Sarah's cordial tone.

The truth had never seemed so daunting, three strangled words that would change both our lives forever. Finding my father had been a lifelong task, one I'd believed would have a concrete result. Like learning his name would give me closure. The treasure at the end of a grueling hunt. This wasn't the end, though. Finding my mother was the beginning. A journey I was ready to start.

Reminding myself how near August was, how full my life would always be, I said, "I'm your daughter."

She sucked a harsh breath. "Gwen?" Gone was her wariness, the tremble in my name hinting at tears.

My vision blurred. "It's me."

"But how?"

"It's a long story." The craziest of birthday adventures. "But the luggage you sent years ago got lost and turned up yesterday. Then I found your journal and the box on Tank Hill. I don't know what to think or do, but…I needed to call."

Sobbing slipstreamed through the line, ragged inhales. "Oh, Gwen. My Gwen."

Each word swelled in my chest, so much hurt and love abrading her voice. Mine couldn't pass the fire lining my throat. I pressed my hand to my quivering lips. It didn't help. My tears fell, hope and regret wetting my cheeks. "I didn't know who you were. I got the cards, but I didn't know."

"How could you?"

"Mom never said a word." Mom. Mary. The woman who gave up her life to raise me.

"I should have called. I shouldn't have assumed, but

Gwen…I just couldn't. I wasn't strong enough. I didn't think I deserved you."

Exactly why I'd pushed August away. Like mother, like daughter.

A sniffly laugh escaped. "I can't believe this."

Her crying intensified. It set me off again, the two of us blubbering shamelessly. Eventually, she gained control over her breaths, each one slowing. Mine calmed as well. A shudder passed from her end. Then, "Happy birthday, baby."

A birthday I'd never forget.

CHAPTER 22

11:11 p.m., 49 Minutes…

Gwen

It was later than intended by the time August and I met our friends. Kissing happened before we left my apartment. Then on the street. In the taxi. Outside the taxi. As much kissing as we could fit in during his last hours.

Talking with Sarah had helped clear my mind slightly. We'd kept the conversation short, both of us too emotional to say much. We'd made plans to talk again tomorrow. I was nervous for that exchange, one that would likely be more jarring. Painful wounds would be opened for us both. Whatever the outcome, it had to happen. She needed to know what my childhood had been like. I needed to know her life. We had to figure out who we were to each other.

I'd never been more thankful to see Rachel and Ainsley.

Their chosen bar was busy for a Sunday night. Industry

night, they called it, for chefs and servers who usually worked while others partied. Hanger 47's tall ceilings gave the room an airiness, the corrugated walls, vintage lighting, and airplane memorabilia super cool.

Before August and I ordered drinks, the girls spotted us and dragged me away from the group.

Ainsley gave me the once-over. "You're late and you haven't returned my texts. What kind of best friend do you think you are?"

Rachel rolled her eyes. "What she means to say is, are you okay? Is everything good with you and August?"

"Right. Yeah. That." Ainsley nodded. Her curvy figure was pronounced in a stunning cream dress with sheer sleeves and a dangerously high hemline. Rachel's risqué cutaway dress was courtesy of Ainsley, too. Personal shopper extraordinaire. I'd have to book her for an afternoon, use her expertise to source a sexy ensemble for my Germany trip.

My sights drifted past the tattooed clientele who frequented this place—most ink depicting a vegetable or cooking utensil on arms or necks—and landed on my guy. August was chatting with Owen and Jimmy. Cameron and Emmett joined them with fresh drinks. August spoke with his friends, but his heated glances cut my way often.

I may not have sipped any wine yet, but a warm path slid down inside my chest. "Everything is amazing with August," I told the girls.

Rachel sighed. "She's fallen in love."

"It's sickeningly sweet." Ainsley beamed at me.

If I looked as dopey as them when they swooned over their men, sickeningly sweet was the perfect description. "I booked a flight to meet him in Germany. We're determined to make this work." I didn't mention August's and my baby talk, our hopes to one day have kids. I felt too fragile. But it sent my mind to my newfound history, how it would feel to give up my yet-to-be conceived child. My insides twisted at the thought.

Rachel touched my wrist lightly. "If things are good, why do you look sad?"

"He's leaving," Ainsley said, pointing out the obvious. "Of course she's sad."

I *was* sad August was going, but excited, too. I would torment the man of my dreams through dirty texts. Seeing him again would be the best kind of reunion. "Saying goodbye to him will be painful, but some other big stuff happened."

Rachel and Ainsley stared at me, wide-eyed, as I laid out my crazy day and the diary details, how August had kept the information from me, that act leading to the biggest case us two Badass PI partners had ever cracked: my father and the woman who'd raised me were dead, but my aunt was my mother…and she was alive.

"You never found your father, but you found your mother instead," Ainsley said, awed. "I'm barely standing after that revelation. How are you on your feet?"

Rachel wiped a tear from her freckled cheek. "Because she's the strongest woman we know."

I glanced down at my body. August had unleashed a sexy growl when he'd seen me in my leather pants, three-inch heels, and red strapless top. He'd said he loved how strong I was.

Standing here, still on my feet after my insane day, wasn't because I could do burpees and box jumps. Growing up in a cold home had toughened me. I'd learned to breathe through stress, repeat stupid movie titles if needed. Play not-very-good guitar. Now I had a man who loved me and the best friends a woman could want. I'd earned this inner strength.

All I said was, "Of course I'm here. I wouldn't miss our birthdays."

The three of us hugged, our twenty-seventh year almost over. Year twenty-eight would knock it out of the park.

"With August gone, we'll have to rally." Ainsley rubbed my arm. "I'll bake you my famous spinach brownies."

Rachel and I traded horrified looks. "It's not necessary," I said.

"Of course it is."

"It's really not."

"Owen loves them. I'll make a double batch."

Those vegan brownies tasted like cardboard mated with grass. If Owen ate them, he either had the palate of a starving prisoner, or he was the best boyfriend this side of Canada.

"I'll make extra for you, too," Ainsley told Rachel.

"Will you look at the time?" Rachel glanced at her slender wrist, which didn't house a watch. "Pretty sure it's almost midnight. We should get back to the boys." Crafty girl, dodging the brownies.

She kissed my cheek before we moved. "But Ainsley's right. Not about the awful brownies, but about us rallying. We're here for you. If you need a breather, come visit me in Napa. If you need me to make an emergency trip here, just say the word."

I squeezed her elbow. "I'd be lost without you ladies. And you realize what this means, right?" When I had their attention, I pulled three folded papers from my front pocket.

They both gasped.

"I forgot we did that," Rachel said.

This time last year, we'd made resolutions that would change our lives. We'd written them on papers to hold ourselves accountable. Rachel and Ainsley had fulfilled theirs months ago. Mine had seemed impossible, the distant hope to know my father having slipped through my fingers when Mary had died.

I may not have met him, but I'd discovered his name, my history, and I'd hopefully be meeting my birth mother in the coming months. "I'd say we rocked the shit out of our birthday wishes."

"Was there ever any doubt?" The pride in Ainsley's voice was contagious.

I gave the girls their papers and pocketed mine. "To another amazing year."

Ten minutes before the clock struck midnight, we joined our men. Jimmy pulled Rachel's back into his chest and wrapped his arms around her. Owen did the same with Ainsley and played with the pendant hanging from her necklace.

August winked at me and picked up a glass of red wine from the bar. "Figured you'd want this."

"You're a mind reader." I did want the wine. I also wanted him. In a simple white T-shirt and faded jeans, he was lickable. My libido revved back to life.

He tucked me into his side and raised his glass to the group. "Is there a birthday wish on tap this year?"

"I don't need a wish to get what I want," Ainsley said. I expected her to make a show of kissing Owen, but she batted her Lancôme lashes at his brother. "If Emmett doesn't tell me what Owen's tattoo means, I'll tell his boyfriend about the gift I'm buying for Emmett's birthday this year."

Emmett narrowed his eyes at her. "Nice try, but this guy"— he flicked his thumb toward Cameron, whose hand was in Emmett's back pocket—"knows what I'm packing below."

Playing along, Cameron waggled his eyebrows. "Any bigger and I'd be in trouble."

Undeterred, Ainsley tapped her index finger against her chin, as though contemplative. "I'm not sure I believe you, and I bet the crowd here might wonder why I feel obliged to buy you a...PENIS PUMP."

She said it loud enough that a few people turned their heads.

I snickered. The fact that Owen had Japanese words tattooed on his ass was funny. The fact that he'd been clueless to their meaning until this year was priceless. The cheeky (pun intended) man now refused to tell Ainsley. Just to torture her.

"Not amusing," Emmett said, then grumbled something under his breath.

"I'm still waiting." Ainsley cleared her throat, ready to crow.

Emmett jutted his chin at Owen. "Just tell her already. She'll only get worse."

"It's true," Rachel said. "She's like a fashionable pit bull."

Owen dashed a hand through his sandy hair and shrugged. He leaned down and whispered in Ainsley's ear. She bit her lip and covered her heart with her hand as she listened. Blue eyes glazed, she looked at Emmett. "You're forgiven for not telling me."

"Now I want to know," I said. Ainsley rarely got choked up.

She ignored me and pressed a kiss to Owen's chest.

"So no real wishes?" Jimmy asked us.

"Come on," August said, jumping on Jimmy's prodding. "Isn't this wish thing a big deal with you ladies?" The way his smolder slid to me suggested he wanted a say in mine.

Rachel studied Ainsley and me, both of us wrapped up in our men, then she clinked her wineglass against Jimmy's. "I think we all have what we need. It's also about that time."

The start of our twenty-eighth year.

We all shrunk into groups of two, happy to celebrate our new beginnings privately, and I had a slew of new beginnings to contemplate.

August pulled me around to face him. My favorite fresh start. "I love you, Possum. I know the last couple days have been nuts, but being with you is better than I could have dreamed." My best friend pressed me against the bar and kissed me deeply, unconcerned by the busy room.

I nipped his bottom lip. "Best birthday yet."

I didn't need a resolution this year. If anything, I'd need as much status quo as possible, considering the changes I'd be facing: meeting my mother, balancing my job and interests with my man and my friends, sustaining a long-distance relationship.

August's warm gaze roved over my face. "You sure you're doing okay?"

Staring up at him, my answer came easily. "Surprisingly, yes. Tomorrow will be a different story, but we have now."

"Our seconds," he whispered.

"Every last one," I agreed.

EPILOGUE

Two Years and Seven Seconds Later

AUGUST

My strut offstage wasn't pretty. I nearly bailed over a set of cables, I accidentally knocked over the water glass I'd had the roadies set out, and I almost dropped my guitar while handing it off. Getting my hands on Gwen trumped a smooth exit.

Fans were great. Performing was a rush. Nothing beat wrapping her in my arms, especially when it had been three long weeks.

She grinned when I stepped backstage, clapping like it was the first time she'd seen me in concert. "You were amazing."

I lifted her up and pressed my face into her neck. "Missed you so fucking much."

She giggled when I bit her collarbone. "I couldn't get here fast enough. Wish I could have caught the start of the show." She said this while covering my face in kisses. I landed a dirty one on her mouth.

My brother wolf-whistled, obnoxiously enough to pull us apart. "You don't get paid more for the peep show."

I snagged a guitar pick from my pocket and flicked it at him. "Might need to amend my contract."

He failed to bat away my pathetic assault and the pick hit his cheek. He curled his lip playfully. "Doubt Uncle Rex will be flexible, but I could book you at Hunk-O-Mania. Bet those women would slide money down your G-string if you show skin."

Having Finch as my manager had invigorated my North American career, enough that I could split my time between Europe and here. Unfortunately, it came with his smart mouth. "The only woman I strip for is right here." I kissed Gwen again.

Finch groaned. "You guys need to keep the PDA on lockdown."

Gwen blew him a kiss. "Not a chance."

Grumbling, Finch marched off, and I breathed in all things Gwen. "Happy birthday, Possum. Sorry it's slightly late."

"Doesn't matter. It's the best one yet."

"You say that every year."

"I mean it every year."

If we were alone, I'd make sure nothing beat this year's celebration. I'd glide her zipper down and slip my hand into her panties, coat my fingers in her wetness and make her shudder. Then I'd make love to her all night. All morning, too. Man, did I miss her.

I'd arrived in San Francisco late this afternoon, had hightailed it to the Blue-Eyed Raven before Gwen had finished work. She, of course, had to spend time with Rachel and Ainsley before making the show. Our whirlwind of a life.

"Where's my girl?" I asked while sneaking a taste of her ear.

"Right here."

Damn straight. "And my other girl?"

"In your dressing room. Sarah's with her."

After much deliberation, Gwen had decided to call her mother and her aunt by their given names. Not Mom and Aunt Mary. Less confusion for her. As awful as Gwen's childhood had been at times, she saw Mary in a different light now. As a woman who'd sacrificed everything to raise her. It didn't undo the damage those years had caused, but it helped. As did getting to know her birth mother.

Another new woman in my life.

Except the only other girl I was itching to see had my nose, her mother's eyes, and the prettiest wisps of dark hair this side of the moon.

Keeping a tight hold on Gwen's hand, I led us to my dressing room. Sarah was reading a magazine while Lola slept in her portable playpen. An eleven-month-old treasure.

I went to reach for my girl, but Gwen tugged me back. "Don't you dare wake her."

"But it's been three weeks." I sounded like a whiney kid.

"I don't care if it's been three years. She has your vocal gift and isn't afraid to show it. I may need a hearing aid."

"But I—"

She pressed her finger to my lips. "...*but I* nothing. You're gonna make little miss's mom happy by taking her for a birthday drink while grandma watches *The Voice*'s future star."

Sarah waved her magazine in a shooing motion toward the door. "I've got my van loaded already. I just need to pack Lola and the playpen, and we'll be off. I'll bring her 'round first thing tomorrow."

Sarah moving to San Francisco last winter had been a godsend. My folks visited from Chicago a couple times a year, not enough to lean on them for support. Having Sarah in town meant Gwen could return to CrossFit and her other pursuits, while someone we trusted watched Lola.

The first six months or so between Sarah and Gwen had been

dicey. Nothing easy about discovering your estranged aunt was your mother. The two had worked hard to move forward, even visiting Ted Mercer's home together. He hadn't had any other children, but they'd talked with his widow, had learned he'd left his criminal pursuits in favor of construction work. A simple life for a complicated man, in the end. The meeting had given Sarah and Gwen some closure.

Watching them together now, how easily they smiled, how Sarah strived to ease Gwen's burdens, spend time with Lola, get to know our family? It choked me up at times.

"I'll agree to whisking Gwen away on a late-night date," I said, "*if* I get to carry Lola to your van." I was needy to smell Lola's baby smell, a mix of springtime and lavender and perfection.

Gwen rolled her eyes. "Fine, but you better not tickle her."

"We have a deal."

Gingerly, I lifted Lola and cradled her against my chest. My fragile sweet thing. She gurgled, the soft sound filling my heart until it nearly burst, and I fought the urge to wake her. I got her settled in her car seat without incident. I didn't tickle or poke her just to see her open her eyes. Vibrant eyes, like her mother's.

Gwen said Lola looked more like me. I thought she looked more like her. My wife. Words I never thought would describe Gwen Hamilton. Other words came to mind, the ones that filled my lyrics these days.

Partner.

Lover.

Mate.

Everything.

And always *fever*. For the rest of my life, I'd burn for this woman.

———

Thank you for reading Gwen and August's story!

Need another delicious escape?
Check out my other novels and enjoy falling in love all over
again.

ALSO BY KELLY SISKIND

One Wild Wish Series:

He's Going Down

Off-Limits Crush

36 Hour Date

Over the Top Series:

The Snowflake Effect

One Degree of Perfect

Slammed into Focus

Showmen Series:

New Orleans Rush

Don't Go Stealing My Heart

The Beat Match

The Knockout Rule

The Bower Boys series:

Fall in love with the Bower brothers! A decade after being forced into Witness Protection, they're finally allowed to return home and fight for the women they lost.

Visit Kelly's website and join her newsletter for great giveaways and never miss an update!

www.kellysiskind.com

ACKNOWLEDGMENTS

This book began with a news story. Actually, this entire series began because I read a wild article about a woman whose lost airline luggage was returned after having been missing for twenty years. Seriously. Twenty years. That happened. Then my writer brain switched on and the beginnings of 36 Hour Date was imagined.

This plot bunny kicked off the entire One Wild Wish series, but it was the last book I wrote. You can imagine my excitement when finally putting pen to the page, or my fingers to the keyboard. Add in the challenge of creating a romance with obstacles and a Happily Ever After over a thirty-six hour period, and I can honestly say this has been one of my favorite novels to write.

Until the next one, of course!

Huge thank you to my writing partners in crime who read for me, call me on the stuff that isn't working, catch those pesky typos, and make my words a whole lot better: Kristin B. Wright, J.R. Yates, Jennifer Hawkins, Heather Van Fleet, Jen DeLuca, Tammy Cole, Shelly Hastings Suhr, Rebecca Williams von Groote, Beth Miller. You all rock my world.

Tamara Mataya, your editing has been indispensable. Sarah Henning, thank you for your keen eye on these final pages. Emily Smith-Kidman. Emily, Emily, Emily…I can't thank you and Social Butterfly enough for helping to get this book into the world. Your tireless efforts are more appreciated than you know.

To all you awesome bloggers: y'all are the best. You are the backbone of this industry. The romance community thrives because of your hard work.

My husband, who listened to me talk about August and Gwen incessantly, deserves a medal for his patience. I love you to pieces.

ABOUT THE AUTHOR

Kelly Siskind lives in the wilds of Western Canada. When she's not out hiking or skiing, you can find her, notepad in hand, scribbling down one of the many plot bunnies bouncing around in her head. She loves singing while driving, looks awful in yellow, and is known for spilling wine at parties.

Sign up for Kelly's newsletter and never miss a giveaway, a free bonus scene, or the latest news on her books.

If you like to laugh and chat about books, join Kelly in her Facebook group, KELLY'S GANG.

Connect with Kelly on social media:
facebook.com/authorKellySiskind/
instagram.com/kellysiskind/
https://www.tiktok.com/@authorkellysiskind

www.ingramcontent.com/pod-product-compliance
Lightning Source LLC
Chambersburg PA
CBHW061610190726
48288CB00007B/2251